ACCLAIM FOR GATEKEEPER AND ARCHER MAYOR

"Infused with a fatalism that gives weight to an agreeably entertaining mystery."
—*Washington Post Book World*

"Mayor's Joe Gunther novels are among the best cop stories being written today."
—*Booklist*

"One of the best contemporary American mystery writers."
—*Providence Sunday Journal*

"The strength of this durable series has always been its insularity: local settings; sharp, small-town characterizations; homegrown police procedures."
—*Kirkus Reviews*

"Mayor is the boss man. . . . He has made an honorable art form of the regional mystery."
—**Marilyn Stasio**, *New York Times Book Review*

"A great storyteller."
—*Maine Sunday Telegram*

more . . .

"Mayor's major strength is his ability to etch personalities in their settings so that they are as vivid as a video."
—*St. Petersburg Times*

"Mayor knows how to keep you turning pages."
—*Trenton Times*

"Lead a cheer for Archer Mayor and his ability not only to understand human relationships, but to convey them to his readers."
—*Washington Sunday Times*

"Mayor's strength lies in his dedication to the old-fashioned puzzle, brought to a reasonable conclusion."
—*San Jose Mercury News*

"One of Mayor's strongest points is his detailed knowledge and application of police procedure."
—*Southbridge Evening News* (MA)

GATEKEEPER

GATEKEEPER

ARCHER MAYOR

WARNER BOOKS

NEW YORK   BOSTON

Copyright © 2003 by Archer Mayor
Excerpt from *The Surrogate Thief* copyright © 2004 by Archer Mayor
All rights reserved. No part of this book may be reproduced in any form or by any electronic or mechanical means, including information storage and retrieval systems, without permission in writing from the publisher, except by a reviewer who may quote brief passages in a review.

Cover design and art by Robert Santora

Warner Books

Time Warner Book Group
1271 Avenue of the Americas, New York, NY 10020
Visit our Web site at www.twbookmark.com

Printed in the United States of America

Originally published in hardcover by The Mysterious Press
First Paperback Printing: October 2004

10 9 8 7 6 5 4 3 2 1

To Ponnie, with love.

Acknowledgments

As many have heard me say, I often write about subjects I know little about. This not only allows me to venture forth and educate myself, it also puts me in contact with many generous people far more knowledgeable than I. To them, as always, I owe an enormous debt. They spend time with me, often take me places to show me what they're talking about, and even occasionally glance at parts or all of my early drafts to let me know where I've inevitably messed up.

That having been said, however, messing things up is part of human nature, and I'm sure that despite the kind efforts of some of those listed below, I have still managed to make mistakes. These are mine alone, and for them, I apologize in advance.

In short, therefore, a mea culpa and heartfelt thanks to the following:

Rick Bates

Bonny White

Stephen Spitzer

Heidi Nelson

Matt Nally

Jim Maxwell

Greg Davis

Wayne Dengler

John Merrigan

Myles Heffernan

Jimmy Cruise
Mike Ruse
Kevin Geno
Dave Schauwecker
Sean Shattuck
Joe Zingale
Nick Marro
Brian and Joyce Morgan
Eugene Wrinn
John Goodhue
Jim Bissland
Mike Gorman
Jesse Bristol

Matt and Nancy Jones
Christopher McLean
Dave LaChance
Steve Eddy
Dave Stanton
Karen Carroll
Abby Mnookin
Maria Ogden
Robin Patch
Jim Davidson
John Martin
Paco Aumand
Julie Lavorgna

Also, my gratitude to:

The Vermont State Police
The Rutland Police
  Department
The Putney School
Youth Services of Vermont
Windham County State's
  Attorney
The Brattleboro Police
  Department

The Rutland Historical
  Society
The Holyoke Police
  Department
The Vermont
  Department of
  Corrections
Book King

Chapter 1

That's five dollars even."

Arnie Weller looked over the shoulder of the balding man holding out a ten-dollar bill and checked on the whereabouts of the young woman he'd seen entering a few minutes earlier.

"Out of ten," he automatically chanted, not bothering to meet his customer's eyes. Where was she? He turned to the cash register, his fingers dancing across the keyboard in a blur. He caught the spring-loaded drawer against his hip as it opened, quickly made change, and proffered it to the man.

"Want a bag?" he asked, back to surveilling the rear of the store.

There was a telling pause from the customer, forcing Arnie to reluctantly focus on him. "What?"

The man smiled. "I bought gas."

Arnie stared at him, at a total loss. "Sorry. Have a nice night."

Shaking his head, the man slipped from Arnie's line of vision, through the double glass doors to the right, and into the night, where his pickup was parked beside one of the gas pumps.

Arnie saw what he thought was the top of the girl's head pass behind a row of stacked boxes and six-packs near the bank of fridges along the far wall. Hardest place to see anyone, he thought angrily, still nursing a grudge. Two weeks ago, he'd asked a so-called security expert for an estimate on rigging the place with cameras. One week later, he'd bought a gun instead. For a whole lot less.

Bastard.

Arnie Weller ran a clean store, paid his taxes, took care of his employees, most of whom were worthless. He dealt with the chiseling gas company, the wholesale suppliers who screwed him out of habit, and the endless state forms issued monthly to make his life difficult. He paid his insurance, although they never settled his claims, donated to charitable causes he didn't agree with, and belonged to a chamber of commerce he thought was as useless as tits on a bull. He even cleaned the bathrooms twice a day, despite and not because of the disgusting condition he found them in, each and every time. If his customers were pigs, it didn't mean he'd join them.

And he put up with the disrespect, the surliness, the petty thefts, and the general offensiveness of the young people and trailer trash who supplied most of his retail business.

All in all, Arnie believed, he was a model business-man, employer, and patriotic citizen.

And he despised every aspect of it.

Three times he'd been robbed in the past two months, once by a man with a hammer and twice by people carrying guns. Arnie had known the kid with the hammer and had told the cops right off. They'd caught him hours later buying drugs with the till money. The little jerk had ended up with barely a scratch, being un-derage. No record, no jail time, just a few weeks in rehab. To Arnie's thinking, hardly the penalty for threatening a man's life. This was Vermont, after all, famously one of the best states in which to break any law you liked.

But Arnie had suffered nightmares for weeks, envi-sioning that hammer coming down on his skull. And that was before the two guys with guns. They had really scared him.

The first had been so nervous, Arnie had worried more about the gun going off accidentally—the ulti-mate irony. The kid had worn a ski mask, dark with sweat, his hand had trembled as if he'd been sick. Even his voice had cracked. If the barrel of the gun hadn't been so real, Arnie might've even felt sorry for the poor bastard. But the gun had been real, and the son of a bitch had hit Arnie across the head with it just before he left, for no reason at all.

They'd caught that one, too—a drug user like the first—and him at least they'd put away. But Arnie still had the scar, along with the flash of realization that had accompanied its acquisition that one of these days he might actually be killed for running this marginal, ball-busting convenience store.

Then the latest one had shown up.

Not a kid. Not nervous. An out-and-out bad man.

The gun had been bigger, the hand hadn't shaken, and he'd worn the hood of his sweatshirt pulled down over half his face, giving him an almost demonic appearance. And he'd clearly enjoyed his work. He'd come around the counter, forced Arnie to the floor face-down, and had emptied the cash drawer himself. He'd even stuffed some Slim Jims into his pocket as an afterthought. Then he'd knelt next to Arnie's head, had shoved the barrel of his gun into Arnie's ear, and had cocked the hammer, chuckling all the while.

"Tell me where you live, little man," the man had whispered.

Arnie had told him, the dread rising up in him, making it hard to breathe.

"Now we both know. If you're planning on calling the cops, you might want to remember that."

After which he'd reached with his gloved hand between Arnie's legs and had given his testicles a hard, painful squeeze. "I got you here, little man. Never forget it. Keep your mouth shut or this'll be nothing compared to what's next."

Arnie hadn't told anyone about him. Not the cops, not his wife, not his buddies. He'd swallowed the loss, had struggled with the fear, had consulted with the security man.

And had bought the gun.

That hadn't turned out too well. Instead of supplying him with the comfort he'd hoped for, the gun had nestled under Arnie's untucked shirt like a tumor threatening his life. He started judging everyone who entered the place in relationship to the gun—would they force him to use it or not? The anger he'd channeled into visions of shooting the hooded man, were he to dare to show his face again, was gradually replaced by the fear that he really might return—and that Arnie would die for having presumed a cold-bloodedness he knew he didn't possess.

Tentatively, as he'd done a hundred times since buying the damn thing, Arnie touched the butt of the gun through his shirt with his fingertips, as if the bulk of it against his stomach weren't enough to confirm its presence.

They were alone in the store, the girl and he, and he knew goddamned well she was hiding back there, biding her time to step forward.

He'd recognized the type, of course, as soon as he'd caught sight of her—underfed, dirty hair, her clothes a mess and probably not her own. Her body language upon entering hadn't met the two standards of legitimacy—either looking around to get a bearing or heading straight for a known product. Instead, it had been like a rat's running for cover—from the door to the aisle offering the most cover from Arnie's view. He'd seen that in shoplifters before. And with both the hammer kid and the nervous man with the ski mask. Although not the last guy.

Still, she was only a girl.

"Miss?" he finally called out, doubtful of the authority he tried to inject into his voice. "Is there something I can help you find?"

"The money," she answered from a totally different direction. And very nearby.

He swung around, startled, stumbling slightly as his feet tangled. She hadn't stayed by the fridges. Somehow she'd circled around, coming at him from behind his own counter, slipping through the narrow gap beyond the hot dog machine at the far end. She was ghostly pale, her red, sunken eyes resting on dark pouches of swollen skin. She looked barely able to stand, much less resist an attack by him.

But in her hand she held a knife, large and glinting in the light, and the gun against his abdomen suddenly felt like an ice cube, sending a deep wave of cold from his stomach out to his extremities.

"Take it easy," he said.

"Give me the money," she ordered, her voice barely a whisper.

"You need a doctor."

She stepped closer and gestured with the knife. What strength she had was clearly being routed to that hand. He had no doubt whatsoever she could harm him if necessary.

And yet, inexplicably to him, staring at another weapon in still another loser's fist suddenly reversed the coldness he'd just experienced, flushing his face with rage and making him at least think of some heroic counteraction.

But that's where it stayed—in the thought process. The impotence remained, compounding his anger. He turned toward the cash register, humiliated, presenting her with his back. "You fucking bastards."

The sound of the till springing open matched the electronic ding of someone crossing the threshold of the store's far entrance—the one near the hot dog machine behind the girl.

Despite it being summertime, the man entering had the hood of his sweatshirt pulled partly over his face.

They were a team.

Seeing his nightmare brought back to life threw Arnie into a second reversal. Yielding to fear and fury combined, he pulled his gun from under his shirt, swiveled to face the girl, who was looking over her shoulder at the man in the hood, and fired.

The explosion was huge, deafening Arnie, reverberating off the walls, dropping the girl like a pile of clothes to the floor, and sending the hooded man staggering back in alarm against the door behind him.

His hood slipped from his face as his head smacked against the glass, and Arnie, his gun now trained on him, his finger tight on the trigger, saw a wide-eyed, pimply teenager he knew well from past transactions.

They stared at each other for a long, very quiet moment before the teenager finally managed to stammer, "Oh, shit. Please don't."

Arnie saw him raise his empty hands in surrender and finally lowered the gun, the realization of what he'd just done settling on him like a fog.

Crumpled and silent on the floor, the girl began leaking a dark puddle of blood.

Joe Gunther didn't bother showing his badge to the Brattleboro patrolman guarding the convenience store entrance. They knew one another. Gunther had once been his superior.

"Hey, Larry. Who's running this?"

"The detective's inside. How'd you hear about it? We barely got here."

Gunther smiled. "Scanner. Hard to break old habits."

The patrolman opened the door for him, and Gunther stepped from a cool summer darkness filled with flashing red and blue strobes into the store's harsh fluorescent lighting, suggestive of an operating room.

Or a morgue.

A tall young man with an oddly hesitant manner rose from behind the counter. His face broke into a broad smile as he recognized the new arrival.

"Lieutenant. Good to see you. God, it's been a while. I didn't think the VBI went in for things like this."

He stuck out a hand, realized it was sheathed in a latex glove, and began struggling to remove it.

Joe Gunther quickly grasped him by the forearm in greeting. "It's okay, Ron. It's not worth the hassle to put it back on."

He didn't bother correcting the other man on his outdated rank. Gunther hadn't been a lieutenant in several years. It was "Special Agent" now, a burdensome title he still found absurd, but one that the political birth mothers of the new Vermont Bureau of Investigation had chosen in a typical effort to impose profundity where it could only be earned over time. "And I'm not here officially—just offering help if it's needed. You okay with my dropping by?"

Ron Klesczewski shook his head in amazement. "You kidding? Just like old times. Not that we need help. This is more like the inevitable finally happening."

"I just heard it was a shooting."

Klesczewski invited Gunther to look over the far edge of the counter at the wide pool of drying blood now spread from one edge of the narrow space to the other. It was smeared and covered with lug-soled boot prints, he presumed from the ambulance crew he'd also heard summoned on the scanner. If not for the slaughterhouse color, it might have looked like the aftermath of a playful struggle in a mud bath.

"Storekeeper shot a nineteen-year-old woman. She's still alive—barely. He used a .357. Real cannon. I don't think he had any idea what he was doing."

Gunther tilted his chin toward a carving knife lying at the edge of the crimson mess. "That hers?"

Klesczewski nodded and glanced at the small notepad in his hand. "Arnold Weller's the owner. He says he's been robbed twice recently, once at gunpoint, once by a guy with a hammer. He bought the gun out of frustration. Said he wouldn't have shot her if he hadn't thought the other guy was involved, but I'm not so sure."

Gunther looked at him briefly without comment. Klesczewski answered the implied question. "Some teenage kid walked in just as these two were facing off. He had his sweatshirt hood down low over his face— it's a fad right now, plus it's a little on the cool side. Arnie swore he thought he was a bad guy, why, I don't know."

"The kid was clueless?" Gunther asked.

"Oh, yeah. Went to the hospital, too. He could barely talk, he was so shaken up. Like I said, the whole thing was just waiting to happen—more and more dopers doing more and more rip-offs. Storekeepers getting cranked by the week. Matter of time before somebody killed somebody. Maybe this one was itching for an opportunity, maybe he was just frazzled to the limit."

Despite the nature of the conversation, Gunther suppressed a smile at his young colleague's seasoned attitude. Ron Klesczewski had been a fresh-faced detective when Gunther had run the Brattleboro squad a few years back. He'd been given command of it upon Joe's departure only because Gunther had taken the most obvious successor along with him to his new job. A natural with paperwork and computers, Klesczewski had been slow gaining self-confidence otherwise, although things had obviously improved now that he was top dog. Gunther's amusement was in adjusting the new to his memories of the old.

"She was on drugs?" he asked.

Klesczewski shrugged. "Blood tests'll probably tell

us before she will—assuming she survives. But she has the look, all the way down to the fresh track marks in her arm."

Gunther gazed once more at the gore covering the linoleum behind the counter—a body's lifeblood diluted with the root cause of its own destruction. Ron Klesczewski was perfectly correct about the inevitability of Brattleboro's increasing dilemma, but he could just as easily have extended it to include the entire state. While bent on pushing the same old romantic, fuzzy image of cows and maple syrup and grizzled farmers muttering, "Ah-yup," Vermont was in fact facing a heroin epidemic. Almost one hundred fatal overdoses had been racked up in the past ten years, and countless more reversed in hospitals and ambulances. Small potatoes compared to Boston or New York, but not so negligible on a per capita basis, in a state of a half million residents. And it was climbing fast. The state police drug task force, which used to count heroin busts in the single digits five years back, was now spending 50 percent of its time on these cases alone.

"What's her name?" he asked, almost as an afterthought.

Klesczewski again consulted his notes. "Laurie Davis."

Gunther became very still, catching his younger colleague's attention.

"You okay? You know her?"

"She a blonde?" Gunther asked.

Klesczewski began rummaging around in a box he'd

placed on the counter. "Hang on. I think I can do better than that."

He extracted a plastic evidence envelope with a driver's license captured within it. Gunther held it at an angle under the bleak lighting to better see the small photo.

"And this was definitely her?" he asked.

Klesczewski nodded. "She's got more meat on her there. I have crime scene photos in the digital camera if you don't mind the small screen."

Gunther shook his head and returned the envelope to him, feeling tired and mournful. "Doesn't matter. I know her."

Two hours later, Joe was staring at the coffee machine in a hallway off the waiting room at Brattleboro's Memorial Hospital, wondering if more coffee at this time of night would qualify as suicide by insomnia.

"Don't do it," came a woman's voice from behind him, as if his thoughts had been blinking on and off above his head.

He turned to see an equally tired-looking Gail Zigman approaching from the doors of the intensive care unit. She gave him a half-hearted smile and slipped her arm through his. "We both need some sleep," she finished.

"How's she doing?" he asked her.

"She's alive. They did what they could, but the blood loss was huge. Basically, she's in a coma and they have no idea if she'll come out of it." She rested her head against his shoulder and sighed. "At least they're getting some brain activity—whatever that means."

In books written a hundred years earlier, Gail might have been called Joe's "particular friend." She was that, certainly—his sounding board, the echo of his conscience, his lover of many years—but she was not his wife. Perhaps because they'd met later in life, or were in many ways too independent, or simply were loners drawn together by instinct, they'd formed an eccentric partnership as solid as that found in a good marriage, but in which they sometimes didn't see each other for weeks at a time. In fact, for half of each year, Gail lived and worked as a lobbyist in the state capital of Montpelier, which under normal conditions was a two-hour drive away.

Not that these conditions applied. Gail had driven down at warp speed following Joe's phone call to her, and had been monitoring Laurie Davis's progress from just outside the operating room ever since.

Laurie Davis was her niece—her sister, Rachel's, daughter.

Gunther kissed the top of her head. "She might get lucky. Sometimes the brain just needs a little nap before waking up, good as new."

They began walking down the empty, bland hallway toward the elevators at the far end.

"You're talking about a previously healthy body," Gail responded. "Not someone already half dead from drugs."

He thought about saying something comforting, as

he would have with anyone else, but that wasn't their way. Plus, they'd both seen the girl, or what was left of her. There was little point pretending she wasn't a train wreck before Arnie Weller's bullet had torn into her skinny chest.

Gail shook her head, her voice hardening as she stared at the floor. "What the hell was she thinking?"

Joe felt uncomfortable. Laurie wasn't his relation. He'd only met her a couple of times. But she'd lived in Brattleboro, having moved up from suburban Connecticut at Gail's urging, and he was wondering now if he shouldn't have known that she'd fallen on hard times. He wasn't on the PD any longer, but he stayed connected. It would have been easy to keep tabs on her. Cops did that for one another's families, even extended ones.

"Thinking probably isn't a huge prerequisite," he suggested vaguely instead. "Seems like it's usually more about dulling the pain."

She looked up at him sharply, and he realized he'd unintentionally turned the tables on her, causing her to question her own responsibilities here.

"Sorry," he added quickly. "I didn't mean it to come out that way."

But Gail wasn't looking for a way out. "You're right," she admitted. "If she had been feeling any pain, I wouldn't have known about it. I didn't keep in touch—barely paid attention to her." She paused to sigh. "My sister's going to fall apart."

"You haven't reached her yet?" he asked.

She shook her head. "Got the answering machine.

They're probably on the town. They do that a lot. It was one of the issues between them and Laurie." She paused again and then added, "Everyone thought Laurie coming to Vermont would give them all a break."

Chapter 2

David Spinney was having what his mom called a space-cadet moment, when your thoughts are miles outside your body. Her line was that those were definitely good-news, bad-news times — good if you didn't like what you were doing; bad if you needed to be paying attention, like if you were running a table saw or something. Being a nurse, she tended toward practical thinking.

But David wasn't worried. He was just riding around Springfield in the back of a car with friends, listening to music, complaining about teachers and girlfriends and parents, the car slipping through successive pools of light as it coasted along the cool summer darkness from streetlamp to streetlamp. It was one of the safest places he could think of to let his mind drift. Not that his mind was too far off—just a few blocks, really, to home and family, and the uncertainties he was feeling there.

"Hey, Dave, pass the six-pack up."

Absentmindedly, he retrieved the beer from the floorboards between his feet and dropped it onto the bench seat between the two young men up front. The older of the two, Craig Steidle, who'd bought the beer and owned the car, extracted a can for himself, handed another to Wayne, beside him, and dangled a third over his shoulder from his fingertips.

"Take one, man."

David shook his head at the eyes in the rearview mirror. "Maybe later."

Craig laughed but didn't move his hand. "More for the rest of us, then. Want one, Little Chris?"

Chris was sitting beside David, his head bopping to the music thrumming throughout the car. "Cool."

The can arched through the air and bounced off Chris's leg, making him jump in surprise.

"You were supposed to catch that, dumbass," Craig taunted him. "Make sure you aim it out the window when you open it."

Chris was the youngest of them, at fifteen, although David only beat him by ten months. Nevertheless, it qualified Chris as the butt of most of their jokes, for which David was guiltily thankful. He'd once been the one catching all of Craig's flak.

Chris opened the beer as instructed, literally holding it outside the car as Craig pulled off the road into the Zoo, the nickname for the Springfield Shopping Plaza and the primary hangout for kids from all over town. Once a marsh poking a blunt peninsula into a bend of the Black River, it was completely paved over now, lined with a string of the usual retail outlets and looking—like the rest of Springfield—a little the worse for wear.

"Don't wave the goddamn thing around, stupid," Craig yelled back at Chris over the music. "You'll get us all busted."

Shamefaced and confused, Chris withdrew the can, spilling some of its contents into his lap. He ducked down and took a surreptitious swig to partially restore his self-respect.

Craig aimed the car for the plaza's cul-de-sac, ostensibly at a small cluster of U-Haul trucks, but in fact toward the Zoo's inner sanctum and well-known place of ill repute—a poorly lit footbridge connecting the back of the plaza to Pearl Street and the old Fellows machine-tool plant on the river's far bank. He drove slowly, checking out the social clusters of kids hanging around parked cars like shipwreck survivors clinging to flotsam. His hand dangled out the window so he could flick his fingers at those he knew in a series of studiously casual greetings. From the back seat, next to pimply-faced Chris and his self-consciously suckled beer, David granted Craig a begrudging respect—as obnoxious and transparent as he could be, Craig did have a certain hard-won bearing. Currently a resident of the town's Westview housing development, down-and-out through several generations, he'd turned his limited talents into something his peers saluted with a measure of respect. He also had a criminal record, if a minor one, which added to his luster among the younger teenagers.

Craig slowed to a halt a dozen yards shy of the foot-bridge steps. These were the key attraction to the place, combined with its isolation and its escape route potential. The steps were seen by the kids as a forum, where like-minded people could privately convene. The merchants and the police saw it differently, of course—as a gathering spot for dopers and drunks and a place where at least one rape had occurred within the last few years.

"Hey, Jenny," Craig called out to a young woman sitting half sprawled across the steps, unaware or uncaring of how her posture and her miniskirt defeated any hope of modesty.

Jenny merely looked at him, scowling slightly.

"Come over here." Craig made to take a swig from his beer can, pausing just long enough to add in an undertone, "Skanky bitch."

Wayne chuckled beside him as Jenny made a show of reluctantly getting to her feet and ambling over to the car, stretching to reveal both her boredom and her bare midriff.

"What do *you* want, Craig?" she asked, emphasizing the "you" as if she were addressing a bad smell.

Craig smiled and placed his hand on her hip, his thumb flicking the silver ring piercing her navel. "What've you got?"

She laughed but didn't move away. "More than you can handle."

In the back seat, ignored by both of them, David watched her through the open window, at once attracted and repelled by the messages she projected. He studied the fit of her clothes, imagined her experience with men, and struggled to balance the stirrings he felt with the knowledge that were he to "get lucky" with her, he'd probably end up disappointed—if he were fortunate enough to get off so lightly.

"You never complained," Craig was saying, his hand slipping a little lower on her hip. "You picked up some new tricks?"

"If I did, they weren't from you."

Craig's hand stopped, and David could see from her eyes that she feared she'd gone too far.

"I could maybe pass them along," she added, her sultry tone sounding strained.

But Craig had lost interest. "Yeah, along with Christ knows what kind of disease. I can live without that."

She straightened, stung. "Fuck you, too, asshole." She turned away as if to move off.

He laughed, letting his hand hover against the outside of the door. "I thought that's what we were just talking about. Hey, hey, come back. Lighten up, for Christ's sake. When did you get so touchy? What else you got for me?"

She paused, and David could sense her weighing her options, which, it occurred to him, might have been a bit of a reach.

"Why're you such a jerk?"

Craig brushed his fingertips against the back of her hand. "Come on, Jenny. You got something good, I can ditch these assholes and you and me can find a place."

Wayne laughed a little nervously, as if he'd been asked to do something he didn't completely understand. No one paid him any attention.

"I maybe got something," Jenny finally admitted.

"All right," Craig drawled. "That's my girl."

She straightened suddenly and took a step away from the car. "Shit."

They all followed her stare and saw a police car slowly approaching.

"Fuck this," Craig muttered, but didn't move.

"What d'we do?" Wayne asked plaintively.

"We pull our guns and shoot it out, moron. What d'ya think?"

Wayne looked crestfallen, as if now he'd catch hell for not bringing a gun.

Their eyes tracked the cruiser as it soundlessly rolled near, the reflections from the plaza's mercury lighting making its windshield glimmer, turning its driver into a vague silhouette.

"Who is it?" Craig asked Jenny.

"I don't know yet. Can't make it out."

In the back seat of the car, Chris took another nervous hit from his beer can, filling the confined space with an audible slurping.

Craig twisted around to glare at him. "Right, genius. Take a fuckin' swig right in front of the cops."

Behind him, the darkness abruptly burst into a pulsing riot of piercing blue and white lights from the cruiser's strobes.

Chris dropped the can. David quickly moved his feet to avoid the splash against the floorboards. After one last wilting glare, Craig turned away without a word and slouched slightly into his seat.

Moments later, an oversized shadow came between them and the throbbing lights.

"Hi, boys. Good evening, Jenny."

"Up yours," she said.

A flashlight blinded them all in turn as the police officer carefully checked them out.

"Turn off the ignition and get out of the car, please. This side only. Keep your hands where I can see them."

Craig opened the door, resuming his earlier, surly tone. "If it ain't Officer Sam. Long time."

"That's 'Sergeant Walker' to you, Steidle. Move over there."

One by one, they lined up against the car. David felt like his intestines were filled with liquid and that the slightest jarring might make them spill over.

"I suppose not one of you knows what the drinking age is," Sam Walker said. An eighteen-year veteran of the Springfield Police Department, he was working on his second and sometimes third generation of repeat offenders.

He put his face very close to Chris's. "Tell me once and tell me straight, son. What's your name?"

"Christopher Williams."

"How old are you, Chris?"

"Fifteen."

"And here's the big one. Was that a beer I saw you drinking just now?"

Chris's voice cracked. "Yes, sir."

Walker smiled. "Good boy."

He stepped back slightly and played his flashlight across David's face. "You're new. You fifteen, too?"

"Sixteen."

Walker remained silent a moment. David became suddenly aware of how quiet everything was. For the first time, he could hear the sound of the river water gliding by over the embankment. He felt like he was standing at center stage in an abandoned theater, sensing but not seeing dozens of eyes peering at him from a hundred nooks and crannies.

"I know you," Walker finally said, making David's heart skip a beat. "You're Lester Spinney's kid."

Lester Spinney opened his eyes and stared blankly at the darkened television screen for a moment, trying to remember where he was and why he was there.

"Les, it's the phone."

He looked over his shoulder at his wife, Susan, still dressed in her nurse's uniform.

"What happened?" he asked.

"You fell asleep watching TV again. Wendy turned it off before she went to bed." Susan offered him the portable phone in her hand. "Anyhow, it's for you."

She sounded tired, which matched her near-haggard expression. She worked at both the hospital and a local doctor's office, and the toll was beginning to show.

He took the phone from her. "Spinney."

"Lester, it's Sam Walker, down at the PD. I picked up your kid tonight."

Spinney sat up, alarmed. "What happened?" Behind him, he heard Susan pause at the door, frozen by his tone of voice. In the worlds they inhabited—hers of medicine, his as a special agent for Joe Gunther and the VBI— news of this sort was seldom good.

"It's no big deal," Walker quickly reassured him. "He was in a car with an underage drinker and one of the local bad boys—scumbag named Craig Steidle. He's not in trouble—blew double zeros on the breathalyzer. But I thought you'd like to hear about the company he was keeping. I have kids—older now—but I would've liked to have known."

Spinney passed his hand across his forehead and then gave his wife a thumbs-up to set her at ease. "No, that's fine, Sam. I appreciate the call. I'll have a talk with him."

Sam Walker's hesitation showed he wasn't quite finished.

"What else?" Lester asked.

"Well, again, it's nothing connected to Dave. I mean, he was just there. But I found some weed on Steidle and one of the others—a loser named Wayne Fontana—and when I drove up on them at the back of the Zoo, it looked like Steidle was about to score some crack with a user-dealer named Jenny Peters. She does a little hooking on the side." He paused again before adding, "I'm real sorry, Les—"

But Spinney cut him off. "It's fine, Sam. I appreciate it. You did the right thing. Is Dave still there?"

"Yeah. I thought you'd like to pick him up."

"I'll be right down."

Spinney slowly pushed the cut-off button on the portable phone, but kept it about chest-high, as if it now contained something valuable, if ill defined.

"What happened?" Susan asked from the doorway.

He forced a smile. "He's not in trouble, but he is at the PD. Someone in the car he was in was underage and had a beer. Anyway, Sam said it didn't look like he'd had a drop. I'll talk to him."

She frowned and looked at the floor. He could almost smell the guilt coming off her like a scent. Lord knows, in that, she wasn't alone, which prompted him to add, "Tough thing to avoid at his age. Sounds like he stuck to his guns, though. You have your shower. I'll go pick him up. Be back in no time."

She left the room without a word, so that when he rose, Lester Spinney was all alone—with only the misgivings he hadn't shared with her.

Chapter 3

Gail paused on the sidewalk, looking up at the four-story building before her. Wooden, peeling, sagging, and vast, it was one of Brattleboro's infamous dens—an eighty-year-old maze of low-income apartments. A doper's haven, a magnet for illegal activities, and a museum of odd and offensive odors, it was also cheap, downtown, and a short stroll from the town's primary twilight-world hangout, the Harmony parking lot, where the "denizens of the night"—real and imagined—surfaced as each day's light faded to darkness.

Which was why she'd chosen noon to visit her niece's last address. It was late enough to hope a few people might be awake, while early enough that they might not have ventured forth on their daily rounds.

This was a slightly skewed and paranoid vision of reality, of course. For all her canniness and experience—Gail had variously been a Realtor, a select-woman, a volunteer at the women's crisis center, and a prosecutor at the state's attorney's office in town—she was also a woman born to privilege. Despite her support of many and sundry causes aimed at protecting and elevating society's disadvantaged, she wasn't one of them, and had an outsider's visceral lack of ease in their company. She hated this about herself, not surprisingly, seeing it as suppressed prejudice and unworthy of her ideals, but it remained. And it sat like a lump in her throat as she eyed the apartment building's dilapidated front door.

Taking a breath, she left the sidewalk and entered.

Immediately, this internal social debate came under stress. The place was dark, narrow, hot, and evil-smelling. She walked along a close-fitting hallway lined with punctured and torn drywall, stained and covered with graffiti, amid the muted murmurings of a dispossessed populace. There were shouts and arguments, small children's cries, the occasional thrumming of music muffled only by a succession of thin walls. Doors slammed somewhere overhead, footsteps could be heard echoing from afar, and yet she saw no one as she slowed to a stop, uncertain of which way to turn. Encased in an invisible turmoil of stirring humanity, she felt utterly alone.

She looked around, wondering how to proceed. Last night, before falling asleep together at Joe's small converted Green Street carriage house just a block away, the two of them had discussed what must have happened to Laurie. Gail had been furious, her frustration and guilt fueling a rage against almost everyone and everything she could think of, from drug dealers, to lousy prevention in the schools, to society in general. She'd also gotten angry at Joe for what she thought was a fatalistic, even complacent attitude. He'd pointed out that technically, Laurie had been committing a crime here and that there was little the police could have done in any case. They had enough on their plates without trying to discover what had pushed Laurie over the edge. Besides, he'd added, not unsympathetically, it was pretty obvious from her condition what her motives had been.

But Gail hadn't been receptive. She hadn't taken it out on him—she was practical enough to know that from his viewpoint he was right: The police were not in the business of probing some young woman's emotional or psychological problems. But Gail could be. For most of her adult life, she'd made such missions a basic tenet of who she was—a person who really did try to do something for society's semighostly population of the poor, the despairing, and the generally marginalized. And her commitment in this had usually involved total strangers, not her own niece. Guilt notwithstanding, it became clear to her that she'd have to be the one to pursue the cause of Laurie's plight. In the end, steadied by that resolve, she'd calmed down and let Joe get some sleep. And the following morning, she'd set out on her course.

However, now that she was here, she was suddenly at a loss. The apartments had no numbers, there was no directory or bank of mailboxes she could refer to. She began to suspect that the door she'd used hadn't even been the main entrance.

"Who're you?"

She turned to find a young girl peering at her from down the hallway, having appeared as silently as a ghost. She was a solid child, seemingly square and round both, with thick, straight black hair cut like a helmet around her head.

Gail smiled. "Hi. I'm looking for Laurie Davis's apartment. I'm her aunt."

"And you don't know where she lives?" The girl's face was almost stern.

Gail decided to play it straight. "I've never visited her here."

"Smart. This place is a dump."

Gail smiled slightly, caught off guard. "You live here long?"

"Long enough to know that much."

"Good point. You know Laurie?"

"I seen her around. Not to talk to, though. Where're you from?"

"Across town."

The girl nodded. "You look rich."

Gail was stumped for a response. She was rich, certainly relative to anyone here. And while it rarely came up in conversation, her money was a subject of some embarrassment to her. She'd earned a great deal of it, true enough, but she'd also been brought up in its comforts—a fact that had clung to her like a confusing mixed blessing.

Gail changed the subject, feeling disappointed in herself. "Could you take me to her apartment?"

The girl also seemed let down by her response, because she made a small frown, turned on her heel, and merely said, "Sure," before heading off in the opposite direction, quickly taking a right and vanishing from view.

Gail trotted along to catch up, following her small guide along a confusing variety of hallways, staircases, and right and left turns. Despite the time of day, the whole place was somber, but without the coolness associated with what felt like an underground colony. It brought to mind the complex rabbit warren of lore, but one baking in the sun, making Gail wonder if, despite the warm weather, the heat hadn't been left on. The air was stifling and stagnant the higher they climbed. By the time the girl stopped in front of a scarred and splintered hollow-core door, a trickle of sweat was coursing between Gail's shoulder blades and she was feeling slightly dizzy.

"This is it. Have fun," the girl said, and began walking away.

Gail wiped her forehead with her palm. "Wait. How do I get in? Is there a super or a maintenance man or someone with a key?"

The girl looked at her quizzically. "Why don't you knock?"

Gail felt stupid, and out of her depths. A woman who had never hesitated to go anywhere or try anything, who was comfortable pitting her brains and abilities against anyone she met, had now twice been brought up short by a twelve-year-old.

She laughed self-consciously, not bothering to explain. "Right. Stupid. I think I'll try to cool down a little first. Thanks for your help."

The girl eyed her skeptically, let a small but telling pause elapse before saying, "Okay," and then took the hint and disappeared down one of the tunnels she traveled like a veteran miner in search of diversion.

Which left Gail pretty much where she'd been when they'd met, even if she now knew which door was Laurie's.

She looked down at the scuffed wooden floor a moment, thinking again about why she was here. She'd told her sister on the phone it was to collect a few of Laurie's things, if only to have something familiar to put by her hospital bed. But the true reason stemmed from her conversation with Joe. Gail wanted to search the apartment, to find something explaining Laurie's descent, maybe even some compelling evidence she could bring to Joe. Gail wanted to set things right and ease her feeling of impotence with some action, all while knowing in her heart that she was basically running in place—right now literally working up a sweat for nothing.

She glanced at the door again, considering how unlikely it would be that this building had a maintenance man standing ready with a passkey. Yielding to impulse, she reached out and twisted the knob.

The door opened.

Surprised, Gail stepped inside. The room was small, square, fetid, and a total, absolute, war-torn pigsty.

In its middle stood a man. Staring at her.

"What do you want?" he demanded.

He was skinny, longhaired, and unshaven, wearing a dirty T-shirt and jeans. Both his arms had tattoos and his gaunt face looked mean.

Gail had been raped years before in what she'd thought was the safety of her own home. She had worked hard to place that experience out of her way if never out of her mind, but now it came back like the release from a dam, in a hot and sickening tidal wave.

"I . . . ," she stammered. "Who are you?"

He took a step toward her. In his hand, he held a small canvas bag. "None of your fucking business."

She suddenly wondered if she hadn't made a terrible mistake—had in fact just walked into this man's home. She looked around in confusion. "I'm sorry. I thought this was Laurie Davis's apartment. A small girl led me here. I just assumed . . ." Then she saw a framed photograph, leaning against the wall, of herself, Laurie, and Laurie's mother, linked arm in arm in happier days, laughing at the camera.

The sight of it cleared her head enough that she recognized other signs that this was a woman's bedroom.

"Tell me who you are or I'll call the police," she said more forcefully.

But he'd recognized the earlier fear, an expression he was apparently well acquainted with. He stepped up close to her, smiling, his eyes narrow and menacing. She could smell his breath when he spoke.

"I'm not gonna tell you shit, and you're not gonna call nobody."

"You're trespassing," she countered, hating the tremble in her voice.

He laughed. "And you're not?"

"No, I'm not. I'm family."

Their bodies were almost touching. She felt like a rope under tremendous strain, as if the slightest touch would be enough to make it burst apart.

But the man was as careful as he was threatening. He sidestepped around her and paused at the doorway. "I wouldn't brag about that, if I were you," he said, and disappeared.

Gail closed the door, locked it, leaned her back against its flimsy surface, and shut her eyes tight, fighting for calm.

Over a hundred miles away, Joe Gunther sat in a small conference room in the Department of Public Safety's headquarters in Waterbury, Vermont, part of a large complex of old institutional brick buildings, the centerpiece of which had once been the sprawling state mental hospital—an association detractors still used with high humor.

The room was dark, dominated by a photographic slide that stuck to the far wall like a luminescent painting. It was the picture of a man hanging by his neck from a bridge, suspended like a sack of clothes over a tangle of gleaming railroad tracks.

"This was taken in Rutland this morning—the River

Street Bridge," said a voice in the darkness. "The victim's name is James Hollowell, and the Rutland drug unit's ID'd him as a local street dealer, mostly crack and heroin."

"Any leads on who killed him?" Gunther asked.

The voice belonged to Bill Allard, Gunther's immediate boss and the chief of the Vermont Bureau of Investigation. A career state trooper, he'd been tapped to head the VBI because of his people skills, his experience, and the fact that the Vermont State Police, housed just one floor below in this same building, hated the idea of the VBI—the brainchild of the current governor and a perceived threat to the VSP's preeminence in state law enforcement. It had been the commissioner of Public Safety's hope that appointing someone with Bill Allard's heritage and qualifications would soften the blow to his erstwhile agency's ego.

But the jury was still out.

Allard turned on a small light by his side to consult some notes. "Not specifically, but things have been brewing in Rutland long enough that this was basically waiting to happen."

Gunther thought back to last evening in Brattleboro, when Ron Klesczewski had said roughly the same thing about the storekeeper shooting Laurie Davis.

"A power struggle?" he asked.

"Nothing so clear-cut," Allard responded, hitting the key on his portable computer to bring up another slide of the same scene. "But the drug unit says things like this do happen, where a dealer tries screwing his supplier out of some product and gets reprimanded."

"I'd say that's being reprimanded," Gunther murmured, but he was beginning to wonder why he'd been asked up here. Dangling bodies from bridges was pretty exotic for Vermont, whose homicide rate usually hovered in or around single digits for a given year, but still, callously speaking, it did look like some lowlifes had merely done in one of their own.

"They must have some ideas," he suggested, extending his private musing.

"They have ideas, all right. Problem is, those ideas cross state lines."

"Holyoke?" Gunther asked. Holyoke, Massachusetts, had been a source of Vermont-bound drugs for several years, and he'd heard from the number crunchers that statistically Rutland had become a primary terminus, which was odd, given both its geographical isolation and its relatively small size when compared to Burlington. But the pipeline was undeniable and well known: Holyoke, Brattleboro, Rutland, with many small stops along the way.

As a result, Allard wasn't surprised by his insight. "Apparently, it's more than the usual scuttlebutt. Doesn't sound like much to me, but there's intel indicating someone's trying to organize the traffic way beyond its current level, which is pretty wide open. And I guess hanging someone from a bridge could qualify as a billboard advertisement. No one's tied it to Holyoke, of course, or to the Hollowell hanging, either, but that's the word from the street."

"Is the Rutland PD having problems handling this?" Gunther asked diplomatically. The commissioner and the governor notwithstanding, both Allard and Gunther saw the VBI as primarily a support service—a major-crimes team brought in only when invited by the local law. The two politicians, naturally enough, had far grander visions of some look-alike, state-level FBI, but the two old cops knew the value of observing turf: You got ahead by getting along, and in the short, two-year history of their new agency, that philosophy had paid off handsomely. Even the state police were unofficially muttering that the VBI was courteous, competent, well manned, and so far, not headline hogs. Rumor had it that Governor Reynolds was most irritated by this self-effacement, which privately pleased Gunther very much.

And which therefore made Allard's response all the more disappointing.

"The PD's fine. It's Reynolds who's having a cow."

"Why?"

Allard hit the key on his computer again. This time the picture was of the inside of a dingy motel room and of a young girl's corpse lying on its side across a rumpled bed, a tourniquet around her arm and a needle on the floor near her dangling fingertips.

"Because of her. She's Sharon Lapierre, or was—granddaughter of Roger Lapierre, former Rutland Town selectman and party bigwig, who's also raised a pile of cash for Reynolds."

He stopped there, letting silence fill in the obvious.

"Ah," Gunther finally conceded, feeling suddenly tired. So much politics in this job—dealing with the public, the press, the municipal managers, and the statehouse folks, and with every fellow police agency in each and every investigation. This, however, was going to be above and beyond the usual. Jim Reynolds was running for reelection, as governors did every two years in this state, and he was facing a tough race. Through inference alone, Gunther already guessed the waters he was going to be asked to enter.

"He wants the VBI, his pet creation, to put things right," he suggested, "with appropriate press coverage."

Allard smiled humorlessly. "You're good. That's almost a direct quote. So far, the media's been so excited by the hanging that they haven't picked up on Sharon's death yet—we're sitting on it pretty tight—but it's not just about Miss Lapierre in any case. That would be too obvious, even for Reynolds. He's about to release a press statement saying the VBI will be tasked as of this week with eliminating the trafficking of heroin into the state of Vermont, so that he looks like he's doing more than just reacting to a pal's personal loss."

Gunther let out a short laugh. "God, I hope he didn't invoke the 'war' on drugs too. That would be way old news." He pointed at the picture on the wall. "I suppose it goes without saying that she died of a heroin overdose."

"That's what it looks like. And the motel room was booked to James Hollowell."

That, Gunther found interesting, his brain instantly weighing what he'd heard so far about politicians, high-profit drugs, and the inkling of an organization making a grab for the local market. "No kidding? What's the story there?"

Allard leaned back in his chair and hit the lights, causing them both to blink in the sudden glare. "That's one of the things you're supposed to find out," he said.

Gunther made a face, despite his curiosity. "Rutland's not only got a good police department, but they share a building with an equally qualified sheriff. Not to mention that there's a state police barracks in town and an FBI substation. And isn't the Southern Vermont Drug Task Force already quote-unquote tasked with handling heroin traffic? Seems like all that would make our showing up a little redundant—at best. My guess is the reception would be frigid, and I'm not sure I'd fault any of them."

Allard shifted in his chair. "This isn't a debate, Joe. It's a done deal. I put in my two cents from the start, but basically we're screwed."

"You know we're about to flush two years' worth of good PR down the drain."

They both stared at the pale ghost of the slide that Allard hadn't yet extinguished.

"You said the governor was about to issue his statement," Gunther finally said, the company man not just yielding to the inevitable but transforming it instead into a challenge to be met. "How much time do we have?"

"Three days, maybe a little more. He's knee-deep in prior campaign commitments right now, he wants to be brought up to speed before he talks to the media, and like I said, he wants some time to elapse between her death and his announcement. So, we've got a little breathing room. But he is hot to trot and he's been known to shoot his mouth off prematurely. Plus, we don't know what'll happen when the press discovers Sharon. Why do you ask?"

Gunther drummed the tabletop with his fingertips. "Because the only way we can get this to work is if we lock something in before he makes it official. If by the time of the announcement we're seen by the other agencies as having something tangible to bring to the table, then we *might* be treated as something more than an uninvited guest. Right now both the Rutland PD drug unit and the task force have legitimate claim, a track record of working together and solid, preexisting intelligence sources. We'll need something to top all that, or we'll end up looking like the weird political creation we've worked so hard not to be. I'm not so worried about the other cops—they'll just ignore us if they want. It's the governor's opponents that could put the limelight on us. After all the effort we've put into this organization, I'd hate for us to be treated like a po-litical football. Our people deserve better than that. And they should expect us to watch their backs."

Bill Allard looked a little taken aback by his vehe-mence. "I don't argue with you, Joe. But what can you do?"

Gunther stood up. "Scramble. And you can help. Get the governor to keep his mouth shut till I give the thumbs-up. Tell him he'll be sinking us before we leave shore and making himself look like a jerk otherwise. And make sure that when the time does come, he does two crucial things: One, he doesn't single us out like he's planning to. He can identify us at that press conference, but only in a laundry list that includes Rutland and the state police and whoever else I can think of by then. And two, he cannot say we or anyone else are going to stop heroin from coming into the state. If he does, he'll lose the election, and I'll be happy to explain to the media why. If he has to say something bombastic, have him stick to Rutland itself—as in 'a major effort will be made to curb the import of heroin there' . . . or something like that."

Bill Allard nodded once. "I'll do what I can."

Chapter 4

Dick Allen lived outside Chester, Vermont, not far from the state police barracks he'd commanded toward the end of his career. A man of legendary stature within the law enforcement community, he'd gained much of his fame through his ability to get along with almost anyone, from the hardened criminals he routinely got to confess, to nitpicking statehouse committee members hoping to tighten his agency's purse strings. As he climbed through the ranks, always shunning desk jobs for field commands, he'd nevertheless been called on by the brass to represent the state police far and wide, garnering respect wherever he went. During his last five years on the job, his reputation had finally so evolved that when a reporter once referred to him jokingly as "Gandhi Allen," no one had thought it a stretch.

And as if to prove the point, as soon as he'd hit his maximum benefits level, Dick Allen had retired without fanfare or fuss—just another warhorse quietly going out to pasture, according to him.

Except that he hadn't severed any of his old ties. Ten years away from the job, he was as influential now as he'd ever been, keeping in touch, lending advice, helping out from behind the scenes—and discreetly wielding influence with the subtlety of an old Mafia don pretending to care only for his garden.

As soon as Joe was briefed by Bill Allard, he knew his first stop had better be Dick Allen.

Another aspect of Allen's fame was as a tinkerer. He built things, repaired things, took things home from the dump for mysterious and dimly defined future uses. When he'd been on the job, fellow officers had gone to great lengths not to tell him their computers or desk chairs or cars had fallen ill. It wasn't that he couldn't repair these objects, but he followed his own timetable, which could sometimes cover quite a period. And, of course, nobody had the heart to refuse him if he did offer his services. He was that highly regarded.

This habit, however, did make his house easy to separate from its neighbors. Located on a dirt road near the tiny village of Cambridgeport, in Rockingham Township, Dick Allen's residence came after a series of nondescript ranch-styles, tucked demurely among the trees and rolling hills that defined the general neighborhood. But his home was huge, made of logs, with a rusting metal roof, and was clearly the project that would never reach completion. Allen and his family had lived there for over twenty years, and it still looked as though the building contractor had just left for lunch. Tools, machinery, and hard-to-define equipment were scattered about the lawn and dooryard, and a half-built scaffold reached ineffectively up one exterior wall, groping toward a huge hole on the second floor that aspired to be a picture window. There was a partially finished deck off to one side, several cars with their hoods up and their engines clutched by tendrils of weeds, and what looked to be an incomplete aboveground pool standing in the back lawn like a wooden boat that had been dropped from a crane with disastrous results.

This was a tinkerer's Valhalla, and from what Joe had heard, Dick Allen only left the place to fetch more supplies and to catch up with friends at the barracks nearby, where he kept current with the latest news.

He came out to the car as Gunther killed the engine, one hand available for a shake, the other predictably filled with a small electric motor.

"Joe, good to see you. I can't believe it's been so long. Not since you jumped ship to become a junior fed."

Gunther laughed. "Ouch—double-damned. I doubt the feds like us any more than the locals."

Allen was leading him toward a large picnic table set up near one of the disemboweled cars under a huge shady maple tree. "That's not what I'm hearing," he said. "Not across the board, anyway. I think you're winning hearts and minds." He added with a smile, "If maybe only one at a time."

They sat opposite one another, and Allen placed the

small motor between them like a talisman, explaining as he did, "Jeanie's blender. Thought I'd take a look at it before she threw it out."

"She know that, or did you get it out of the garbage?"

Dick Allen looked hurt. "Busted. So, what's the number two man of the VBI doing way out here on a workday?"

"Looking for advice," Gunther admitted. "Maybe some help. You hear the news about the guy they found hanging from that bridge in Rutland?"

"James Hollowell? Yup. I'm impressed you've kept the lid on Sharon Lapierre this long, though. Pretty devious."

Gunther accepted this small show of bravura. Allen was establishing that he was still within the loop.

"It's not us. That's Rutland PD's doing. Didn't take you long to hear about it, though."

Allen shrugged. "Some people thought I'd find it interesting. I do, too. Is your bureau involved?"

"Not yet, but Reynolds is about to make a statement that'll throw us right into the middle."

"Without an invitation?"

"Would you have asked us in?"

Allen thought about that for a moment. "Maybe, depending on what you had to offer and on how tough the case looked. I don't have the details on this one yet—only the rumor mill headlines. But to be honest, that's just old broad-minded me. I think you're right, otherwise—there's still too much pride out there to ask for help from the likes of you guys, especially early on.

Which I guess means you're about to land on a bunch of toes."

Gunther appreciated his old friend's canniness. It spared him having to be subtle about the truth. "I hate this, Dick. Our charter says we can initiate investigations, but this doesn't even qualify. It's flat-out party crashing and I can only see it coming back at us. I was telling Allard the only way I see getting any cover is if we're somehow seen as an asset, like you said. What *have* you heard about this case?"

"That Hollowell didn't commit suicide, that he was probably murdered where they found Sharon Lapierre, and that whoever snuffed the one probably did in the other. Nobody's told you this yet?"

"I haven't asked. I didn't want to be seen sniffing around. They're saying Lapierre was overdosed by force? How was Hollowell killed?"

"He was whacked on the head. And despite the deal with the tourniquet and the syringe, Lapierre didn't even have a fresh needle mark, so they probably killed her some other way, too."

Gunther was surprised, given what Bill Allard had told him about the girl. So much for Allen having heard only rumors. "Both the hanging and the overdose were staged? Why?"

"Beats me. I guess I should say beats them, since I'm just a fly on the wall and forensics is still doing their thing. But a wild guess would be to make a statement to someone who understands the body language, so to speak."

"And who's making the statement?" Gunther asked.

Allen picked up the motor and spun the central shaft between his fingertips, as if he were launching a whirligig. "That, I haven't heard. Don't think they've dug that deep yet. Does sound like someone rippling his muscles to make an impression, though, which isn't the norm for either the place or the drug trade in general, at least the way it's usually practiced up here."

"I was told there were underground rumblings that the Rutland scene might be getting organized. You think that connects to Holyoke somehow?"

Allen pressed his lips together thoughtfully. "I heard there's been an increase in traffic, and certainly Holyoke's the number one supplier, next to Hudson Falls, New York. Plus, the police chief down there is putting on a serious squeeze, trying to push the drug business out of his jurisdiction. He was quoted the other day as saying, 'I don't care what city they go to as long as it isn't Holyoke.' So, maybe somebody is getting something going. I've always wondered why no one's thought of that before. All these losers driving into Vermont to quadruple their money just so they can put the profit up their nose. It would seem that anyone with any sense would see the advantage of keeping clean and getting rich, fire-breathing police chief or not. It's a no-brainer."

"But you haven't actually heard they're doing that," Gunther stated.

"Nope. Does raise an interesting angle, though. One that could play to your advantage—and to the boys who don't think you're worth much right now. The Southern Vermont Drug Task Force is people-poor and overworked at the moment. They communicate well with the Holyoke PD, but basically they're country cousins begging for favors—they don't have anyone on the ground working solely for them. Your outfit would be a real asset there, especially if you're right about a Holyoke link. In a lot of these things, where the same people have been working the same problem forever, sometimes the addition of one small advantage can make the difference. Even with their prejudice, the task force will value that. Could be key, if you mind your manners."

Joe mulled that over, weighing the possibilities. "It would give us something to trade, and I already asked Allard to tell the governor not to single us out when he makes his announcement so we don't come off as a bunch of gold diggers."

"Extra money wouldn't hurt, speaking of that," Dick Allen suggested. "Coming in bearing gifts is always a safe bet." Allen smiled and shook his head. "Jesus, I can't believe I'm helping you do this."

"Why are you?"

He thought about that for a moment. "Because it's time. The majority of your guys used to work for us. They moved over because there was a chance for advancement and experience. Maybe they were right and maybe not, but it would be nice if they got a shot at it. Don't get me wrong, I still think the Vermont State Police is the best we have, and I was pretty unhappy when the VBI showed up. But the VSP can be a little hidebound and frustrating, and sometimes gets a little full of itself. And, hell, you know? Nothing lasts forever—

even New Hampshire's Old Man of the Mountain finally fell off his perch—and I've seen the benefits for other states that went with an investigation bureau. Could be we're due for a change, whether we like it or not."

"That's pretty generous, Dick."

Allen tilted his head and turned devil's advocate. "Okay, but it's from a dog with no teeth. You might want to consider that handing out money like a miserly rich uncle could backfire in the winning-friends department."

Gunther shook his head with frustration. "I know it. I just don't know what else to do. I don't want us to be the ones bringing gifts to the party just to be shut out right after we sit down. We'll earn whatever respect we get, but we have to be able to participate."

Allen straightened slightly and gave Gunther an appraising look. "You said at the top that you wanted advice and maybe some help. I take it this is the help part. You want me to put in a good word?"

Gunther leaned forward, placing both hands flat on the table before him. "Dick, we've known each other a long time, worked cases together. I'm asking you to do whatever you think is right. Of all the people who've been watching the VBI, I figure you're one of the few who really understand what we're trying to do. Sure as hell, when I think back to past conversations, you and I were pretty consistent about how we would all benefit from a lot less rivalry."

But Allen already had both hands up in mock surrender. "I hear you, Joe. Keep in mind, though, that my influence has been greatly exaggerated and barely exists among the younger generation." He got to his feet as Gunther was doing, and took up the small motor in the palm of his hand—a man only truly at ease when holding something mechanical.

They walked together toward Joe's car as Dick Allen added, "But I will keep an eye out and do what I can."

That couldn't hurt, Joe thought as he drove back down the dirt road. He didn't underestimate for a moment the true value of Allen's influence. What rankled him still, however, was that he was having to do this in the first place. As valuable as he truly believed his agency to be, he hated that it was being treated as a political pawn, and imperiled in the process.

His longing for credibility wasn't just so others would see the VBI as something of value. It was also so that its members could be awarded the respect they'd worked so hard to acquire.

In this world of self-interest at the cost of almost everything else, where the invocation of the "good old days" was too often a veil to hide inefficiency and blind chauvinism, this debate about creating a better law enforcement model had become an issue with Joe—something he hoped he could see taking root by the time he retired.

Except that like an aging knight of some idealized but mythological Round Table, he was growing both wary and weary of the ceaseless assaults of closeminded and manipulative selfishness.

*   *   *

Back in Springfield, on Summer Street, Lester Spinney gently closed the door to his car, as he did on surveillance when he didn't want to attract attention. Except that this time he was in his own garage, in the middle of the afternoon.

He walked through the door connecting the garage to the kitchen and stood there for a while, listening. Susan was at work, Dave at his part-time summer job, Wendy was spending a couple of days at a friend's house in Chester. The house was totally empty. It suddenly occurred to him that he might never have experienced this before—being the only one here. When they'd bought the place ten years ago, they were already a family, and despite some routine comments from him about never having a moment alone, he had never seriously pursued it. Now that he had, and without telling a soul, it made him feel devious and underhanded.

He'd taken a detour from work, driving from a court appearance in White River back to Brattleboro, taking advantage of the opportunity to do something he hated to do.

Slowly, walking so his heels didn't strike the floor with any sound, Lester left the kitchen, crossed the living room, and headed toward the staircase leading upstairs. He imagined this was what it felt like to burgle someone's house, being attuned to every sound, and especially to the off chance that somebody might walk in. The fact that he knew every inch of the place, however, and could connect a dozen memories to every item in it tainted the fantasy and only increased his discomfort.

He climbed the stairs to the second floor and turned left, passing by Wendy's open door on his way to the end of the hall. He paused to glance in on her bedroom, as he'd done so often following a late night assignment when he'd missed dinner yet again—not to check on her so much as to simply listen to her breathing and take solace in her peacefulness, her barely discernible shape just visible under the covers in the night light's feeble glow.

This time the room appeared oddly disarrayed, missing its crucial element, its dolls, books, clothes, and posters merely support players on an otherwise empty stage. As with the house, Lester realized he'd never seen this room looking so utterly abandoned.

He continued to the end of the hall and the closed door barring his progress. It was covered with bumper stickers and pictures cut from snowboarding and car magazines, along with a No Trespassing sign to which the owner had added in red letters, "This means you."

This was David's room, where the door was always closed. Lester took the knob in his hand, twisted it, and pushed the door back on its hinges.

He hesitated at the threshold, as he might at the edge of a cliff, before stepping inside—a cop about to conduct an illegal search. A father about to start wrestling with an obsession.

Sammie Martens looked up from her desk as Gail Zigman entered the office. "Hey, you looking for Joe? He's not here. Sorry."

Gail opened her mouth to respond when the phone rang. Sam held up an index finger in apology before answering it and launching into an arcane procedural discussion Gail paid no attention to. Instead, she wandered around the small office like a visitor to an office-life exhibition.

In fact, she was a semiregular here, to the point where Judy, the secretary in the tiny entryway they all pretended was a reception area, knew to let her through whenever she dropped by.

She enjoyed this office. Unlike most such places, with divider panels, cramped work nooks, a kitchenette, an interview room, this was all there was: four walls, four desks, the usual paperwork decorating the walls, and some standard office equipment. Bare bones. Joe's desk was no different in style from that of the newest member, Lester Spinney, who had come to VBI via the state police and AG's office, instead of the police department downstairs, as had the other three. It was, she thought, the way an investigative squad should be laid out, and probably a good many other offices as well—fewer places to hide or provide opportunities for envy and resentment.

Of course, she knew that none of this had been by choice. For the VBI, it was purely a matter of economics. Most cops saw this kind of arrangement as mostly a pain in the ass. Cops like their privacy, which is why, when they are forced to set things up in this fashion, they usually place their desks so they don't face one another.

Here each occupant sat in a corner, looking out,

which struck Gail as interesting for its implied double message—they did face each other this way, true enough, but only from behind a barrier. It seemed a perfect encapsulation of the sometimes contrary emotions that made a good unit work.

Waiting for Sam to get off the phone, Gail reflected on how each desk spoke of its occupant: Sammie Martens, hers a frantically arranged landing zone for reports, directories, forms, faxes, notebooks, scattered pens and pencils, and a computer that looked threatened by it all; Lester Spinney, his desk supporting some official detritus, but mostly dominated by family photos, children's drawings, an NFL coffee mug, and a scrawny winged animal hanging from the ceiling with a sign around its neck labeling it the Spinneybird, a credit to its owner's cranelike physique; and Gail's own Joe Gunther, the one she knew best, his desk almost bare—one closed file folder, a worn pad used for taking notes while on the phone, a mug from her full of pens, a rarely used computer, and an assortment of odds and ends lined up like mystic icons. Among these latter were a smooth and weathered metal tapping spout used for maple-sugaring, a memory of his late father; a matchbox car from the fifties, the era from which his brother collected cars for real; and a uniform button from Joe's time in combat—a memento as simple in appearance as it was complex in meaning.

That accounted for three of the four desks. The last one was in the far corner, away from the door and the single row of windows, placed catty-corner so its owner could watch all aspects of the room, even though it made reaching the chair difficult. Its surface was littered with catalogs and magazines, some clearly unread paperwork. It was messy in appearance and looked neglected overall, as if its owner didn't visit often and, when he did, didn't attend to office work. That much was certainly true, since it belonged to Willy Kunkle, the one member of Gunther's team Gail could barely tolerate. To her, Kunkle represented all that was bad about law enforcement. She thought him an insensitive, prejudiced bully, quick to condemn, impossible to debate, and flat out rude to boot. A boor, in the fullest meaning of the word.

And he was there because Joe had all but moved the earth to get him there, seeing qualities in the man Gail had never glimpsed. The fact that he was also Sammie Martens's boyfriend—which to Gail ranked among the craziest of notions—did make, she conceded, for a typically human contrariness she couldn't help but applaud.

She was still staring at Willy's desk when Sam's voice asked from behind her, "You okay?"

She turned and sat on the edge of Joe's desk. "No," she admitted. "I just came from Laurie Davis's apartment. There was a strange man there."

Sam stared at her blankly for a moment. "Right," she finally said, "the shooting from last night. Sorry. It's not our case, so I guess I zoned out. What were you doing there?"

"She's my niece."

Sam's brows furrowed. "Ouch. Too bad."

Gail stared at her. No "I'm sorry to hear it" or "Gee,

tough break." That was it: "Too bad." It was the kind of reaction Gail imagined Sam had worked long and hard to make instinctive—a tough guy's response. One of the boys.

And yet she knew Sam wasn't one of the boys. Through her own observations and from what Joe had told her, Gail saw Sammie Martens as very much a self-made woman: From a lousy childhood, to some tough military training where she'd volunteered and succeeded at everything she'd tried, to a street cop who'd made detective in record time, and now to the VBI, she'd made it a point to make sure no one regretted passing her up the ladder.

And, of course, she'd paid the price.

Gail knew Sam wasn't as hard-bitten as she pretended. She knew about the string of loser boyfriends, the loft she called home that was full of exercise equipment and cop training manuals. She also knew there were times when Sam came to Joe for comfort and solace, responding to what Gail suspected was a commingling of father image and hero worship.

But just as Gail could see Sam in the almost dreary, black and white light she'd chosen for herself, she could also see the younger woman in more complex terms—as someone almost to envy on one level and to pity on another. In limbo. And painfully aware of it.

"Did the man do anything to you?"

Gail blinked at the question, still lost in her musings. "No. It was all implied—the way he looked at me, the way he stood too close just before he left."

"You get a name?"

Gail again thought of Sam's lack of spontaneous warmth. Not "How horrible" or "I hate it when they do that."

She shook her head instead of answering.

"But you knew he wasn't supposed to be there."

It wasn't a question, nor was it an accusation. It merely hovered between the two, challenging Gail to go into more detail. She began wondering if this conversation was such a great idea, coming straight on the heels of an encounter that had stirred a repressed nightmare. She worried she was reading too much into everything now.

She looked at Sam a little haplessly. "I know it sounds stupid. I hadn't seen my niece in a long time. But to find out she's been shot, is an addict, lives in poverty, and tried to rob a place at knifepoint. It's a little much, I guess. I suppose you're right. The guy was probably just someone living down the hallway." She laughed uncertainly. "Came by to borrow a cup of sugar, right?"

Sam's professionally neutral expression changed. She shook her head slightly, as if confused, and then motioned to the guest chair between the two desks. "Have a seat, Gail. I didn't say this guy was legit. I wanted to know if we could nail him with anything. What did he look like?"

Gail took the chair and gave the best description she could, feeling a resurgence of the fears that had gripped her at the time. As she recited his features and Sam took notes, Gail became sensitive to an odd but familiar mix of emotions building within her, not the least of which were anger and resentment that she'd been put in this position once again.

She'd almost lost her bearings at the time of her rape, her brain twisting away from her bruised body, her mind going on journeys of its own, far from her friends and the events unfolding around her. She'd worked goddamned hard to get it all back and to rebuild a life loosely based on what had predated it.

As she spoke to Sam, she saw not only the man she'd just met—and the ghost he represented—but the circumstances that had led her to him: her niece, what she must have gone through before trying to rob that store, the fact that she'd had no one to turn to, as Gail had had in her time of need.

By the end of her recitation, after Sam had said, "I'll get this downstairs to the boys in blue. They'll probably know this jerk right off. We'll get him for you," Gail found she was barely listening.

She got to her feet. Despite Sam's reassurances, Gail now felt remote from this conversation. The news of Laurie being shot, Joe's fatalism about it, the man at the apartment, the very details she'd cataloged entering this office, had all intertwined to cut her loose from the logical, reasonable world she usually inhabited with ease and comfort. With Sam's words barely an echo in her ears, she moved toward the exit feeling alone and distracted, in dire need of a course of action.

And utterly responsible for doing something on Laurie's behalf.

Chapter 5

Joe Gunther sat on the windowsill and hitched a leg up, wedging his foot against one frame and his back against the other. The VBI office was on the second floor of Brattleboro's old Municipal Building, once a high school and built in the 1800s. It looked pretty ugly from the outside, had lousy heating and cooling, was poorly laid out and crammed with people, but its windows were huge, could be opened, as this one was now, and had really comfortable sills for taking in the summer sun.

It was late in the afternoon. There was a unit meeting planned for half an hour from now, but for the moment, the office was empty. Joe knew that Sammie Martens was downstairs consulting with the PD and would be back momentarily, but that didn't diminish his pleasure at having the place to himself, even if briefly.

Joe was a loner by instinct. Married once as a young

man, widowed not too many years afterward, and left without children, he'd gone through a long period getting used to a life alone before meeting Gail at a political function. At the time—and often to this day—people thought them an odd match. He an old-fashioned, lifelong cop, born on a farm some sixty miles farther north up the Connecticut River, and she a New York–born, hypereducated rich liberal. But they had their common ground. Both were independent, hardworking, committed to their jobs or causes, and armed with a strong sense of right and wrong.

And both seemed to need as much time apart as time together.

He'd wondered about this once, even fretted a little in the early days, thinking of the unlikeliness that two halves of a couple could actually share this particular trait for more than a few months. But he didn't worry about it anymore. They'd gone through so much by now, including living together briefly following her rape, that they'd found a comfortable niche they could share, despite it being both unconventional and perhaps inexplicable even to themselves. All that counted was that it worked.

As if the topic had been visibly hanging in the air, Sam walked into the office as Joe was musing along these lines, and announced, "Gail dropped by a while ago." She crossed to her desk, rummaged around its paper snowbank for a couple of seconds, and extracted a single sheet, which she then consulted. "Said she'd gone to her niece's apartment and bumped into a guy the Bratt PD's since identified as Roger Novelle—local bad boy specializing in crack and heroin, both the using and selling of same."

She tossed the piece of paper back onto the pile and sat in her chair. "Nothing happened between them, by the way. He was just there when she opened the door. He probably did a lick-his-eyebrows number to impress her with what a ladies' man he is, which I think freaked her out a little, but other than that, nothing."

Joe had no trouble imagining what aspect of the encounter had freaked her out. If Gail hadn't suffered a flashback meeting such a guy in such a setting, she couldn't have been considered normal.

"Was she okay?" he asked.

"Yeah. A little distraught. No surprise. I never did get what she was doing there. I'd say collecting some personal effects if I didn't know the girl was in a coma."

"I don't think that matters," Joe said. "Gail tries to think the best of things. She'd want Laurie to have something of her own near her bed. You know if she went home? I ought to call her."

"No clue," Sam answered. "I did ask them downstairs to pick the guy up on an illegal entry charge if they could, though. I thought you might like a chat."

Joe swung off his perch and reached for the phone. "Thanks." He dialed Gail's number, reached the answering machine, and said, "Hi. I just heard what happened at Laurie's from Sam. Hope you're okay. Give me a call when you get this."

He hung up the receiver and glanced at Sam, who was still watching him. "Did she say what Novelle was doing?"

Sam shook her head, admitting, "It wasn't a super-straightforward conversation. Like I said, she was a little out of it. She didn't mention anything, though, so I guessed maybe he was just there."

"Probably retrieving some goods for resale," Joe mused. He checked his watch. "The others are about to arrive, but I wanted to ask you something first. When you were undercover at Tucker Peak last winter, chasing that drug dealer, did you ever pick up on any Holyoke connections?"

She turned to her computer and began punching keys as she spoke. "Yeah. I don't remember names since that's not where we ended up, but I did have a conversation where . . ." She paused to concentrate. "I wrote it down just in case . . . Here we go. Miguel Torres. I was told he was the go-to man if I wanted primo stuff."

"Coke or heroin?"

"Everything, from what it sounded like."

"Is your source still available?"

"The guy who told me about Torres? I guess so." She switched to another program and ran a check. He watched her wandering through the machine's brain with casual expertise, amazed at how easy she made it look. She finally sat back. "He's not dead or in jail, so I suppose he's still operating."

"What's his name?"

"Bill Dancer. He was very hot to get me in the sack. Funny how the attraction wasn't mutual." She smiled crookedly. "God knows why not, though, given my luck. Why all the questions?"

"The governor . . . ," Gunther began, but was interrupted by Lester Spinney entering the office. Spinney was routinely so cheerful, his glum expression caused them both to stare at him.

"You all right?" Gunther asked. "You look a little down."

Spinney tiredly dropped the book bag he favored over a briefcase onto his desk and slumped into his chair. "White River was a pain in the ass."

"It go okay, though? It was just a deposition, right?"

Lester waved his hand dismissively, regretting he hadn't better disguised his feelings. "Right. No problem. Guess it's just that time of the month."

Sam threw a pencil at him.

"Sexual harassment," came a voice from the door. "Call a lawyer."

Willy Kunkle crossed to his desk, squeezed between it and the wall, and wedged himself into his chair, looking, as Gail had noted earlier, ready to hold off hostile headhunters. His useless left arm, its hand as usual tucked into his pants pocket so it wouldn't flop around, seemed uncomfortably pinched between his body and the arm of the chair, but Willy didn't notice or care. The result of a sniper bullet years earlier, the incapacitated arm was more an extension of his attitude than a part of his body—and was routinely used by its owner to throw people off.

"Very short briefing today," Gunther announced as soon as Willy settled in. "But it is a heads-up. I guess everyone's heard about the hanging in Rutland?"

"Nice of the scumbags to police their own garbage," Willy commented.

"Maybe," Joe continued, never one to let Willy derail the proceedings, "but it looks like we'll have to chip in as well. The governor will soon be announcing that in an effort to stop the flow of heroin into Vermont, the VBI will be called to the trenches."

"As what?" Willy demanded. "I thought your big deal was for us to play backup to everybody, including the village constable."

"Let the man talk," Sam said wearily.

Joe nodded in his direction. "No, he's right. Crude, but right on target. This is going to happen mostly because there's a second drug-related death that hasn't made the news yet, involving a relative of one of Reynolds's key backers. Our biggest job, however, will be to find a way not to look like the governor's flunkies."

"Nice try," Willy grumbled. "It's what we are."

"Not if we deliver something the others don't have. Then his choice looks reasonable and we maintain credibility."

"How do we do that?" Sam asked. "The Southern Vermont Drug Task Force has years more experience than we do."

"I'm working on that. They are strapped for help right now, Allard is maneuvering to give us exclusive access to extra money, I got Dick Allen weighing in with his old buddies on our behalf, and I'm hoping for one extra piece of leverage, which is to get in on some of the action at the source."

"In Holyoke," Sam suggested, bringing their earlier conversation to bear.

"Right. The task force will probably have to commit

more time than they'd like on this Rutland double homicide. If we can build up something fast with a Holyoke
connection, it might make us more useful, not to mention more acceptable. 'Cause don't get me wrong here: I
don't just want to look good. We need to be a real asset."

"Why Holyoke?" Kunkle asked. "We've known
about them for years."

"True," Gunther told him, "but while most of
Rutland's drugs have been and are still coming from
there, there's now a very vague rumor that someone in
Holyoke may be organizing how things are being done."

"Shit—that was bound to happen."

"What's the plan, then?" Sam asked.

Joe glanced over at Lester Spinney, usually a much
more involved member of the general conversation. So
far, he'd done no more than distractedly poke at the
small framed family photos on his desk with the end of
a pencil.

"Homework," Gunther said. "I've already got Sam
started. If you all coordinate with her, dig into your personal files, have talks with your informants, and see
whatever you can come up with that has anything to do
with Holyoke, that would help. I've typed up what I got
from Allard about the Rutland deaths and will print it out
after this—it has dates, names, and details that might be
helpful. If you have any ongoing cases that can be put on
the back burner for the next couple of days, put them
there. This gets top priority for now. And it's basically a
no-lose deal for us—if we do tumble to an organizer, so
much the better, but given that the trade originates in

Holyoke regardless, any foothold we gain on the inside will have merit. Problems?"

The general silence spoke for itself. As unpleasant as was the way they were being brought in, the mere scent of a major case was an adrenaline rush for these cops. Joe was sanguine they'd get results.

But he did have one last question of his own. "Willy, you're the expert on local lowlifes. Ever hear of Roger Novelle?"

Sam looked at her boss sharply as Willy answered, "Sure. Real scuzzball. Looking at habitual offender status next time he faces the judge. No Holyoke connections that I know of, though. I doubt he has the brains to read a map. Why?"

"Name came up."

Officer Henry Jordan drove slowly down South Main much later that night, only vaguely aware of the open street ahead of him, his attention all but entirely focused on the parked cars and sidewalks to either side, the houses beyond, and the narrow streets and alleys in between. Of all of Brattleboro's sundry neighborhoods, this was the one perhaps best qualified as the land that time forgot. Not time, really, not literally, although most of the buildings here dated back to Brattleboro's industrial heyday, when this area was one of its larger employee housing clusters. But certainly most social service organizations saw it as a backwater. The houses were generally run-down and in need of paint, frequently broken into multiple apartments, and host to a larger group of transients than elsewhere in town. Brattleboro's good fortunes followed its major commercial arteries, not surprisingly, and South Main Street was definitely not one of those.

Jordan slid along at close to twenty-five miles an hour, his windows open both for the cool night breeze and so he could better hear what was going on. He kept the two-way radio volume to a murmur. It was at times like this that he felt most empowered as a cop, as if he were the good shark slipping through the dark water, watching for those elements wishing harm on society. Which is what he really believed. He was a young man, a patriot, proud to wear a uniform, and saw his role more as a defender of the weak than did many of his older colleagues, whose fatigue-tinged cynicism both irritated and concerned him, making him fret it might be contagious.

He slowed to a stop between two widely spaced streetlamps and hid in the shadow cast by an enormous maple tree. Slowly, as if fearful his actions might throw off an audible sound, he killed his headlights. He saw far ahead of him, caught in profile from some distant glimmering, two people moving around the outside of a parked car.

Jordan hadn't been on the Brattleboro force for more than a couple of years, but he'd mostly worked nights and had developed some time-saving instincts, along with a feel for what types of activities were likely to occur at what time. He knew in his gut that what was going on up ahead would be of interest to him.

He quickly looked around him. For the moment, he

was alone. He gently let his foot off the brake and resumed rolling at a snail's pace, bringing the shadows around the distant car more sharply into focus.

It had all the makings of a drug deal—one man at the wheel, looking passive, in control, the other man hanging on the door, his butt swinging to and fro with nervous anticipation, shifting his weight from foot to foot. Jordan could see the man's arms occasionally gesticulating, as if pleading or bartering. Like a hunter creeping up on his prey for a clean shot, the young officer crawled forward, unaware by now that he was even holding his breath.

The car's motor was running, or at least the ignition was on, because its parking lights were glowing red, and along with them the license plate light. Jordan had a pair of binoculars in the back seat, but by now he knew he had only a few more feet before the plate numbers, obscured by grime, became readable.

Which was when the man outside the car suddenly straightened and stared right at him.

Jordan gunned his engine, leaped forward a few yards, and simultaneously hit both his headlights and his strobes, instantly flooding the scene with a pulsing, multihued light show.

In that snapshot of a moment, the man at the wheel of what was now clearly a Chevy sedan stuck his head out the window and looked back, just as his companion took to his heels and fled across the street. The driver was Roger Novelle, whose mug shot Henry Jordan had carefully stuck to his dashboard at the start of his shift.

Jordan reached for his microphone and switched over

to the cruiser's loudspeaker. "You in the car. Stay put and stick both your hands out the window."

He might as well have fired a starter pistol. With barely a pause, there was a screaming of burning rubber, an acrid, dense plume swirled into the air, and Roger Novelle took off like a mechanized jackrabbit, with Jordan in close pursuit.

Jordan switched the radio back to the transmit frequency. "Dispatch, one-twenty. I'm in pursuit of Vermont 128F4, heading south on South Main at approximately"—he paused to get his bearings—"Oak Grove. Requesting backup."

The response was immediate but calming. "Ten-four, one-twenty. Will do. Please keep advised."

By this point, Jordan had hit his siren, fearful one of the kids who lived along the street, many with little or no supervision, might come running out to watch the entertainment. After that, he focused only on the taillights before him as they dipped and swerved, Novelle's car picking up speed.

Ahead, there was a Y-junction, the left hand dipping to a steep drop toward Route 142 and the town of Vernon beyond, the right hand heading slightly up and into a curve, eventually leading to the high school and the south end of Canal Street, one of Brattleboro's commercial strips. Jordan tensed himself for the lurch he knew would come from the first choice, convinced Novelle would do as he would have and head for the dark, open road. Instead, he had to pull quickly on the wheel as Novelle did just the opposite and cut right, causing them both to skid into the curve in a slippery spray of loose gravel.

Breathing fast from the surprise, Jordan struggled to key the mike again. "One-twenty. We're heading for Fairground Road."

"Ten-four. Units are responding down Canal to intercept."

As Fairground Road began flattening out and broadening to both sides, first by the town garage and then in anticipation of the vast high school parking lot, Jordan found himself caught in a moral quandary: The correct procedural thing was to continue what he was doing now, keep pressure on the pursuit and let the others box the guy in, but the young man in him was demanding otherwise. If he could do this right, Henry Jordan might end the chase and get the collar on his own—here and now.

He hit the accelerator as the road took its general sweep to the right, pulled up alongside the Chevy, and began sheepdogging it into the dirt parking lot, aiming for the line of trees in the distance.

But Novelle would have none of it. To Jordan's terror, he abruptly cut left and collided with the cruiser's right fender, making Jordan veer off to go bounding and skidding across the road.

Gasping, Jordan fought the wheel, regained control, and now fueled with rage, pointed straight at the other car, catching it just behind the left rear door.

But either Novelle was a better driver or the Chevy more sure on the road, because the impact of this second collision was minimal. After a small fishtail, Novelle was back in front as before, with the young cop now feeling humiliation mixing with his anger.

They were coming to where Fairground intersects with Canal Street at a traffic light. It was technically a T-bone, since opposite Fairground was the entrance of the Price Chopper parking lot, but given the chase so far, Jordan wasn't laying bets on Novelle's choice of routes.

Sure enough, Novelle again defied logic and cut right, onto Canal, ignoring both the interstate entry ramps to the left and the highway leading to the town of Guilford beyond them. He was driving straight toward downtown Brattleboro and into the oncoming blue lights of two patrol cars.

"He's heading right at you," Jordan shouted needlessly into the mike, making the corner with one hand on the steering wheel and bouncing off the far curb. He was blessing his luck that there was no other traffic.

Novelle had no trouble with the other two cruisers. He merely went straight at them, picking up speed, trusting to both their drivers' lack of suicidal tendencies and their fear of damaging their cars to make them get out of his way.

Which they did. Like a sharp knife running through paper, Novelle sliced cleanly between them, with Jordan still on his tail.

Now the radio was jammed with chatter, and Jordan didn't bother competing. He kept both hands on the wheel and dedicated himself solely to bringing his quarry to a halt, regardless of the cost.

Canal at this point was broad, empty, and downhill, following the geographical influence of the Whetstone

Brook, which over the centuries had carved a meandering but significant ravine along the town's east-west axis. Both Novelle and Jordan took advantage of all this to hit sixty-five miles an hour past the hospital and down the gentle S-curve to the flat stretch paralleling the brook farther down.

At that point, Jordan again pulled up next to the Chevrolet and attempted to push it off the thoroughfare, this time toward several parked cars. Novelle countered by hitting the brakes suddenly, letting the cruiser slip before him, and then cutting right and accelerating, hitting Jordan broadside and causing his car to spin into a three-sixty as Novelle squealed away.

Now spewing his own twin plumes of burned rubber, Jordan swung cursing back into alignment and resumed chase, his attention sharpened by the two additional cruisers who were coming up from behind. Like a runner with only the finish line in his sight, Jordan fixated on the Chevy's rear bumper.

At the end of the flat stretch, Canal veered right, following the top of the embankment, while Elm Street went straight across a steeply angled bridge and the Whetstone Brook below, heading for Frost Street at the bottom of the ravine. It was the bridge Novelle chose to take without slowing, leaving the ground at the top of the hill and coming down half on the road and half on the sidewalk, causing a shower of sparks to rooster tail behind his car, accompanied by bits and pieces of muffler that pinged off Jordan's windshield as he followed suit.

"Henry, what's your twenty?"

Jordan became aware the dispatcher had tried to raise him several times, finally resorting to his first name.

"I'm in the fucking air," he muttered through clenched teeth, watching the Chevrolet slide expertly at the bottom of the hill into a nicely executed left-hand turn onto Frost Street, now away from downtown. "And I'm getting tired of this shit."

Frost was quiet and residential, following the brook toward West Brattleboro and changing its name to Williams Street beyond Union. Usually a leisurely drive filled with views of steep verdant hillsides and precariously perched old homes overhanging the ravine, this time it was fast, dark, noisy, and scary as hell. Despite the cool air whipping in through the open windows, Jordan was drenched in sweat by the time they roared by Brannen Street in a blur, and was all but ready to concede defeat, eat his pride, and let the others finish this for him.

Until he saw Novelle almost lose control just shy of the tiny bridge after West Street. In that split second, Jordan saw his chance. He stamped on the accelerator, braced himself for the impact, and hit Novelle's right rear fender head-on.

The effect was like riding a merry-go-round on rocket fuel. Jordan heard more than he saw—a cacophony of tearing metal, screeching tires, and the dull thuds of large objects coming violently to rest. He felt weightless at times, totally disoriented, and as if he were watching the world go by in short photographic snippets, each one having no relation to the next. At the end of it all, much to his surprise, he was left in darkness and silence, aside from the soothing gurgle of running water.

By instinct, he reached across and undid his seat belt, realizing only then that he was up to his waist in the brook, which was flowing through one window and out his own.

Shaking his head, smiling from the relief at simply having survived, he opened the door with unexpected ease and swung his feet out onto the stream floor, still feeling as if he were dreaming. Then, yielding to much the same impulse, he cupped his hands in the water before him and splashed it over his hot, sweaty face.

He took in a deep breath, blinked a couple of times to adjust to the darkness, and found himself staring straight at Roger Novelle.

Novelle was hanging halfway out his car's shattered windshield, his face bloody and torn, one arm looking absurdly twisted. But he was alive. And in his good hand, he held a gun.

The two men watched one another for a long couple of seconds. Overhead, the tree branches reflected the blue and white lights of the two cruisers that ground to a halt on the road above. Over the water's rush and the hum in his head, Jordan could barely hear the familiar chatter from the distant two-way radios.

Then a huge, bright flash exploded from the end of Novelle's gun, and Jordan felt the impact of a sledgehammer smash him in midchest.

Chapter 6

Hi, Tony. What the hell happened?"

Police Chief Tony Brandt rubbed the side of his nose thoughtfully. Despite the late hour, he was neatly turned out as usual, looking like a slightly bemused college professor on leave from some midwestern ivory tower. A lifelong cop, he'd never managed to affect any of the typical cop trappings, from his manner to his taste in clothes.

"Real mess, Joe. High-speed chase, police shooting, one man dead. Shades of Dodge City."

"The dead man one of yours?" Joe asked, feeling a sudden dread.

Tony waved his hand dismissively. "Henry Jordan caught a round in the vest. He's being kept for observation with a really good-looking bruise. If the shooter had aimed higher—or used a Teflon bullet—we'd be looking at a whole different story."

"Who was the shooter?"

Brandt looked at him curiously. "That's why I called you down here. Sam dropped by this afternoon and asked us to bring the guy in so you could have a chat with him. Apparently, Gail found him hanging out in Laurie Davis's apartment—Roger Novelle?"

Gunther's brow furrowed. He'd tried contacting Gail several times tonight to ask her about that encounter. All he'd gotten was her answering machine, and when he'd driven by her house, none of the lights had been on.

"You call her about this?"

Brandt shook his head. "Didn't have a reason to. After Novelle took his potshot at Jordan, two other officers opened up and killed him. I didn't see what Gail could do for us, not right now, in the middle of the night. The state police will be running the investigation, and I don't doubt they'll want to have a chat—with her and you both, for that matter, given your relationship—but I don't think it's too complicated in any case. We found heroin in Novelle's car, and we've tracked down the user who was buying from him when Jordan surprised them."

Gunther nodded at the sound of the magic word. "Heroin again," he murmured. "Well, I guess that guarantees the cat getting out of the bag."

Tony Brandt gave his ex-chief of detectives a questioning look.

"The headlines will tell you," Gunther partly explained.

"The governor's going to try to milk this for all it's worth."

Gail's house was still dark when Joe pulled up opposite it a second time. Of course, at three in the morning, he wasn't expecting otherwise. He'd called again from the hospital, hadn't bothered leaving a message, and this time was determined to be less delicately self-effacing.

He left his car, crossed the driveway to the kitchen door, igniting the battery of motion detection lights Gail had had installed following her attack, and applied his two keys to the locks she carefully set every night.

He felt odd entering the house, and not just because of the circumstances. He'd once lived here with her, although he'd never felt truly at home. It had been bought with her money and decorated according to her taste, but his lack of comfort had stemmed more from the incentive than from the decor. She had needed him to be nearby, to watch her back emotionally and physically as she struggled to rebuild. He'd been happy to help, of course, had considered it a privilege and a natural extension of his love for her, but he'd also known it wouldn't last, and that despite her protests to the contrary, she'd eventually become firm-footed enough to start longing for her independence of old. His moving out had actually come as somewhat of a relief to both of them.

Still, it felt funny to be "back home," where, as with

a long-delayed visit to a grandparent's house, familiar smells and sights commingled and got confused with foreign ones. The pull between feeling like an intruder and standing on safe ground was palpable, and Joe proceeded quickly through the darkness upstairs to Gail's bedroom hoping to end the awkwardness as fast as possible. But he also couldn't lie to himself—by now, he'd become alarmed by her silence.

He paused on the threshold of her room, the moon through the skylight revealing a shape in her bed.

"Gail?"

He half held his breath to better hear some sound from her, watching intently, until the merest hint of a movement finally gave him relief. Only then did he step inside and cross over to the bed.

"Gail. It's Joe."

He sat by her side and gently laid his hand against her head, noticing as he did so the prescription bottle and glass of water on the nightstand.

"Gail," he said, his voice still soft. "Wake up."

With his other hand, he reached behind the phone and hooked a finger around the cord, pulling it free from where it dangled unattached to its nearby outlet. That explained why she hadn't been answering his calls; only the downstairs machine had been picking up.

He leaned over and kissed her cheek. "Come on, sweetheart. It's Joe."

Finally, she stirred, moaning briefly.

He took advantage of that to roll her onto her back, sweeping her hair clear of her face as he did.

"Wake up, Gail."

Her eyes fluttered and opened slightly.

"Joe?" Her voice was groggy and clotted with induced sleep.

"Yeah. It's me. Everything's okay. I had to see if you were all right."

She blinked several times, clearly trying to understand what was going on.

"Everything's okay?"

"I hope so," he told her, kissing her cheek again. "I heard you had a tough time yesterday afternoon at Laurie's place. I'm sorry I wasn't there."

The eyes closed again, hoping to shut out the memory. "He was horrible."

"You don't have to worry about him. We got him. What happened, anyway?"

She had all but surfaced by now, her breathing more rapid, her responses close to normal. He could still sense the effects of the sleeping pills, but his mind was at ease that she'd obviously only taken enough to knock herself out for a while.

She rubbed a hand across her face. "Nothing really. I mean, nothing you could point at. I just had a bad flashback is all. The guy . . . something about him. He was creepy and insinuated what he wanted to have happen, but it was his smell more than anything that brought me back. He never touched me, but I almost felt it had happened all over again. I felt . . . violated. And scared. Humiliated."

She suddenly raised both her arms and encircled Joe's neck, pulling him down to her and sobbing into his chest. "I thought it was behind me. Even when I was with him, I thought maybe I still had it under control. But then all afternoon I got pulled lower and lower."

He let her cry for a while, rubbing her shoulder, his face half buried in her hair and her pillow, breathing her in.

Eventually, she quieted enough that he could straighten slightly and look at her. "I've been worried about you. Called a few times, drove by earlier. Couldn't figure out where you'd gone. Sam said you came by."

"It's not just that, Joe. It's Laurie, too. I can't get what she went through out of my mind. I feel responsible. Of all people, I should have known to watch out for her. I know how things are out there."

Joe was shaking his head. "Gail, you can't do that. We all have our own lives to lead. We can care for each other and try to help when the going gets tough—you did that when you suggested Laurie come up here in the first place. But she came with her own baggage. You're not responsible for that. Don't forget why you made that initial offer. Her life was a mess back home."

"It doesn't help, Joe. I've told myself all that."

"Where are her parents? Right now."

Gail looked at him, startled. "I . . . in Connecticut."

"They're not here? They didn't come up?"

"They will," she said weakly. "They're making plans. They know she's safe . . . that I'm here with her."

He let his long silence speak for him.

"I've got to put things right," she finally murmured.

"You're not seeing her as a victim only, are you?" he asked eventually.

"What do you mean?"

"That the Lauries of the world, no matter their backgrounds, do have some responsibility for how they end up."

"I know that," she said, her voice tensing.

"It's not just good and evil," he continued, ignoring the warning. "Most dealers are users, and most users end up as thieves, prostitutes, mules, you name it. It's a mixed-up mess, but it's a mess most of them acknowledge right up to the end. That's why some of them actually beat it and get better—because deep down they know they can. They're the only ones accountable."

She was angry at the condescension she heard in his words—the platitudes that allowed him the distance he needed to function in his job. But she also knew what he was attempting, and so merely placed her hand against his mouth and said, "Stop."

He straightened, caught off guard, and studied her closely.

"I don't care about all that," she explained. "I don't care how people rationalize their way clear. I saw how that works when I was raped and reduced to an unidentified victim in the paper. I see part of me in Laurie, Joe, in ways you'll never understand, and I won't put up with it any more now than I did back then."

Gunther was vaguely confused by parts of what she

was saying. He thought about asking her what her plans were, knowing how capable she was of setting almost anything in motion.

But he also finally recognized the anger in her eyes, and with it an extra element he thought might be pure bewilderment. There was a shift going on here he'd never before seen in this woman he thought he knew so well.

He stroked her shoulder instead of responding, and simply informed her, "This probably isn't the right time, but I mentioned that the guy you met in Laurie's room had been caught. He was actually killed in a shoot-out with the PD. I didn't want you to hear that on the news."

"Who was he?"

"Roger Novelle. Meant nothing to me, but Willy knew him. Local bad boy. He was dealing heroin when he was shot."

Gail stared into the darkness of her bedroom for a few seconds before asking, "He was Laurie's supplier?"

"We don't know yet. Sam's talking with Tony Brandt, and VSP is doing the shoot investigation. Right now everyone's playing connect-the-dots. I wouldn't be surprised, though."

Gail laid her head back against the pillow, her expression implying that she'd come to some sort of decision. "Thanks, Joe. And thanks for coming by."

He hesitated and then stood up, hearing the dismissal in her tone. He was anxious about what he'd just witnessed, and a little irritated at being shut out. The only saving grace, if it even qualified, was that he thought she might know less about what was going on inside her than he did.

For the moment, though, he would let things lie. He leaned over, kissed her, and retreated through the dark, empty house the same way he'd arrived.

Sammie Martens turned on the car's dome light and checked her makeup in the rearview mirror. She hadn't worn the stuff since the last time she'd been under-cover, at Tucker Peak, and harbored a neophyte's inse-curity about how long, or even if, it would stay put. Not that she was slathered with it—just some eye shadow, a little mascara, a touch of blush, and, of course, lip-stick—but it still felt like she was wearing clown paint. She then twisted the mirror to see her hair. That, she was more comfortable with—a simple blond dye job—even if the effect still startled her.

She switched off the light, drove the last eighth of a mile down the road, pulled into the driveway, and cut the engine.

She was beyond Guilford, south of Brattleboro, near the Massachusetts border, parked in front of a his-torical memento even her parents would have found quaint. It was an old-fashioned, 1930s motor court, the kind that mushroomed all over the country with the new rage of the affordable automobile. A string of sep-arate wooden cabins, now swaybacked, peeling, and looking as if the earth were about to reabsorb them, still reflected the culture of their time, when people in

their black Fords pulled off after a grueling day's drive
up from the city and set up in their homes-away-from-
home, complete with barbecue pits, glider swings,
fireplaces for those chilly evenings, and individual
front porches from which to socialize with the neighbors.

Once well tended and tidy, the grounds of this place
had been left to disintegrate, helped along by a scrag-
gly line of rusting eighteen-wheeler boxes standing
guard alongside the road, partially blocking the view
and the remnants of the long-dead neon sign advertising the place. Weeds choked what had probably been a
neat lawn and colorful flower gardens, and all that was
left of the curved gravel driveway was a rutted dirt
trail, lumpy with tree roots and rocks, that ran ill defined before the row of cabins.

Sam got out of her car and pulled her tight sweater
down over her hips, feeling constrained in a pair of
stretch jeans two sizes too small. She'd felt less uncomfortable in a flak jacket, combat boots, and a forty-
pound pack.

She surveyed the string of buildings fanned out before her. Once identical to one another as motel units,
they'd been remodeled here and there as detached
rental apartments, some with extra bedroom wings,
others with a carport. A few had been destroyed altogether, leaving a jarring gap in the row, like a broken
tooth. In all cases, they amounted to as cheap a form of
housing as she knew—a north country version of tar
paper shacks, meaning they had to at least hold up
under a snow load.

Despite the late hour, she wasn't surprised to see some lights on. The place was no magnet for the nine-to-five crowd.

She walked slowly, fearful that she might twist her ankle wearing high-heeled boots. Not naturally statuesque, she'd had to compensate beyond the makeup and the clothes with a little padding in the appropriate places, making her feel like the Michelin Man on stilts.

About half way down the row, she found the number she was looking for and stood quietly for a moment, taking her bearings.

The old porch to this unit had been dismantled, so access to the crooked front door was an uneven stack of cinder blocks. From what she could see through the uncurtained windows, the door led directly into a kitchen, with what looked like a bathroom in the back. On the left was a small bedroom. All the lights were on and she could hear faint music leaking out onto the grass.

She stepped closer to the bedroom window after checking around for any movement from the neighbors. Inside, stretched out on a disheveled bed, was an unshaven man in his underwear, his head propped up on pillows, his face bathed in the ethereal glow of a TV set Sam couldn't see.

She studied his expression for several minutes, trying to gauge his frame of mind, before moving to the front door and quietly knocking on it.

She had to do this several times before a male voice finally called out, "Who's there?"

"It's Greta, Bill. From Tucker Peak. Last winter."

She heard him stumbling to get up, bouncing against the wall as he hurried to get his pants on. As she'd told Joe earlier, Bill Dancer had done everything he could in his very limited repertory to get her into bed when she'd been pretending to be a ski instructor and he'd been a grease-smeared mechanic. She had no doubts whatsoever about what fantasies had electrified his mind at the sound of her name.

In fact, when he finally tore open the door, she noted he'd put on a clean shirt, still creased at the fold lines, and was chewing a breath mint of inordinate strength.

"Greta Novak, my god. What a surprise. I mean, wow. I never thought I'd see you again."

"Which means you're going to let me stand out here all night?"

He leapt backward, making room, and almost fell over a chair pushed up against the wall behind him. "Oh, shit. No, come on in. Damn, you look really good."

She felt like crouching so she could replace her padded breasts with her face in his line of sight, except that he was already looking lower, smiling like a poleaxed cow.

"God," he murmured again as she swept past him into the tiny kitchen.

"So you said," she answered, looking around.

He followed her glance and immediately started to move things around on the cluttered counter near the sink, which was itself stuffed with dirty dishes. "I'm sorry about the mess. I don't entertain much. I wish

I'd known you were coming. I would've cleaned up a little."

"Don't worry about it," she said. "I'm not staying long."

He stopped in midmotion, as if that were one surprise too many—a stunning disappointment he tried to cover with a show of hospitality. "Well, sure, would you like something to drink? I got beer, some Scotch, if you'd like." He dove at a sorry-looking armchair and cleared it of some clothes. "Have a seat, too. Take a load off."

He added a small one-liner to test the waters, always the smooth talker. "Not that your load isn't totally perfect."

Sam chose the least dangerous of his libations as she settled down, crossing her legs with a flourish and rubbing one hand along her thigh. "Give me a beer."

He opened the undersized, rusty fridge and extracted a six-pack. He tore two off and handed her one, which she merely stared at. "You wash the lid on that?"

He stared at her for a split second, as if interpreting a foreign language. "Oh, right," he then said, and made for the crowded sink. He wedged the can under the faucet, rattling the stack of dishes, scrubbed the top energetically, dried it with a quick swipe against his shirtfront, and tried handing it to her again.

She even took some pity on him at that point, accepting the can. "You just never know where these have been."

He perched on the edge of a barstool, his own beer

forgotten on the counter beside him. "Greta Novak. At my house. Unbelievable. I didn't even know you lived around here. I thought you were from Europe or some-place."

Sam took a swig of beer. "Yeah, right."

"No, no. I mean it. You have to admit, the name sounds foreign."

"I don't even have an accent, Bill. And the name's made up. I changed it so I could sell myself better."

He laughed nervously, still amazed this was happen-ing. "Holy shit, you hardly need that. Don't you know what you look like? I mean, Christ, you're . . ." But his voice died off as she gave him a hard look.

"Sorry," he continued in an abashed tone. "But you're a fox."

She frowned. "Don't fuck with me, Bill. We both know what I'm talking about. Getting ahead means a shit-load more than getting laid, and you can't get ahead on looks alone."

He looked confused. "Right."

"You need an edge, an angle, you know? Something they can remember about you besides a nice ass."

"Like a catchy name," he suggested, clearly groping.

She paused to let him soak up her condescending roll of the eyes. When she resumed, however, she didn't elaborate but moved the conversation along. "That's a start. But there's an attitude, too. You have to show people you're a winner."

Sam purposefully let a drop of beer fall from the can to her sweater, and made a small show of stroking her breast, ostensibly to wipe the moisture off. His eyes followed the action longingly.

"Which is what brings me here tonight," she added, drawing his attention by waving her hand where he could see it.

He flushed and self-consciously stared her straight in the eye.

"I need your help, Bill."

"Sure. Anything."

"Remember when we worked together on the mountain? All the dope that was floating around?"

He smiled. "Oh, yeah. Lots of good shit."

"Right," she agreed, "and lots of money being made, too, but not by you or me."

Again, he gave her a blank look.

"Come on. That's what I'm talking about, Bill. Turning the tables. People like us doing dope, getting nowhere fast. Time to play the other side."

She could almost see him pull back. "I don't know, Greta. I run some stuff—"

"I'm not talking running, stupid," she cut him off. "I'm talking dealing."

"Oh, shit. That can get dangerous."

Sam stood up quickly and took a step toward the front door. "Yeah, you're right. I'll go find someone else. I was just looking for a name, like a reference, but hey—no sweat."

To her disappointment all he did was hang his head and say, "I'm sorry. I wish I could help."

Her hand rested on the doorknob. But that was it. He seemed crestfallen. She switched tactics.

Leaving the door, she crossed over to him, fitting herself between his splayed-out knees as he sat on the barstool. "Am I moving too fast?"

He looked up at her, not sure what to do with his hands, which from their resting place on his knees were almost touching her waist. He swallowed. "You've been here five minutes. It's hard to get used to."

Her fingertips brushed against his upper thighs. Her face was inches away from his, making her grateful he'd taken that breath mint. "I'm sorry, Bill. You know what it's like when you've been waiting for something a long, long time, so that when it finally arrives, you can barely control yourself?"

"Sure."

Sam dropped her voice to a near whisper. "It's like sex. The person you've been after is right where you want them at last. They're spread out, clothes off, can't wait to get it on, but waiting is the one thing you can't do. You're too worked up. The moment of a lifetime is ruined."

Her fingers dug into his legs. She leaned forward so that their noses brushed and their lips almost touched. "Ever had that feeling?"

His forehead was beaded with sweat. With agonizing slowness, his hands slid off his knees and just barely touched her hips.

She slipped free of his legs, ostensibly to retrieve her beer from the arm of her chair and take a swig.

He could barely breathe, much less respond.

"Well," she resumed, "that's what this is like for me.

I can't wait to get laid, but instead of a guy, I'm talking money. I want to get rich so bad, I can taste it."

"What can I do?" he just managed, his throat constricted.

"A name, Bill. I want to find out how it works, learn the ropes, you know? Be an apprentice or something. Maybe Holyoke'll have the person I'm after." She crossed the tiny room and put her hand back on the doorknob.

Out of the mess of mixed messages she'd thrown him, he latched onto the one key word. "I know people in Holyoke."

She moved back toward him, but not as closely as before. "You're kidding. See? I knew I was right to come here. You think I could meet them?"

Dancer looked nervous. "Greta, I want to help. But these guys are really dangerous. I can work with them. I've been doing it for years. But even so, I have to be super careful. For one thing, being white counts against you, big time. They hate our guts. If I tried to set you up with one of them, no telling how it might end up."

Sam made a baffled expression and once again slid in between his knees, taking his face in her hands. "Bill, I wasn't talking about going solo. I want you to be with me. I want us to do this together." She touched his lips with her fingertips.

He could barely sit still. She could feel the heat coming off him as from a radiator. "Greta," he half moaned, "you never gave me the time of day before. I can't—"

She kissed him very lightly. He leaned forward to

get more, his hands landing with more confidence on her waist, kneading her through her thin sweater. She pulled back enough to address him. "That was then. I didn't know what I was doing, and maybe I don't now. But I want to try. I'm tired of my life. I need a change, and I need your help."

His face flushed, he managed to say, "I've done stuff for one of them—been a help. I can make a phone call."

She rested her palm on his chest. "Thank you, Bill. I knew you were the right man for this. What's his name?"

"Miguel Torres. He's one of the big movers down there. They only have three or four, so that means something. He's real good."

She gently stepped back once more, smiling and grateful. "You're a sweetheart. I wish I could stay."

He looked like she'd just stamped on his foot. "You can't?"

"Not tonight. I told you, I only dropped by for a little while. I'm so sorry, though. I didn't realize we'd hit it off so well, so fast."

"Fifteen minutes," he suggested, almost pleading.

She returned to the door, but this time she opened it and stood on the threshold, from where she blew him a kiss. "I'll call you tomorrow. See how you made out. Okay? Don't let me down."

"No, no," he said, standing awkwardly. "I'll make sure you can meet him."

She closed the door and walked into the night, crossing the wrecked front yard to her car rapidly, before he had time to summon any questions. The trick to these things, she knew from past experience, was to let the contact come up with most of the story.

She fired up her car and drove a few miles north before pulling off the road and dialing Joe's home number on her cell phone, unable to resist sharing her success.

"Hello?" Gunther's voice had the false sharpness of someone who was trying to sound wide awake.

"It's Sam. I just left Bill Dancer's place. Pretended I was Greta Novak. I think I just got an interview lined up with Torres in Holyoke."

There was dead silence on the other end.

"That's our in with the task force," she explained, surprised and a little disappointed. "Like you said, we bring an inside connection to the Holyoke crowd—something they've never had before."

"Okay," her boss said slowly. "I see what you're saying. You set a date and time yet with Torres?"

"Dancer'll call him tomorrow and nail it down. I hope."

Gunther seemed relieved at the qualifier. "So it's not a done deal. You moved right in on this, Sam—without backup."

It was her turn to pause a moment before saying, "You said time was wasting."

"Right. Well, get some sleep and we'll talk in the morning. I'm glad you didn't get in trouble."

*   *   *

Joe remained holding the phone receiver after Sam had hung up, staring thoughtfully into the darkness of his bedroom. He'd been short with her, which he knew she'd take hard. But he didn't feel bad about that. It was typical of Sam to charge off this way, almost in righteous pursuit. She was ambitious, obviously, but she was also one of the true believers, and that, he'd often pondered, could be dangerous—depending on the circumstances.

And these circumstances were not of his choosing.

Chapter 7

Lester Spinney sat in his car, watching a three-story house about halfway down the block. He knew the owner of record, a local garage mechanic who also ran a wrecker service. Except that his knowledge of the man came more from his history of petty drug busts. Nathan Sherman, nicknamed Natty for no reason related to his appearance, had been a steady customer of the Springfield police since his early teens, and he was in his mid-forties now.

But as popular as he was with the cops, he was genuinely so with the local teens. Two of these were his own sons, the older of whom had begun to build a record all his own.

Not hard-core stuff. The son, Jeff, had been charged with disturbing the peace, petty vandalism, loitering with intent, multiple vehicular offenses. And in a per-

fect example of a father-son tradition, minor drug offenses. Never heroin or crack or even the higher profile
pills. But certainly, a lot of marijuana, called weed by
the kids, had passed through the house, and that was
only what the police could actually prove. The law of
averages dictated that what they'd missed was the vast
majority.

Spinney's problem was that his own son, David, was
now inside.

He checked his watch in the dark, using a nearby
streetlight to see. He wasn't in his own car. He'd borrowed a neighbor's on some flimsy excuse. He hadn't
wanted Dave to see him staking him out.

It was almost ten o'clock.

He rubbed his eyes with his fingertips. He knew he
wasn't acting rationally. He knew that the solution to
all this was to talk to Dave and to ask him what was
going on.

And yet he now sat in a borrowed car, running a surveillance as if he were building a case.

He hadn't found anything incriminating in Dave's
room when he'd searched it earlier that day. Just a
growing guilt, clinging like a sticky cobweb to all of
his son's belongings. He had discovered hidden pictures of nude women, one stashed pornographic book.
But instead of being touched by his son's normalcy and
discretion, Lester only felt increasingly burdened by
his own sense of failure. His son was acting on the hor-
mones of any sixteen-year-old boy, while Lester had
somehow jumped the tracks, ignoring everything about

Dave except a vague and unsubstantiated possibility of drug use.

And now he was sitting in the dark, watching the shadows play across the curtains of the Sherman home, worrying about what might be occurring inside.

What had his own father been like? An icon of sorts, albeit a working-class one. Spinney had been born and brought up in Springfield, the heart of Vermont's so-called Precision Valley. Things had been invented in this region that became mainstays of the whole world's daily activities, from interchangeable gun parts, to the steam shovel, to the common spring clothespin. Early Vermonters were practical, hands-on problem solvers, and had bred a generational string of like-minded people. Over time, Springfield became the cradle of huge, expensive, very exacting machine tools—the type of equipment that manufacturers across the country and elsewhere needed to make their own machines. These were tools made to almost infinitesimal tolerances, and the workers who produced them carried their expectations to all aspects of their lives. When Lester's dad bought a car, he drove it around for a while, discussed its attributes with his friends, and then jacked it up onto a lift to perhaps rebuild the transmission to his own standards. He was a man in blue jeans and a white T-shirt who walked with the respect of his peers in a town whose various boards were dominated by engineers wearing pocket protectors. The 1950s lasted forever in Springfield, it seemed, preserving the town and its residents in a protective time bubble.

Until it all fell apart with a crash.

There are various debatable reasons for this, depending on who's got the podium. The economy, the fallout from the sixties and Vietnam, the unions and the strikes against the local plants, the flight of corporations for foreign shores, life in general, the Democratic Party.

Whatever.

In any case, Springfield's machine-tools market drained away, and with it, the town's lifeblood. What Lester remembered most, however, was how baffled the whole place became, almost overnight, like a huge ship whose rudder had been suddenly blown off. Friends fell out, relatives became polarized, the bars began doing a booming business, and domestic abuse became a recreational pursuit. The sons and daughters of those T-shirted men spun out and away from the cocoon everyone had taken for granted, leaving behind a stunned community.

As for the Spinney family, the once-admired, benignly taciturn father became dour, anxious, and clearly directionless, leaving a leadership void his wife couldn't fill. Lester gave it his best, being firstborn, trying to be cheerful and supportive as the household unraveled. He got so good at steering people to look on the bright side that he was the last one to come to grips with his parents' divorce and his father's struggle with alcoholism. By the time he woke up, all he had left was a reputation for being upbeat, an attribute he felt had all the fragility of an orchid.

But it became his signature characteristic. It got him jobs, friends, his wife, and the fondness of his children.

And for most of the time, it even worked, especially since things had more or less gone his way. Working for the state police, then the AG's office, and finally the VBI, Lester Spinney had led a charmed life.

Only when he hit the occasional adversity was he reminded of the shallowness of this vaunted optimism. Normally, all it took was a few hours to rebuild. But this time, right now, whether it was his age or David's age—the same as his own at the time of his family's collapse—or perhaps his growing exposure to drugs and their destructive effect, Lester wasn't bouncing back. From the moment he'd received that phone call from Officer Walker, the emotional pull on his psyche had been comparable to quicksand. He was feeling alone and speechless, his only visible resource being his training as a cop.

He passed his hand across his forehead, struck anew by the realization of what he was doing—sitting in the dark, substituting communication with surveillance.

He caught sight of himself in the rearview mirror. "You are one crazy son of a bitch, you know that?" he murmured.

He started the car and headed home, not casting a further glance at the Sherman home.

Holyoke, Massachusetts, is the home of the Volleyball Hall of Fame, an incongruity lifted to Olympian heights by an actual visit to the city. For if ever there was an image associated with a sport, it couldn't be more at odds with this city. Holyoke is, in a sequence of contrasting images, a stalwart, brick-and-granite icon of faded nineteenth-century industrial might; a city trying to adapt by building duplexes where once there were factories; a monument to the arsonist's craft, with enough rubble-strewn empty lots to recall newsreels of bombed-out Berlin of late 1945; the proud parent of one of the largest shopping malls in New England; the near title holder in Massachusetts for high crime and unemployment; and a case study in how outdated the region's WASP reputation had become, with a now nearly 50 percent Hispanic population.

In short, the portrait of Holyoke presents like a splayed-out collection of unrelated postcards: genteel, leafy suburbia; gutted urban relic; lofty, graceful Victorian mansion; and embracing, blue-collar, 1950s neighborhood. The jarring thing is that these contrasts often fit into a single city block. Schools are next to crack houses, which are opposite tourist stops that overlook ruins. To the casual onlooker, this sociological chaos is only punctuated by the gap-toothed look of the place—there are so many missing buildings, prey to either fire or the wrecker's ball, that the eye can see much farther than expected, all the way to countless walls of boarded-up or bricked-over windows.

Holyoke is startlingly eccentric as cities go, and despite the bright face its chamber of commerce advertises, a place of staggering disadvantages.

It was also where Sammie Martens, once again as Greta Novak, arrived in the company of Bill Dancer the day after she'd dropped by his cabin to tantalize him with her proposition.

Not that he'd been wholly converted to her vision of
an economic bonanza. He was still worried about the
company they'd be keeping. "Greta," he said as they
entered downtown, as bustling a place as any, if more
down-at-the-heels, "you don't know these people.
They're not like the woodchucks or highfliers we had
at Tucker Peak. This ain't no ski resort. These sons of
bitches'll cut your heart out as soon as look at you."

"Give it a rest, Bill. You sound like a bad movie."
Sam looked out the passenger side window at an un-
usually large number of Hispanic faces slipping by before her eyes. She knew Holyoke had been a big Irish
town back when it was king of the hill in the early
1900s. To her, coming from the whitest state in the
Union just an hour's drive away, the difference was
both surprising and confusing, defying explanation.
History—much less the nation's ethnic migratory
trends—had never been of interest to her, who far pre-
ferred equipment catalogs and police intel printouts.
She was feeling like she'd been dropped into a totally
different world, which also made her a little less sure of
what she was doing.

She was now flying solo, again without having told
her boss. Were she to disappear down here today, nobody would be the wiser.

"Where's Torres live?" she asked, mostly to get her
mind elsewhere.

"A few blocks down. We won't be seeing him,
though."

She took her eyes off the scenery. "What d'you

mean? That's why I'm here, for Christ's sake. You jerking me around?"

Dancer made as if he were swatting away flies. "I'm not. Damn. You get worked up fast. I keep telling you: These people do things different. There's like, you know, a pecking order. You gotta pass muster."

"Meaning you've never set eyes on Torres."

"I have, too," he complained, turning off Appleton just shy of the discordantly large and modern police department building. "A lot of times. But he's not gonna take too kindly to my bringing some girl to see him first time, right off. You could be a cop, for Christ's sake."

"And you could be a genius. Fat chance," she retorted, but she could feel the blood slowly rising to her cheeks.

She was here out of pure ambition. Not for herself—at least not to where she'd admit it—but for the bureau. She'd convinced herself, in that odd way people have when they've turned away from the obvious, that she needed to seal a connection to the Holyoke crowd before telling Gunther of her plans. She'd sensed his apprehension that she was moving too fast when she'd told him of meeting with Bill Dancer, just as she'd known that after a night's sleep, Joe would make sure she didn't do anything impulsive.

But time was of the essence here. When he'd asked about what drug contacts she'd made at Tucker Peak last winter, he'd all but told her that. He needed the VBI to have credibility as the governor dumped them into the task force's lap, and she was going to give it to him—whether he liked it or not.

"So who are we going to meet?" she asked Bill.

"Guy named Carlos. He's like a lieutenant. You make an impression on him, you get to meet Torres. Why're you being such a bitch? Last night, it was like you couldn't wait to get it on. Now I'm like some piece of shit."

She let out an exasperated sigh and blurted out the simple truth. "This is a big deal to me, Bill. It means a lot."

He didn't answer, staring straight ahead. She suppressed her irritation and touched his cheek with the back of her hand. "I'm sorry. I shouldn't take it out on you. You're my passport here—like my guiding light. I'm just wired is all. Do you forgive me? I'll make up for it later."

Dancer's face pinked up slightly, and he smiled despite himself. "It's okay. I been there. This is it," he announced, pulling the car over to the curb, surprisingly near downtown and police headquarters.

A young man approached the car on Sam's side, smiling as he caught sight of the car's license plate. He squatted down on the sidewalk to see them both through Sam's window. "Hey. You guys from Vermont. You here to score?"

"All set," Bill said in a loud voice. "We're late for a meeting."

The young man glanced at the address across the sidewalk from them. "I'll sell to you cheaper."

"Christ," Bill answered him. "Back off."

The dealer straightened and said, "Sure. Fuck you,

too," and wandered away, his eyes on the passing traffic.

They got out of the car, Bill looking sour. "Only reason anyone from Vermont comes down here is for dope. And we're like sugar to cockroaches." He nodded toward the dealer. "That guy works for Carlos—only reason he can be this close to the front door—and still, he's trying to undersell his own boss."

He motioned to a large beige brick apartment building with a recessed and arched front entrance—straight out of the 1920s—but stained, cracked, tired, and decorated with a waist-high band of continuous graffiti. "These people are something else."

As they crossed the sidewalk, another young man wearing a tank top and two gold chains appeared, this one standing in the doorway. He was looking at Sam as if she were made of ice cream. One of his chains had a large pendant in the shape of an Uzi machine gun.

He made a show of reaching toward the small of his back, as if resting his hand on a real weapon. "What do you want?" He kept his eyes on Sam as Bill did the talking.

"We're here to see Carlos."

"He's not here. You gotta talk to me." He smiled and raised his eyebrows, still not acknowledging Bill by sight.

"We have an appointment. Concerns Miguel."

This time he shifted his gaze. "What about?"

"That's our business."

Sam gave Bill credit. He did seem to know how the protocol worked. The young man stepped back, just barely. "You better hope it don't get to be my business. Apartment 8, straight ahead."

They had to squeeze by him, and he closed the gap even more when Sam got close, his chest bumping into her arm and jostling her. He smiled and put his hand on her ribs, just under her breast. "*Hola*. Careful. You don't wanna fall."

She stared right at him. "Not with you, I don't."

He laughed. "What do you know?" His face hardened slightly as he added, "You stand against the wall. I gotta check you out."

"Come on, man," Bill protested.

"You, too. Hands on the wall."

The phrase startled Sam, given the role reversal. She wondered how many times she'd given the same order. But she also heard the tone in the man's voice. He needed to save face. And she needed to comply.

"It's okay, Bill," she said, and put her palms flat against the wall. "These folks can't be too careful."

To pay him some credit, the man checked out Bill first, even if the search was sloppy and for looks only.

When it came to Sam's turn, though, the whole point of the exercise became clear. He ran his hands all over her, carefully, slowly, between her breasts, between her legs. It was only when he lingered in the latter place that she finally turned, swatted his hand away, and asked with a smile, "Satisfied?"

He smiled back, his self-image reestablished. "For now."

They proceeded down the hall to room number 8.

The door was open. They saw a man sitting at a

rough wooden table, calmly apportioning white powder Sam guessed was heroin from one package into a series of much smaller pale blue baggies. The scene reminded her of when her mother used to put the sugar she bought in bulk into several glass jars. Except that the room here was a pigsty.

"I help you?" he asked, measuring carefully. He was wearing chains, too, the seeming accessory of the moment.

"Hey, Carlos, it's me," Bill said, entering with a faux-familiar swagger, designed, Sam thought, solely for her.

Carlos looked up, both surprised and at a loss to remember who Bill was.

Sam smiled and couldn't resist explaining, "Bill Dancer, from Brattleboro. He said you'd sold him stuff a couple of times."

Carlos nodded. "Right—Bill. You want some more?"

Sam figured now was as good a time as any to step out from behind Bill's shrinking shadow. "Much more. I want to talk with Miguel about setting up an operation in Vermont."

Carlos's reaction was unexpected. He sat back in his chair as if pushed and stared at them under furrowed brows. "Set up an operation? In Vermont? Who're you trying to fuck with here? Johnny send you two assholes?"

Bill threw his hands up. "Jeez, Carlos, lighten up. I don't even know anybody named Johnny."

But Sam picked up on the implication. "What's wrong with dealing in Vermont?"

Carlos considered them a moment in silence, before stating, "You guys really are as dumb as they say. Get the fuck out of here."

He returned to his measuring as if they'd already left.

Bill opened his mouth to say something, but Sam laid her hand on his arm. "Come on, Bill. Money's no good here."

As they walked back down the hall, Bill shook his head. "What the hell was that all about? What a loser. And what's this shit about Johnny?"

"Shut up, Bill," Sam said quietly as they approached the lobby. "And keep it shut while I find out. In fact, wait for me on the sidewalk, right at the bottom of the steps, okay? Not too far off."

Bill looked at her in confusion. "What're you talking about?"

The man who'd greeted them at the door reappeared from outside, having heard their voices. He smiled at them, once again focusing on Sam. "Hey. So soon? That was fast business. You're a quick operator."

Sam smiled back. "Little do you know." She turned to Bill. "Wait for me. I want to talk to . . ." She glanced at the young man in the gold chains.

"Don Juan," he leered.

"Don," she finished. "I'll only be a second."

Doubtful and clearly put out, Bill followed instructions, looking over his shoulder as he left. "I'll be right out here."

"Whatever," Sam murmured, just loud enough for the young man to hear.

He laughed. "What's a slick bitch like you doing with such a yo-yo?"

"He drives the car," she said, leaning back against the wall. "You really named Don Juan?"

A small flicker of the kid leaked through as he admitted, "Nah. It's Ricky." He placed a hand against the wall beside her head so his body was almost leaning against hers. The flicker was gone. "But I can be Don Juan to you."

She quelled the obvious rejoinder inside her head and answered instead, "Yeah, I bet you have your moments." She reached up and hooked one of his chains with her index finger. "This is pretty."

"Not as pretty as you."

Christ, she thought, what thirteen-year-olds have you been hanging out with? "You should know," she said. "You got a good enough feel."

"You complaining?"

What the hell? she thought. Since we're replaying bad movies: "You didn't do any harm. I like a man who knows what he wants."

"Damn," he said softly. He placed his other hand against her stomach and leaned in to kiss her ear gently.

She rested her fingers on his wrist to stop him from moving up her torso. "Doesn't mean he always gets what he wants. Right away. Who's Johnny?"

He straightened, caught off guard. "What?"

"Carlos told us to go see Johnny," she said, expanding a bit on the actual message.

His eyes widened. "He did? No shit. Must've been bullshitting you."

"Why's that?"

Ricky leaned in to touch her neck with his nose. "You smell good."

I bathe, she told herself. "He a bad guy to work with? I don't want to get in trouble."

He gave her a less lascivious look. "You going to *work* with him?"

"I'm from Vermont. That's where Carlos told me to go."

Ricky tilted his head appraisingly and then laughed softly. "Yeah, well, that's right. Vermont's Johnny's turf now. I'm just real surprised Carlos sent you there, 'cause Johnny, he's like shit around here."

"Bad blood?"

"Shit yeah. Miguel used to run junk into Vermont, like a bunch of 'em do. Johnny took it over, a couple of weeks ago. Got ugly, too. Some shootings. A few people beat up. I don't know if Miguel might not get him back, or one of the other top shits around here, for solidarity. They're still pretty hot about it. Johnny might have to pay big-time if he wants to see tomorrow, you know? I mean, live and let live, but you gotta show respect."

"Right," Sam agreed, hoping to keep him rolling. "Maybe they could work something out. Is Johnny smart enough for that?"

Ricky seemed to have almost forgotten his lover routine in exchange for being the answer man. "Johnny's plenty smart. He figured out how to get a piece of the pie, didn't he? Cutting out a hunk of Vermont for himself? That's smart, if you ask me. Maybe he pissed a few people off, but now he's a big shot when he was just a street guy before, and he didn't have to face off with any of the bosses around here for stealing local turf—that really would've got him killed."

"You all but said Miguel wanted him dead."

He took his hand off her stomach and waved it dismissively. "Yeah, yeah. Miguel can't just lie down, you know? Plus the others're mad, too. They all have to save face. It's kind of like Johnny ripped 'em off a little, too." Ricky cupped his groin. "But he has *cojones*. You gotta respect that. They'll work something out. They always do. Maybe some people'll die, there'll be a little trouble, but Johnny's got protection, and like I said, Vermont's not the biggest deal in the world or anything. It was like he took over a side business or something. There's still enough to go around."

"But it's not settled yet, right? There could still be a fight."

He nodded seriously. "Oh, yeah. It's like they say on TV, you know? 'It's a fluid situation.' I love that. 'Fluid situation.' " He suddenly seemed to remember a forgotten line, because he slipped on the leer again and put his face close to hers. "Like us, right, baby? A fluid situation."

She allowed herself a genuine laugh then, patted his cheek with her hand, slipped down and under his arm, and walked toward the open door. "You never know,

Ricky. You like older women?" she asked over her shoulder.

He took her rejection in stride, which she was only hoping he'd do, and laughed back at her. "You can't tell by now? I'm losing my touch."

She paused on the threshold, faced him, and put her hands on her hips, suddenly realizing how close this kid was to the type of man she often did fall for—a little dangerous, a little lost, dangling between being clueless and far too knowledgeable for his own good. "Don't you believe it. What's Johnny's last name and where do I find him?"

"Rivera," he said, and gave her the address, adding, "You be careful. I want you back without bruises."

Chapter 8

Gail sat at a small table overlooking the Harmony parking lot in downtown Brattleboro, nursing a cup of cold coffee. Across from her, operating from what used to be a retail shop, was a drug counseling outreach center, its former display windows now plastered with colorful art and upbeat, antidrug slogans. Both the irony and the courage to locate such a place in the heart of the town's most visible marketplace for illegal substances had made for lively discussions in this debate-happy community. Neighboring merchants hated it, advocates loved it, the selectboard waffled.

Gail, no surprise to those who knew her even slightly, was among the advocates. On this occasion, however, she wasn't sitting in admiration of other people's handiwork. She was waiting for someone to appear from the center's door.

Earlier that morning, fresh from the sleep that Joe had disturbed to check on her well-being, Gail had called on old friends and contacts in the therapy and drug rehabilitation business, until she'd found one who'd dealt with Laurie Davis. This approach from an outsider would normally have met with a professional stone wall, of course, patient confidentiality being the hallowed thing it is, but Gail had paid her dues with this group of people, through her friendships, her backing, and her political might when she'd been on the selectboard. She therefore not only confirmed that Laurie had unsuccessfully been treated for a drug dependency but also got the name of the girl acknowledged to have been her best friend—another addict, named Debbie Holton.

And Debbie Holton came to the Harmony drug outreach center for a regular appointment.

A thin, nervous girl with dirty blond hair and rumpled, baggy clothes appeared from inside the center and paused on the doorstep, taking in the parking lot before her. The Harmony lot is a unique and well-known Brattleboro icon. A large, tree-filled courtyard, accessible through an arched porte cochere at one end and a gap between two buildings at the other, it is wholly reminiscent of a medieval marketplace, walled and protected. Surrounded by buildings both commercial and residential, it is perforated by the back doors of retail businesses and thus allows for a multitude of discreet avenues to the busy streets beyond the walls.

A drug peddler's dream.

Over time, the surrounding merchants had complained and been answered with stepped-up police patrols, surveillance cameras, neighborhood meetings, and hot tip phone numbers for the reporting of suspicious activity. All to little avail. Like rodents reacting to bright light, the pushers would vanish until things settled down, only to reappear as before.

Debbie Holton stepped away from the center's threshold into this familiar territory, instantly blending into a small group of similarly dressed young people who were sitting on the curb chatting and smoking cigarettes.

Gail watched her carefully as she cadged a smoke, shared a few laughs, and took a sip from someone's Coke before finally standing up and shuffling toward Elliot Street, visible between two building blocks.

Gail got up, left a generous tip, and followed her.

Elliot is one of the town's funkier streets, especially here, in close proximity to Main. It hosts one of Brattleboro's quaintest restaurants—a tie-dye, sixties throwback named the Common Ground—right opposite Peter Havens, one of the ritziest. It has bookstores, bars, music stores, an Indian eatery, the fire department's central station, and one of the town's more dilapidated rooming houses. It also boasted the retail birthplace of Tom and Sally's Chocolates, a typically Vermont phenomenon. Akin to Ben & Jerry's ice cream—where two people blended a high-class product with the aura of its down-home, romantic home state—Tom and Sally's made a success of selling, among other things, chocolate cow patties.

Elliot is an anthropological snapshot of what makes Brattleboro the unique Vermont landmark it is.

Gail followed Debbie Holton west, studying her drooped shoulders, the way the bottoms of her jeans dragged behind her heels. She looked like a waif, only vaguely connected to the world around her, and even, Gail now realized, a little like her niece, Laurie, also pale, thin, and blond. That similarity, made Gail all the more resolved in her quest.

Holton suddenly cut through an opening in the railing to her left and made for a long, steep, open-air flight of stairs that connected Elliot to the Flat Street parking lot some forty feet below. All of Brattleboro covered or bordered three significant waterways and was, as a result, spread across a topsy-turvy of hills, gullies, steep slopes, and ravines.

Liking the relative privacy afforded by a staircase hanging between two busy streets, Gail took advantage of her quarry's choice of routes to make her move.

"Debbie," she called out, she hoped in an upbeat voice.

The young girl turned and glanced up, her expression mute at the sight of a complete stranger. Gail read in her eyes the look of a refugee—hungry, fearful, resigned, but also faintly feral.

"What?"

Gail approached, meeting her on the first landing, where the stairs doubled back on their journey to the bottom. She stuck out her hand in greeting, mostly to force Holton to make physical contact with her.

"My name is Gail Zigman. I'm Laurie Davis's aunt." The girl barely touched Gail's fingertips with her own, which were damp, warm, and seemingly without musculature. "Hi."

She had a soft, high voice, clearly lacking in curiosity.

Gail was caught slightly off guard by the bland reaction. "Well, I just wanted . . . I mean, I got your name . . ." She laughed self-consciously. "Let me start again. I heard you and Laurie were good friends."

"Yeah."

After a long pause, Gail continued. "So I wanted to meet you. Find out how you were doing."

"Fine."

"It must've been a shock, though. I mean, I didn't know she was in such a jam."

Debbie was starting to look around, as if hoping for a distraction. "Yeah, well . . . whatever."

Gail pulled at an earlobe. "Look, Debbie. I know this is kind of weird, but I feel a little responsible for what happened. I am her aunt. I should've looked out for her."

"She talked about you."

The statement came out matter-of-factly, without inflection.

"Really? What did she say?"

"That she had an aunt. A big-deal politician. That you?"

To her own surprise, Gail was disappointed. "Not really, but I suppose I'm who she meant. What else?"

"That was it. That's all there was, anyway, right? You doin' your thing, Laurie doin' hers. What's more to say?"

A silence fell between them. Gail usually prided

herself on an ability to speak with anyone. This girl was proving to be an exception.

"Do you want to see her?" she finally asked.

Debbie shook her head. "See myself in someone else's body? Don't think so. I'll get there quick enough on my own."

Gail was startled at both the depth and the starkness of the comment. "Is that what you want?" she asked.

Now it was the young girl who seemed caught off guard. She looked straight at Gail—the first time she'd actually done so. "Sometimes."

Gail pursed her lips for a moment, trying to think of the right way to respond, knowing a misstep now could break the wispy, hair-thin bridge they were building toward one another.

"It must be hard."

Debbie smiled just barely. "It's what it is."

Gail nodded. "If I promise not to bug you about it—not even talk about it, if you want—could I buy you lunch?"

"Now?"

"Yeah."

Debbie Holton looked uncertain. "I don't—"

"I promise," Gail repeated, holding up her hand, as if in a pledge.

Debbie laughed a little. "You gonna put that on a Bible or something?"

She didn't actually accept Gail's invitation, but the two of them started down the stairs side by side.

*   *   *

"What were you doing in there?"

Bill Dancer was clearly put out, trailing behind Sammie Martens as she walked quickly toward their car.

"Getting an address on Johnny Rivera," she said without looking back.

"That's his name? Rivera? I never heard of him. That can't be good. The guy must be a punk."

She circled to the passenger side and opened the door, getting in. He joined her in the car, his face closed down with frustration and anger. He was supposed to have been the main operator here—the guy to depend on. The guy who got the girl, even. Now he didn't know what the hell was going on.

"He might've been a punk once," Sam agreed, "but lover boy in there says he's come into his own as of late."

The reference fired Dancer up again. "What the hell was that, anyway? What did you do with him?"

Sam laughed. "What d'you think, Bill? A fast fuck against the wall? I asked the man a few questions. I stroked his ego. Made him feel like a real dude. You gonna give me shit for that? So we can drive back to Vermont with nothing but the shit on our shoes? That's not why I came down here."

He stared straight ahead, not saying a word.

Repressing a heavy sigh, Sam reached over and laid her hand on his upper thigh. "Billy," she said softly, feeling like slapping him instead. "We came down here to get something going—to give us a jump start to something better. You want that to happen, right?"

"Sure," he conceded, adding, "It just made me feel weird, you know? You doin' that."

She brushed the back of her finger against his cheek. "That's sweet. I didn't know you felt that way."

He stared at her. "Shit yeah, I do. What do you think? I mean, damn. Since I known you, I told you that."

She laughed. "I thought you were just horny."

He smiled awkwardly. "Well, sure. That, too. But . . . you know."

"Yeah. I do. It's okay, Bill. Let's just see this through, okay? There'll be time for us later."

His face lightened at that, and he started the engine. "Cool. First things first. You said you had an address?"

She gave it to him, happy to have him back on track. In the long run, Bill Dancer was disposable, probably the sooner the better. But for right now he gave her the best cover she could ask for—not too bright, locally known, and with past history of purchase and sales. All she had to do was be his bimbo long enough to get in under the tent flaps.

"Tell me about all the head honchos they keep talking about," she said as he pulled into traffic. "The doorman said Johnny Rivera had stirred things up when he made his move."

Dancer was back in his element, feeling good again, at the wheel in more ways than one. "This town's run by about four of 'em, and each one's got turf spread over three areas—the Flats, South Holyoke, and Churchill, which is basically downtown. Those are the screwed-up parts of town, and the best placed, 'cause what with the Mass Pike, I-91, and I-391, complete with on- and off-ramps—not to mention the river and Chicopee and South Hadley on the other side—gettin' away from the local cops is pretty easy. You should look at a map of Holyoke, Greta. It's a laugh. The city's laid out so it looks like someone flipping the finger. I shit you not. Holyoke says, 'Fuck you, America.'"

"Cute," Sam murmured. She had seen a map. The image was there, but only if you were looking for it.

Dancer nodded, lost in his patter. "Yeah. Thought you'd like that. Anyhow, even though there's enough trade to go around, they chew on each other out of habit, you know? It's the macho thing." He lapsed into some indistinguishable accent. "Hey, man, you dissin' me? You insulting my mudda?" He laughed at his own theatrics. "So they cut each other and try to steal each other's turf. Kind of like warlords. Each head guy has maybe thirty or forty street guys, depending, and some of the street guys have people, too. They work it different ways, but it's the corporate thing all over again. Friggin' AT&T. That way the boss never gets dirty, never puts his hands on the product, and supposedly never gets busted. 'Course they do—all the time. Cops grab 'em for one thing or the other. Never sticks for long, but it keeps things stirred up at ground level. I don't know this Johnny dude—probably an independent, 'cause there's a shit-load of them, too—but I bet that's how he did his thing: moved when the powers-that-be were busy, if you get my drift. Happens all the time. They huff and they puff. They do some drive-bys and rough a few competitors up. Sometimes it works and sometimes it don't. Maybe somebody gets killed now and then. But it's all showing off. There's so much money changing hands, nobody has time to fart around with a real gang war. Plus, sounds like Johnny did it the smart way, grabbing business that nobody owned in particular."

He pulled over to the curb. "Here we are."

Sam looked around. "Pretty nearby."

"Whole goddamn town's pretty nearby. Shit, I mean two of the bosses I was talking about? They live a block and a half apart. The turf's pretty clear cut, but you can see one from the other. Holyoke's a small place. Oh, oh—here we go."

He was looking out his window at a short, stocky, twenty-something man who was approaching them from one of Holyoke's interchangeable brick housing blocks carrying a metal baseball bat. Instead of chains, this one had opted for fat shiny rings on all his fingers.

Bill rolled down his window. "Hey, man."

"What're you doin' here?" the bat wielder asked.

Sam leaned over to look up at the man, allowing him a view down the front of her V-neck sweater. "We're here to see Johnny. From Vermont."

"He know you?"

"Miguel Torres knows me," Bill answered. "I used to do business with him. Word is Johnny's the new man, so screw Torres, right?"

"Yeah, well, screw you, too, you don't have no appointment."

"Hey," Sam protested in a high voice. "Come on. We're lookin' to buy quantity here. Johnny's setting up business. We're here to help him do it."

"He don't need no help."

"You sure about that? You telling us to bring our business someplace else?"

She kept her eyes glued to his, driving home the implication.

He blinked. "Get out of the car."

They did as ordered. The man escorted them into the lobby of the building, where a number of others were standing around looking watchful. The hands-against-the-wall routine was followed again, but with none of "Don Juan's" blatant self-interest. This doorman was all business.

"Follow me," he told them afterward, and led them deep and high into the building, not just along staircase and hallways but also through several wall openings that had clearly been made with sledgehammers. Sam had no idea where they finally ended up, or even which wing of the block they were in, but she had a good notion they were at the heart of a modern day fortress, specially customized to both ward off attack and create a multitude of ambushes. If Johnny's enemies were interested in putting him out of business, they'd have to do it away from here.

Their escort finally knocked loudly against a steel-reinforced door. It opened a crack, he exchanged a few words in Spanish with a man inside, and then the door swung back.

The room they stepped into was square, small, windowless, and had five young men in it, all armed with semiautomatic weapons, all decked out in jewelry and designer clothes nobody could appreciate. They said nothing to the new arrivals, and Bill and Sam kept silent, waiting for directions about what to do next.

A door on the wall opposite them opened, and a slim, attractive man in jeans, a designer shirt, and a single thin gold chain around his neck appeared. He smiled pleasantly, nodded to both of them, and said in a quiet voice to Bill, "So, you used to work with Torres."

"Till I heard you were running things."

"He send you to me?" he asked dubiously.

Bill opened his mouth, but Sam answered, "No. He told us to drop dead. We found out about you from one of his people."

The smile widened. "And how did you do that?"

"The same way we got up here. I showed him my tits."

Johnny Rivera laughed. "Tits and brains both. Come on in."

He turned on his heel, leaving the doorway empty. Bill and Sam glanced at their escort, got nothing from him, and followed Rivera's invitation, stepping into a moderately clean, large, furnished room—half living room, half office—where every window was blocked by a steel plate reaching halfway up its length, permitting only a view of the sky from a standing position—a compromise that allowed sunlight but not sniper bullets.

"Have a seat," Rivera offered, settling into a beat-up armchair.

Bill and Sam shared a couch opposite him.

"I hear you've come to help me set up my new business."

Sam glanced around until she saw the intercom on a small side table. Very efficient.

"We've got something to offer, yeah," Sam answered him.

"And what would that be?"

Sam jerked a thumb at Bill Dancer. "His contacts, my business savvy, and our skin color."

Rivera narrowed his eyes as Bill shifted uncomfortably in his seat. "What's that supposed to mean?"

Sam smiled. "You're a good lookin' guy, but you're the wrong color for the whitest state in the whole country. You want to pull this off, you're going to have to fly under the radar—have someone who'll blend in."

"Who says I haven't already pulled it off?"

Sam waved her hand around the room. "This what you call the big time? If it is, we're in the wrong place."

"Pretty full of yourself."

"I'm full of potential," Sam answered. "I'm also full of being treated like a piece of meat who's going to end up with nothing at the end. I'm full of the assholes making promises and delivering jack, and I'm full up to here"—she touched her forehead—"with other people's bullshit. I can be an asset to you. You want to blow that off and miss out on a golden opportunity, fine. It's a free country. But I'm making my move, and I'd like to make it with you."

She worried that last line might've been a little hokey and watched his expression as if he were a drama critic.

But he was fascinated. The women in this line of work rarely looked and spoke like Greta Novak, and he knew for a fact that she was right about the skin color issue. Profiling or not, cops in Vermont took a very close look at nonwhites traveling their roads with out-of-state plates.

Johnny Rivera gave her an approving nod. "Okay. That all sounds pretty good. What's your plan?"

"For years, Vermont's heroin pipeline has started here, gone through Brattleboro, hung a left just below Springfield, and ended up in Rutland. That's where I'll go. I know you're there already, trying to keep the locals in line. I also know you're not having much luck."

"Says who?" he asked, obviously irritated.

She took the plunge, blindfolded, but kept her exact wording carefully vague. "Says the guy hanging from the bridge. Real subtle way to quietly infiltrate a town. You know who the chick was they found dead in that motel room?"

She paused to force him to ask, "Who?"

"The daughter of a bigwig politician, that's who—a guy who gives shit-loads of money to the governor. If you did have anybody working for you up there, you can bet your ass they'll either be in the slammer soon or as far from Rutland as a tank of gas will take 'em. The heat's on, Johnny—you got people all around you down here looking to knock you off, and now you have your little start-up operation staring straight down the shit hole. You don't think you need help, fine. But I think you're wrong."

It was the perfect time for Rivera to throw them out in a fit of bluster, or at least let Sam know that she was blowing pure smoke. Of course, she wasn't sure she wasn't. She had no idea how the deaths of James

Hollowell and Sharon Lapierre were connected to Rivera, if at all, much less anything about Rivera's Rutland operation.

Which made his response all the more satisfying. "How do I know you won't just rip me off?"

"You try me out," she told him, sitting back against the cushions. "After all, how do I know I can trust you? We need to do a little business first. See if we like it."

Her tone of voice with these last words was purposefully ambiguous, letting him wonder if she might not be interested in more than just a business relationship.

"I sell you some shit at a discount, you stick it in your veins, and I never see you again? Great plan," he said, although she sensed it was more ritual than a challenge.

She arched her eyebrow at him, willing to keep playing. "I'm going through all this for an ounce of horse? Get real. Tell me straight, Johnny: Do you use the product?"

He looked at her in surprise. "I'm no junkie."

"Well, I'm not, either. That puts us above almost everybody else in the game. This is about money, and I'm ready to make some."

There was a lull in the conversation as Rivera turned in his chair and gazed out the top half of one of his armored windows. Sam felt like she'd just pitched a truck full of used cars to the man.

Finally, he turned back to them and pointed at Bill Dancer, whose grasp of all this was still undergoing development. "What about him? He your boyfriend?"

Sam laughed. "He'd like to be."

Bill looked confused as his face turned bright red.

"But he's better as my contact man," she continued, being more truthful than Rivera knew. "Been at this for years. Got a good little black book. I can put the moves on people, get them working together, but he's my passport."

Rivera nodded, paused a moment, and then said, "Okay. We give it a shot. I sell you some junk, you show me your stuff."

Two hours later, Joe picked up his office phone. "Hello?"

"It's Sam. I'm in. You can tell the task force and everybody else that Johnny Rivera has a new Vermont operative, and I'm it."

Gunther could almost see the shine in her eyes from her tone of voice. "Sam, slow down. What the hell've you been up to? Where are you?"

"Holyoke. I didn't want you to say no, so I just went ahead and did it. Rivera's having me run a test flight— which'll cost us two thousand bucks, by the way—but I'm pretty sure he's hooked."

Gunther grimaced as he stared out across the empty office. He hated the way this was going—had hated it from that first meeting with Allard. Every corner, it seemed, was producing people bent on pulling the rug out from under him. Politicians were dictating policy, Gail had fallen into some outer orbit, and now Sammie was setting up an undercover operation without clearance or consultation. It seemed everyone he knew was going maverick.

It was time to catch up, to apply a little steadiness, and to mold into something of value the bits and pieces he'd been handed.

"Nice work, Sam," he said to keep her in good spirits, even though he had no clue who Johnny Rivera was. "Come on in so we can put it all together."

Chapter 9

I've been following Dave, putting him under surveillance, going through his room—like I was getting ready to arrest him."

Susan Spinney put her things down on the kitchen table and sat opposite her husband. It was late. She'd just returned from the hospital and had found him sitting in the glow of a single lamp, staring into an empty coffee cup as if it held an oracle's solution.

"Why?" she asked quietly, a chill settling in her chest. "What's going on?"

"That call I got from the PD, when I had to pick Dave up? I told you it was just an open container bust and that I'd talk to him. Well, it wasn't, and I didn't. I mean, I asked him if he knew what he'd done wrong, and he said he did, and I asked him if he'd do it again, and he said he wouldn't. And that was it. Got us both off the hook. But there was more. Stuff I didn't tell you."

He paused. She resisted pounding the tabletop to get his attention, asking calmly instead, "What stuff?"

"The driver was a loser named Craig Steidle. He had some pot on him as well, and when the cops drove up, it looked like he was about to score some crack off a local hooker who hangs out near the Pearl Street walkway."

Susan felt her irritation growing. Despite Lester's profession, she'd always felt she was the family cop, having to enforce the rules and mete out the punishment. Being the bad guy while he came off as the Dad from central casting.

"And you figured you wouldn't tell me for what reason?" she asked, unable to disguise her anger.

He continued addressing the coffee cup. "I don't know, Sue. I'm sorry. It wasn't 'cause I was trying to duck the issue. I searched his room when no one was here, I staked him out when he was at the Sherman place last night. I can't get it out of my head."

"You staked him out? What the hell does that mean? What's he been doing?"

Spinney finally met her eyes. "Nothing—not that I know of. That's what I realized last night—why I quit and came back home. I saw I was losing it over this."

Susan furrowed her brow, trying to sort it out. "Les, for crying out loud. You were losing it because you thought maybe Dave was getting into stuff like crack cocaine? What's not to lose? Do you think he's been doing this for long? What did you find in his room?"

Lester was already shaking his head. "Nothing, and I have nothing to make me think he's done anything other than hang out with the wrong kids."

Susan sat back in her chair and looped one arm over its back rail. "No shit. I feel like wringing his neck."

Lester said barely audibly, "I felt like wringing my own neck."

Susan sighed with exasperation and stood up, looking for something to occupy her hands. She poured some water into a cup and placed it in the microwave. "Jesus, Les. Sometimes I can't believe you. How the hell do you figure that? That this is somehow your fault? Or are you including me, too?" She punched the microwave's keypad angrily, setting it to humming.

Lester reacted instantly, straightening and waving his hands in protest. "No, no. That's not what I meant. It's not a fault thing. Not exactly. I just meant . . . It's just that when you think your own child has made that big a mistake, you gotta wonder." He paused before adding, "It started me thinking about my dad and what happened to him—how it affected me. I don't know. Maybe it's like what they say about how you're going to act in a crisis—you never know till it happens."

He passed a hand across his face. "Christ, I shot a man last year when he sicced that dog on me and Joe." He snapped his fingers. "Just like that. But this time . . ."

Susan sat back down across from him and took up his hand, her frustration quieted by the anxiety in his voice. She knew what he carried from his childhood, and had watched him deal with it—very well for the most part—from the first day he'd become a father himself. "Les, you're muddling it all up. You carry so much around inside, never letting anyone see what's going on, I'm not surprised you get confused sometimes. This is not rocket science." She smiled suddenly. "We just corner the little bastard and beat the crap out of him."

Lester stared at his wife for a split second before they both burst out laughing. It was a tension breaker, of course, and typical of her abilities in that department. It was partly what made her a good nurse. Nevertheless, through the laughter, they watched one another carefully.

Joe entered the conference room late, having gotten stuck behind a truck on the road from Brattleboro to Rutland. He was in the modern brick building on Wales Street housing both the sheriff's office and the police department. Sitting around the table were representatives of both those agencies, Rick McCall, the VSP sergeant in charge of the Southern Vermont Drug Task Force, and Mara Coven, the task force prosecutor. He knew them all, thankfully—some better than others—from his decades on the job. In the center of the large table, pointedly angled so Joe could read it upon crossing the threshold, was a copy of the *Rutland Herald* with the headline "Gov Declares War on Heroin."

"Sorry I'm late," he apologized, pulling out a chair. He'd seen the Brattleboro paper's treatment of the same news earlier, noting with relief that Bill Allard had apparently done his job. Despite the headline, Reynolds had "declared war" only at the very end of his statement, after specifying that the opening salvos would take place in Rutland. Sharon Lapierre's death was also revealed, as an overdose only and not in connection to Hollowell. Her fate was simply described as accidental, the investigation as ongoing, and the family—"close political allies of the governor"—as grieving. Apparently reversing his initial strategy, Reynolds was up-front about Lapierre's death being a major catalyst in his decision—a move no doubt designed to beat his political opponents to the punch. Most interesting to Gunther, however, was that the VBI was mentioned but once in the article as a support unit only.

So far, his struggle to maintain discretion—and therefore acceptance—was working. Today would be the acid test.

"I just got here myself," Mara Coven admitted, "and when I walked in, they were all talking motorcycles. Don't let them tell you otherwise."

"She cranked up the volume there," McCall protested. "Saying Harleys aren't worth a damn. Jeez, Louise."

They laughed and traded a few more barbs as Joe pulled out a chair. At least the mood was looking good, he thought.

"Okay," McCall finally spoke up again. "Much as I'd like to debate this topic at length, I guess we're here to earn our living." He pointed at the newspaper.

"Looks like with their usual leadership style, the politicians are leading from the rear, telling us stuff we've known about for years and promising the voters what we probably can't deliver. It also looks like they're pretending this whole heroin epidemic is centered here in Rutland, when we also know that Rutland's just a hot spot, like Burlington or Brattleboro or even around St. Johnsbury, for that matter."

"Except those places aren't where Sharon got whacked," Peter Bullis said softly. He was a short, square, muscular man, one half of Rutland's small but effective drug squad. An ex–task force member himself, he was a New York transplant and a true believer about the widening spread of drugs. One of the reasons he worked here instead of in the big city was that he thought—just maybe—that places like Vermont might have a chance in stemming a tide he'd seen drown his old hometown. The Rutland PD's drug team, now two years old, had been his idea, although Gunther had heard rumors that Bullis was beginning to despair. Vermont might have the opportunity to avert disaster, but the manpower and the money were lacking—the disadvantages of being one of the tiniest states in a country beset by this plague, standing last in line at the federal trough.

"True," McCall agreed, "which brings us to why we're here. The way things have developed ever since we found Hollowell swinging from the bridge and Lapierre dead in his motel room, we're now facing three situations. The first I hope we can do something about, the second we might be able to do something about, and the third is a pure pipe dream."

He paused for theatrical effect—always a bit of a ham—before explaining, "Of course, I mean the double murder as the first, putting a dent in the Rutland drug trade as the second, and ending drugs in Vermont as the third. Fortunately," and here he picked up the newspaper and held it up, "the governor put his mouth behind the second and only paid lip service to the third, so maybe—just maybe—we might have a chance."

No one else said a word. Joe was biding his time before representing his agency's role in this whole scheme, waiting until he'd tested the waters some more.

"When Sharon was killed," McCall went on, "we were told to call it an accidental and to throw Hollowell at the press to keep them busy. In the meantime, her old man went to the governor, who went to the commissioner of Public Safety, who went to my lieutenant, who, of course, went to me. That was predictable enough. At the same time, though, the governor apparently thought that we could do with a little help from the VBI, which explains our friend Joe being here, too." McCall bowed in Gunther's direction. "Of course, we always appreciate extra manpower, but that makes for a pretty crowded playing field." Here he addressed the two Rutland agencies. "Especially when the home team's already been at it for a while."

This was clearly Joe's prompt to jump in and explain

his presence in concrete terms, except that an investigator from the sheriff's office, named Tom, spoke first. "If it's okay, I'd like to speak for the sheriff on that. Our office is ready and willing to supply equipment, manpower, intel, and material support whenever it's requested, but we're not here to get in the way. We're entirely support, straight down the line, unless you specifically ask us to be otherwise."

Joe still didn't speak up. He could have ridden Tom's coattails, saying much the same thing, but he was curious that McCall had used the VBI's presence to avoid explaining his own agency's role here—or why he was the one running this meeting. Technically, the task force's charter was much like VBI's. They ran their own investigations, but a certain diplomacy was expected when on someone else's turf. Like now. Joe sensed that privately, Rick McCall felt he was standing on thin ice.

In the awkward pause following Tom's comments and Joe's silence, that issue obviously remained to be addressed.

"That's great," McCall began, caught off guard. "Always good to hear. I guess that brings up a chain-of-command question we should probably kick around a little. In the past,without this kind of political pressure, we've always worked the Rutland drug cases through the PD, either by acting as backup or by letting them know we were operating in their backyard."

Gunther glanced at Peter Bullis, expecting and getting the slight grimace he saw. It was no secret that while the task force probably intended to be as clear-

cut in its arrangements as McCall had just described,
the truth was often a bit more tangled. More than once,
Joe knew, Bullis had felt muscled out of the way either
by the task force's greater brawn or through the overly
aggressive personalities of some of its members. It had
never developed into any large bone of contention, but
it allowed Gunther the comfort of not being seen as the
only outsider, which was exactly what he'd been hoping for.

"In this situation, though," McCall was saying,
"since our marching orders come straight from
Montpelier, I had to meet with your chief earlier"—he
focused on the Rutland City cops—"to figure out how
best to proceed. It was his feeling—on paper only, of
course—that the Southern Vermont Drug Task Force
take the lead on the drug investigation, leaving the
homicides to the detective squad and relying on you
and your partner, Pete, to help us out with any local
contacts and information that might come in handy."

McCall didn't give Bullis time to react before
adding, "But I did say 'on paper,' meaning that, in fact,
I'm hoping we'll just basically work as an integrated
unit."

"I don't mind you taking the hot seat, Rick," Bullis
said with a small smile, riding the current Joe's silence
had put into motion. "My unit was designed to get rid
of drugs in Rutland City only. We don't have the time
or money to run a big operation. You've got half the
state to cover, so you're used to this. I'm a happy
camper the way things are."

Faced with Joe's stubborn unwillingness to explain

VBI's role, McCall was forced to reveal his own view instead.

"So, last but not least," he therefore dutifully resumed, "we also have the help of the VBI, who will be bringing in more money, people, and resources than we usually have, which'll be a big help once the heat builds up." McCall finally laughed and shook his head at this point, caving in and candidly admitting, "I got to be honest, though. I know it's part of my job to make sure everybody's happy and nobody's toes are being flattened, but, Joe, when I heard you guys were being thrown into the mix, I had a hard time figuring out why." He held a finger up for emphasis. "Until I got a call from Dick Allen. He was pretty clear we'd only benefit from your involvement, which was really good to hear."

Joe gave him a big smile, happy they'd finally stopped dancing around the issue. "I appreciate that, Rick, and like Tom"—he nodded toward the sheriff's investigator—"I want to stress that we're here entirely as a support group. I don't know what the grapevine might have told you, but Governor Reynolds first had it in his head that VBI was going to do this all on its own, since he sees us as his private caped crusaders. But we put the kibosh on that. It's not who we are or how we function.

"However," he added, shifting slightly in his seat, "we did think we might be able to do more than just supply cash and troops, so one of my people went down to Holyoke to sniff around a little, having heard there might've been changes in how the strings were being pulled up here. Is that true, Pete?"

"Yeah," Bullis admitted. "Could be this double homicide ties into it, too, but we're not sure yet. We've only been able to grill the locals, and they've only told us that something's going on in Holyoke. But it's still really vague." Bullis indicated the room with a sweep of his hand. "One of the problems we all have, being stretched so thin, is that we can only look after our own backyards. Plus, there's not much intel that crosses the border. Some, but not a lot, and it can be pretty dated."

McCall nodded silently in agreement.

"The name Johnny Rivera ever come up?" Gunther asked.

"The name Johnny has. One of the runners we pinched last week talked about somebody named Johnny as if he might be a player, but we weren't sure what to make of it."

"I've heard the name," McCall said. "He's a street dealer down there, I think. One of Torres's crew, maybe?"

"Was," Gunther corrected him, having spent two hours that morning debriefing Sam. "Johnny Rivera decided to move up, but instead of starting a turf war, he just grabbed Torres's piece of the Holyoke, Brattleboro, Rutland corridor, or at least is in the process. Nobody's happy with his screwing up the status quo—in fact, he lives in an apartment with armored windows—but for the moment at least, Vermont's his shot at the big time."

"That's some sniffing around," McCall commented. "How'd you get that?"

Gunther smiled ruefully, careful of how he played this. "New informant we dug up."

McCall gave him a sharp look and then made a show of checking his watch. "Well, we can always stand for a new one of those. I'm really sorry, but I've got to make a phone call in a couple of minutes. I couldn't get out of it, but it won't take long. Be all right if we took a ten-minute break?"

They all stood and either stretched or made for the bathroom or the coffee machine outside. McCall made a discreet gesture to Joe to follow him into an office down the hall, unnoticed by the others.

"Nice piece of swordplay in there. You are a crafty old bastard."

Gunther patted him on the shoulder. "Just keeping you honest."

McCall laughed. "That'll be the day. So what the hell're you pulling now—outsider to outsider? No way I'm swallowing the 'new informant' bit. You got something cooking."

Joe nodded his concession. "One of my people went a little over-the-top when it looked like we'd be brought into this case. I didn't sanction it—said we should take more time to set it up—but as things've turned out, I think we now have someone on the inside."

"We're not talking just an informant, are we?" McCall stated, his surprise evident.

Gunther shook his head. "A cop—undercover, working for Rivera."

McCall's shock was understandable. Popular fiction notwithstanding, running an undercover was a rare, risky, stressful undertaking, and not one that most Vermont law enforcement agencies had tried in decades. It was common to use an officer to make a buy, and not unheard-of to have one act as a bad guy over a period of days from time to time, as in pretending to be a fence for stolen goods. But as Sam and Joe had constructed it early this morning, largely on Sam's insistence that she be allowed to run it on her terms, this was a deep-undercover assignment—she was to commit herself to the role of Greta Novak for however long it took to nail Rivera and his operation.

"Full-time?" McCall persisted.

Gunther nodded. "It's Sammie Martens, which I'd like to restrict to you, me, Peter Bullis, and the Rutland chief and deputy chief, if that's all right."

"You bet," McCall said without hesitation. "Loose lips we can live without." He shook his head. "Christ. I can't believe you set this up so fast. It's amazing. How far along is Rivera to replacing Torres?"

"Just beginning. That's how Sam got in. She gave him some razzle-dazzle about setting things up along more business-oriented lines, and he bit—or I should say, he's in the process, since she hasn't shown her stuff yet."

"So was Hollowell his, or did Rivera take him out because he belonged to Torres?"

"That's one of the sixty-four-thousand-dollar questions. We're not sure yet."

McCall let out a short laugh and scratched his head. "Wow. This is cool. Sam is something else."

Joe was a little more rueful. "She has her moments."

McCall put his hand on Gunther's shoulder. "Okay. Well, thanks, Joe. I appreciate it anyhow, even if it did creep in the back door. And rest assured, there's nothing we'll do to compromise her. You need anything, you got it. We better get back in there."

Gunther kept his pleasure to himself. He'd ducked being seen with suspicion, resentment, or envy by this group. Whether because of Dick Allen's influence, Joe's clearly stated support role, or most likely because working an undercover was too good to resist, Rick McCall had obviously accepted the bureau as an integral part of the team.

Joe let out a small sigh of relief. Now all he had to worry about was Sam not getting herself killed.

Back in the conference room, McCall placed a briefcase on the table and opened it up. "Thanks for your patience. Bureaucratic bullshit, but has to be done. I've drawn up some preliminary paperwork on how to divide the labor and duties among us." He began handing out packets to everyone. "As you can see, we've been labeled the Heroin Task Force. Not too original, but it gets our purpose across. After we hash out the details and make sure everybody's happy—or maybe just equally pissed off—notifications will be sent to all law enforcement agencies statewide, announcing our existence." He paused and pointedly looked at Joe. "That does bring up something, though. If we are to refer to all this outside this room, it might be useful to have a less obvious code word, for discretion's sake. Any suggestions?"

"I thought about that," Gunther answered him. "At the risk of sounding corny, how 'bout Gatekeeper?"

McCall hesitated a moment before smiling. "I like it."

Chapter 10

Gail checked her watch again. She'd arranged to have brunch with Debbie Holton an hour ago, and still the young woman hadn't appeared or left word. Gail was sitting at the window of Walker's Restaurant, on Brattleboro's Main Street—and once again had consumed enough caffeine to set her nerves up for a week.

"More coffee?"

Gail started and turned to look at the waitress holding a thermos and a sympathetic expression—a veteran of broken dates plainly yearning to share her advice with the lovelorn.

Gail smiled and shook her head. "No thanks, I think a bathroom and a walk is what I need now."

She paid her bill, used the bathroom, and stepped out onto the sidewalk, lost in the effort of remembering the West Brattleboro motel Debbie had referred to as home for the time being. Debbie had said the name the day before when they'd gone for lunch at the Food Co-op after meeting for the first time on the wooden staircase between Elliot and Flat Streets. But she'd tossed it off incongruously, Gail had thought, since it hadn't been in any context. As a result, it had drifted into the darkness of Gail's subconscious.

Which wasn't a place from where it would likely be retrieved. In Gail's present state of mind, only the here and now, along with a barely hopeful future, were holding sway. She was bent on righting the imagined wrongs of the past and wasn't inclined to cast a reflective glance over her shoulder. Not at the moment. Maybe later, once she'd found some footing in an act of redemption, might she truthfully face her responsibilities regarding Laurie. But right now it was full speed ahead on a tank full of guilt.

At least it was a beautiful day, sunny but not hot, and the weather seemed to imbue the pedestrians she passed with a lightness and grace. And there were a fair number of them. Brattleboro's heart, unlike those of other, more spread out downtowns, is almost channeled in its layout, forcing its frequenters to be corralled down a sloped, slightly curving length of road between two walls of sturdy, dependable, embracing red brick buildings. Throwbacks to an earlier commercial might, garnished here and there with now quaint architectural flourishes, these stolid, flat-roofed buildings, none much higher than five stories, had exchanged an older muscular aura for something gentler over time. Soot-stained, slightly worn, and more filled with reminiscence than relevance nowadays, these side-by-side behemoths had gently sideslipped into something softer—like grandparents whose authority had yielded to bulk and wrinkles and the impression of wisdom and protectiveness.

Suddenly recalling her destination's name against all odds, Gail continued on Main Street across Elliot and descended the steep sidewalk leading to the town's primary "malfunction junction," where four arteries and a large parking lot commingled in anarchy. Shy of that, however, just beyond the Army Navy store, she cut right onto Flat Street to retrieve her car.

She took the backstreets to what the locals called West B, avoiding the major bridge linking the town's halves—sliced by the interstate as surely as by a canyon—and tucked into Western Avenue by Living Memorial Park. There she stayed, clocking the miles, watching the town peter out, until she finally came abreast of the battered, threadbare motel whose name Debbie had mentioned.

Gail parked, got out of the car, and tentatively approached a shedlike office. Given the whole place's appearance, she had no doubt the rates were reasonable and the rooms available by the minute or the month.

Her hand was barely on the screen-door handle when a woman's voice asked, "Who do you want?"

Gail saw a vague, heavyset shadow in the darkness

of the office. She didn't open the door. "Debbie Holton."

"Eighteen," came the immediate response.

Gail was about to retreat but then suddenly asked, "How did you know I wasn't looking for a room?"

All she heard was a throaty, incredulous laugh and the slamming of an unseen inner door.

She walked along the ranks of cheap, hollow-core doors, imagining the lives they'd barricaded only poorly. She finally stopped and knocked loudly on number 18.

The door opened after a minute to reveal a thin young man, his eyebrow pierced with a silver post, his cheeks swathed with a wanna-be beard, wearing an expression that changed instantly from surly to lascivious as his half-opened eyes took her in. "Hello, Mama," he said, drawing out the first word.

Both the look and the line were hammy enough that Gail felt none of the fright she'd experienced in meeting the late Roger Novelle. Also, this one had a joint dangling from his lips, which tended to ruin his Lothario image. Nevertheless, this wasn't whom she'd expected to see, and so she stammered as she admitted, "I'm sorry. I think I made a mistake."

Debbie's voice circled around the young man, who was taking his time admiring their caller. "That you, Gail? Come on in. That's Nelson. He likes to be called Kicker, but no one calls him that."

Nelson opened the door wider but didn't move back. He was probably close to twenty, maybe older, but his demeanor remained pure teenager. Gail placed her hand against his chest and gently shoved him out of the way, broadening his smile.

The room was predictably awful—small, cluttered, and messy. The walls were decorated with some magazine pictures and a couple of stolen road signs. The furniture was sparse and in need of a trip to the dump, the bed was a stained, bare mattress. Debbie sat in its middle, her legs crossed, her back against a pile of clothes and pillows. She, too, was holding a joint and a lazy smile.

"Welcome to home sweet home," she said cheerily, a watt and a half too bright to be believable. "Grab a piece of floor and take a load off."

Gail glanced around, feeling Nelson still standing too close for comfort. "That's okay. I just dropped by to see how you were. I thought we were going to have brunch today. I started getting worried."

"No worry," Debbie said. "Everything's A-okay."

"Yeah," Nelson said from right behind her. "Stick around. Want some weed?"

She shifted her weight, leaning away from him, keeping her eyes on Debbie. "No. Should you be doing that?"

The young woman's eyes grew round. "What? This?" She brandished the joint.

"Doesn't it violate the agreement you have with the treatment center?"

Debbie laughed. "God. I guess so. But what they don't know won't hurt them, right?"

Here her eyes narrowed slightly so Gail would get the message.

Nelson moved a couple of inches closer and said in a seductive near miss, "Yeah. Our little secret. Sure you don't want a hit, at least?"

She faced him squarely, giving in to her growing annoyance. "Sit down, junior." She turned toward the bed. "And listen up. This is not about my being your buddy and winking while you ruin your life. I've got one too many on my conscience already. But I can help, and I will help if you meet me halfway."

Nelson had moved across the room, his expression closed.

"Chill out, Gail," Debbie said tiredly. "I'm not ruining my life. You want to know the truth, I'm getting it back together." She dangled the joint between her fingers. "This is nothing—it's like you having a beer. I am getting counseling. You said that yourself. I'm fine."

Gail had a sudden memory of herself at nearly the same age, sitting in a similar setting, albeit on a farm near Marlboro, smoking pot and spouting the same nonsense. To her, as to Debbie right now, the comparison between alcohol and marijuana had been benign and reasonable. But Gail had grown up, become a teetotaler, and no longer saw any benefit to either substance. If weed was a gateway to more addictive drugs, then beer was a gateway to liquor, in her hardened view.

But she knew she couldn't take that line with this

girl, especially given the company she was keeping. Nelson might have been as big a threat as he was a ladies' man, but Gail seriously doubted he had Debbie's best interests in mind.

"I'm not going to argue the point here," she said instead. "Not with him around, and not with that crap in your system. I have something to offer you—I can be a guide to the other side, if you like. But you're going to have to come to me next time, and you better be clean."

With that, she turned on her heel, left the room, and slammed the door behind her, making sure they could hear the slap of her heels on the sidewalk as she retreated toward her car.

But her heart wasn't in it. She knew some of the techniques, had seen them used in her volunteer counseling, and didn't need telling that what she'd just laid down was part of a tried-and-true process. But none of it held against her mental snapshot of Laurie lying in that hospital bed—along with the caption that Gail had played a role in putting her there.

She knew full well that if Debbie didn't seek her out in short order, Gail would be back at this motel trying something else. It might be an obsession in the making, but a worthwhile one.

Or so she told herself.

Joe hung up the phone on Gail's machine without leaving a message. He'd already left two, and worried he was back where he'd been before his midnight visit. Her niece had affected her like a tectonic shift. Gail may have *still* been walking and talking, albeit under stress, but who knew what had changed underneath?

He was *still* in Rutland, the meeting having run for hours. They had hashed out everything from procedures and responsibilities to how to prosecute any arrests they might make. They'd even talked about various forfeiture strategies, in case they picked up any money, cars, or valuable property along the way. Notes had been taken, graphs produced, deadlines established, communication webs and chains of command. The most satisfying aspect of it from Gunther's perspective was that the VBI would be playing the support role he'd asked for, across the board, from the Rutland PD, to the state police drug task force, to merely picking up slack where necessary. In all things concerning Sam and whatever she might encounter, however, they were autonomous, free to act spontaneously and instinctively, the only proviso being that McCall be kept inside the circle.

Which was both good and bad news. For, beyond a couple of unsolved homicides, a governor's political pressure, and the overall goal of denting the drug trade, they were primarily responsible for the care and welfare of a single cop. What Sam had done of her own volition now made her the top of the proverbial iceberg, leaving them all to make sure she stayed upright.

Their hopes were that she might open the doors through which they could complete most of the tasks before them. But Joe Gunther's biggest fear was that, were the slightest thing to go wrong, everything could collapse, and he could lose someone as close to him as his own flesh and blood.

He stared at the phone again, thinking back briefly to Gail, wondering what she was up to.

So many loose strings, he thought. So much at risk.

Chapter 11

Sammie checked herself in the cracked mirror, pondering the symbolism of seeing herself reflected in two halves.

"About right," she murmured, and turned off the light.

She stepped out of the bathroom and moved to where Johnny Rivera was packing up bundles of heroin with latex-gloved hands, sitting before a set of electronic scales, a razor blade, a pile of rubber bands, and an assortment of small plastic bags, each stamped with the symbol of a lurking panther, clearly his trademark.

"Ready for your maiden voyage?" he asked. He followed that with a suggestive glance. "I guess your maiden days are pretty long gone, though, huh?"

"That's for me to know," she said, watching him expertly scraping and cutting the drug into the baggie-sized quantities he'd proposed she sell in Vermont in order to prove her worth. He had the heroin separated into three groups: the highly compacted "plugs," which arrived from New York looking like oversized pieces of chalk; the baggies, with so little drug in them—just .025 gram—that it almost resembled the fluff from a dandelion; and finally, the bundles, made up of ten bags apiece.

Each plug was enough to create forty bundles, or four hundred bags. Sammie figured that Johnny, depending on his haggling skills, maybe paid $1,200 to $1,500 for each plug. From what Bill Dancer had told her, she knew such an amount, broken down into bags, might fetch a mere $2,000 in Holyoke—that's what she'd paid him to buy into tonight's run. In Vermont, the same amount could go for $14,000. No surprise that Johnny had seized this as an opportunity. The surprise was that his competitors hadn't taken him out yet—except that business was perhaps still so good in Holyoke, claims from the police chief notwithstanding, that even at low local prices, enough money was being made to exceed demand.

"Who're my contacts going to be in Bratt and Rutland?" she asked casually.

He paused in his work to look up at her. "What did you just say? 'That's for me to know'? This is a test, girlie. You don't get contacts. You make sales—a lot of sales real quick—and my contacts, as you call them, will report back to me how good you did. You do that, and bring me back the money, and we'll see about what else. We talked about this yesterday. You said your boyfriend Dancer had all the contacts you need. Your bullshit beginning to show?"

She shrugged. "My efficient business sense is beginning to show. I got lots of people to go to, but you want to waste time doing a dog-and-pony act, that's fine with me. I'll jump through a few hoops for you, but you better be serious. What's my cut going to be?"

He laughed. "Your cut? For a test run? Your cut is you get in if you do the job good."

She stared at him incredulously. "I don't think so, Pancho. I don't even fart for free."

His jaw tightened at what she'd called him. "You be very careful, chica."

"Then don't call me girlie."

Slowly, his eyebrows furrowed. "That's it? I call you girlie and you get all pissed off? Jesus."

"What's my cut?" she repeated.

"Two thousand."

"Four. That's only double my investment."

He shoved his chair back and stood facing her. "Four? You outta your mind? No fucking way I'm paying you four thousand bucks for a virgin run."

"You'll be getting ten grand after expenses, Johnny." She dragged out the pronunciation of his name and threw him a pout at the end.

His eyes narrowed in anger. "You little bitch. I kill you right here, nobody knows, nobody cares."

She smiled and almost whispered, "Except you. With the cops crawling all over Rutland, looking into that hanging and forcing whoever you have up there underground, this is the closest thing you have to a cash cow—my pretty white Vermont face. Three thousand. As a gift from me to you—a show of faith."

He held her gaze for a full thirty seconds before turning away and sitting back down at the table. "Deal."

It was dark by the time Johnny, Sam, and Bill Dancer, who'd been cooling his heels downstairs all afternoon, stepped into the street and crossed over to Bill's car. Lounging against its fender was a slim young man with a malevolent air.

"This is Manuel," Rivera announced, handing him the paper bag full of heroin he'd been carrying. "He's going with you."

"Bullshit, he is," Sam answered. "He's the exact reason you can't do this without me. I get seen driving around with him, the first cop we meet'll stop us."

Rivera stared at her contemptuously. "Then push his face into your lap, hot stuff. Show him what you got. You come from a state where boys marry boys. They can live with one poor lucky turncoat who can't keep his hands off white meat." His face turned mean as she opened her mouth to protest, and he concluded, "He's going—*girlie*. Lie back and enjoy it."

She shifted tack then and stepped very close to him, daring him to pull back, which he knew he couldn't do and save face. Her mouth almost touching his, she said softly. "Maybe I will, Johnny. In your dreams."

She then moved back abruptly and ordered Manuel,

"Get in the back, then, and don't sit too high up, or they'll be on us like flies on shit."

Manuel stiffened and closed his fists. Sam smiled at them both. "Ooh. Speaks English. That's a start."

Johnny said something quick and unintelligible to his sidekick, who sullenly got into the back of the car, slamming the door behind him. Rivera looked at Sam seriously, all posturing gone. "Greta Novak, I know you think you're very hot shit and that I'm going to be making you into my number one guy, but be careful. Don't push it too far." He tilted his head slightly in the direction of the car. "People like Manuel don't have the management skills I have. He don't know that some assholes can sometimes be handy. He just kills them— it's worth it to him to get in trouble after."

Sam read his expression, considered a retort worthy of Greta, but then stopped, seeing in Johnny's eyes not just deadly earnestness but even an element of real concern.

She reached out and touched his forearm. "Don't worry, Johnny. We'll get along fine, and we'll bring back some money." She smiled. "Like the movie says, this is the beginning of a beautiful friendship."

Sammie Martens wasn't happy, but she didn't feel boxed in, either. Having Manuel along as a watchdog, she finally rationalized, staring through the side window as Bill Dancer drove through the night toward Vermont, might even play to her advantage. If she was impressive enough, the report to the boss could only

help, especially coming from a source she'd made no
effort to win over.

Although that last part did concern her. In her effort
to get Manuel out of the trip, she feared she'd overplayed her dismissiveness of him—he could mess her
up in Johnny's eyes just as easily as he could help.
Perhaps more so, given the stony silence that had
drifted over from the back seat like a cold fog since
they'd headed out.

"Hey, Manuel," she therefore said in a conversational voice, slinging her arm up on the seat back in
order to half turn in his direction. "Hope you didn't
take what I said back there personally. I'm just trying
to keep us out of trouble and make a pile for everybody,
you know?"

Manuel stared back at her, unmoving, expression-
less.

"I mean," she continued, "it's kind of like a con
job—you gotta dress and act like the people you're
planning to rip off. Dumb, but that's the way it is."

But even Bill had gotten her first message loud and
clear. "Give it a rest, Greta. You called the guy a slime-
ball. All the sucking up in the world ain't gonna change
that."

She gave one last glance at Manuel's unsettling
poker face before turning back toward the front again.
"Up yours, Bill. I mean it."

The green "Welcome to Vermont" sign loomed up
into the car's headlights by the side of the interstate and
flashed by like a specter. Show time was nearing.

She placed her hands flat on her thighs. This was

where the fabric of her design would be tested, beginning with Bill Dancer's involvement. She'd needed him for access to Miguel Torres. But now that Torres was no longer a factor, Dancer had suddenly become the odd man—not out necessarily, but certainly not in. Rivera assumed, as did Bill, that they were a team, but Sam knew that Dancer, far more than Manuel, was the loose cannon.

Joe had pointed this out during her debriefing the day before, asking if there might be a way to get him out of the picture. She'd bluffed her answer then, eager enough to impress her mentor that she casually dismissed the problem. "I got him where I want him" was the line, or something equally obvious in hindsight.

In fact, she had no idea where she had him. He behaved like a lapdog, so pleased to be in her company that he was willing to do anything, but during this very drive, she'd begun to wonder at the truth of that. He seemed different heading into the drug dealer's equivalent of battle—either more self-possessed than she'd expected or perhaps simply more adrenalized. The tone of his voice during that last comment caught it well— there was a new edge, and she wasn't sure what it meant.

"Pull off at Exit One," she told Bill as Brattleboro drew closer, her confidence sounding tinny to her own ears. "I want to use a pay phone at the gas station, to line up the first buy. I got people itching for this good shit, all their beepers waiting to flame on."

Bill dug into his pocket, squirming in his seat. He handed her a small phone. "Use my cell. Easier."

She looked at it, surprised he had one, and didn't take it. "Forget it. Don't you know? They're starting to pick up on those things—radio waves or something. Give me a pay phone anytime."

He laughed, his hand still outstretched. "You shitting me? In Vermont? We don't even have state police coverage around the clock. You think they have fancy crap like that, sniffing the air for illegal cell phone chitchat? You are definitely smoking something, babe."

She looked at him hard, struck again by his tone, and especially the nickname. That was a first. "You want to screw this up from the start, be my guest. In the meantime, pull off like I said. I already got this locked in. I put out the call, they all know to show up behind a certain building on Canal. We deal right from the car window, and we're back on the interstate, heading for Bellows Falls—no muss, no fuss."

Dancer put the phone back into his pocket. The exit was coming into view. Sam let out an inward sigh. She had video surveillance arranged at the pay phone so they could document this buy from start to finish. She could have used the cell. It wouldn't have made any difference. All the buyers that were to show up were either cops or paid informants. But again, she'd been triggered by Bill's attitude and thought it a good time to take him down a peg.

"Suit yourself," he said, without the resentment she'd expected.

He aimed the car at the downhill exit and swept onto Canal.

"Right there," she pointed at a battered phone under a nearby streetlight, the better to photograph by.

But Dancer kept up his speed. "Change of plans," he said, oozing the pleasure of someone springing a surprise. "I got a deal going that'll look like Fred and Ginger all over again. We'll be so hot, Rivera'll shit his pants."

He drove past the gas station and turned right on Fairground Road.

"Pull over, Bill," Sam yelled at him. "Don't you screw around with this. This is our shot, goddammit. Pull over." Out of the corner of her eye, she saw Manuel sit forward in his seat, getting ready to act if necessary.

Bill pushed Sam's hands away from the steering wheel. "I know it's our shot, stupid. That's why I'm doing it. I'm the contact guy, remember? This is my job. I'm not going to screw around selling to a couple of needle freaks in town after town all over southern Vermont. That's stupid. Score once, score big, and blow Rivera's socks off. He won't even be on his second sitcom before we drop a bag of cash at his feet in an hour and a half."

He laughed and glanced at her. "Face it, Greta, you got the brains for some of this—I give you that. But I know this turf. I set it up while you were jerking around with Johnny boy, or whatever the hell you were doing up there." He patted his pocket. "Cell phones work just fine, and nobody is listening in. Trust me."

Unfortunately, she did. There wasn't a snowball's chance in hell that any agency in Vermont had the cash, the equipment, or even the know-how to grab a cell phone signal and do anything more than triangulate its source. Their first buy on their first outing on her first detail as an undercover was just about to go wild.

"Joe," the voice crackled in his earphone, "they just blew by the pay phone. Gatekeeper didn't look happy."

Joe straightened in his seat and pressed the earphone to his ear. He was sitting in a van parked nearby. They'd agreed to use Gatekeeper instead of Sam's name just to be safe. "Define unhappy."

The voice belonged to Lester Spinney. He and Joe were the only ones on this detail, testing the waters and lending Sam moral support. Traditionally, a deep undercover is on his or her own, except for checking in with control on a regular, preset basis. This time, however, because the operation had come together so fast, Joe had asked Rick McCall if he could baby-sit Sam's first outing. McCall had agreed but had limited them to Brattleboro only, not wanting to risk exposure.

"Just that. Dancer's at the wheel and he turned right onto Fairground. I think she's just pissed off. There's a third rider, by the way. Somebody in the back seat. I'm following them now."

Joe slid in behind the wheel of the surveillance van and pulled into traffic, driving down Canal toward South Main, which eventually looped around to meet up with Fairground Road. That way, he and Spinney were coming in from opposite directions.

"You get a look at the third rider?" he asked.

Spinney's voice was calm, as always, almost conversational, despite everyone being off the game plan by now. That was one thing about Spinney. Gunther had no idea what had been distracting him lately, but in a crunch, the man was as steady as a tree trunk.

"Nope. Just a shadow. We've passed the high school and the town garage, now heading toward the far end of South Main."

This was the same street where Henry Jordan had first spotted Roger Novelle—a magnet for this kind of activity. "I'm coming in from the far end," Gunther told him. "Don't crowd them."

Bill Dancer pulled over to the side of the street and extracted his cell phone again. Sam watched him, torn over what to do. He did have contacts. It was possible he had set something up that would reflect well on them. Her plan had been to deal to people she and Joe had set up all down the line, hoping both to keep the heroin out of circulation and to cover themselves legally—even deep undercover, she was still a cop and could not sell drugs personally. But this was now Bill's play. She was off the hook in the eyes of the law.

Maybe this could work.

"Hey, Bobby," Bill was saying into the phone. "How's it hanging, bro? I got the stuff if you got the time."

He laughed at whatever response he heard. "No problem, dude. Be there in five. Start countin' out the money."

Dancer put the car back into gear and resumed driving down South Main, but slowly, his eyes on the house numbers. "There it is," he said finally, pulling over, killing the engine, and, Sam noticed, leaving the key in the ignition. "Everybody out."

Sam and Manuel stepped onto the sidewalk and looked around as Bill popped open the car trunk and retrieved Rivera's bag. South Main was an interesting mix of homes and apartments, some middle-class, many far less fortunate. This entire part of town was largely overlooked by Brattleboro's citizenry, acknowledged only when one of the street's several bordering cemeteries was put to use or when a high-profile crime was committed here. But unlike many low-income neighborhoods, this one was also low-profile—the signs and symptoms of its status were easily missed by motorists who used South Main as a shortcut to elsewhere. There were no boarded up or gutted buildings, no gangs of kids loitering around spruced up BMWs. This wasn't Holyoke. It wasn't a hot spot. It was a remote way station on misery's course into the hinterland. Too many of the people who lived here were either victims or transient opportunists, with no more plans of empire building than making enough bucks to see them through the day—or buying enough dope to minimize the pain.

With a bright, cocky smile, Bill Dancer strode by them with the paper bag, heading toward a ramshackle, two-story building with a sagging front porch. "Let's go make some money."

For the first time, Sam and Manuel shared a connection, glancing at each other, he with raised eyebrows, she with a shrug, followed by simultaneous smiles, before they swung in behind the subject of their nervous amusement and climbed the steps to the porch.

They were met at the door by a grim-faced bearded man with his hand under his shirt and his eyes on the street behind them. He placed his free hand flat against Bill's chest and stopped him at the threshold.

"Not so fast."

Bill sounded incredulous. "I just called, for Christ's sake. Lighten up. Bob said to come ahead."

"And now you stop," the man said, "until I tell you different."

He looked at the other two. "You stay outside while I check him out."

He grabbed Bill by the shirtfront and began dragging him inside.

"The bag," Sam quickly said.

Catching her meaning, Bill back-passed the bag to her as he vanished through the door.

In the few moments it took the bearded man to check Bill for weapons or wires, Sam whispered to Manuel, "I don't like this divide-and-conquer shit. If anything goes wrong, we grab the product and run."

Manuel spoke for the first time since they'd met. "What about your friend?"

"If this goes wrong, he's on his own. I got bigger fish to fry than that loser."

The door reopened and the doorman motioned to her. Sam handed the bag to Manuel. "See ya."

The bearded man pulled her by the arm into a small

room off the entryway and pushed her up against the wall, holding her there with one hand hard against her breast.

"You're cute."

She smiled back. "You're not. You want to get this done?"

His expression froze. He extracted a .40 Glock from under his shirt and shoved it painfully into her stomach, making her gasp for air. "I had a wife with a mouth like yours. You don't wanna know what happened to her."

Sam spoke through gritted teeth. "She probably got bored."

The bouncer's search was thorough and painful, leaving Sam at the end of it walking bowlegged for several minutes. He pushed her by the scruff of the neck into an adjacent room, where Bill was waiting.

"You okay?" he asked.

She glared at him. "You are a total moron. You know we're going to get ripped off here, right?"

His voice climbed to a plaintive pitch. "That's not true. Bob and me go back."

She held up her hand. "Shut up." She moved to the door she'd just entered by, paused a moment to listen, and then walked through fast and low. Ahead of her, his gun to Manuel's head, the bouncer had just torn the bag from his hand. At the sound of her entrance, he turned and began swinging the gun in her direction. He was too late. Crossing to him quickly, Sam grabbed a lamp off a small table and in the same gesture smacked him across the side of the head, breaking the lamp, exploding the bulb in a bright flash of light, and bringing him to his knees. She kicked the gun from his hand and finished him off with a chop to the side of the neck. He fell over without a sound.

Manuel stared at her openmouthed, as did Bill, entering behind her.

Through the open door to the entryway, they heard footsteps descending the stairs. A fat man in a stained T-shirt and electric-green sneakers appeared, looking shocked and apologetic in the remaining light from a dim lamp in the far corner. He spread his hands wide to his sides, looking at Dancer and shaking his head. "Jesus, Bill, what the hell happened? That crazy bastard didn't try to rip you off, did he?"

Bill was still staring at everyone wide-eyed and mute. "Bob," he finally said, "what's the deal? You and me go back—"

But the fat man interrupted him, approaching and patting his arm with one meaty paw. "No, no, Bill. I'm real sorry. The guy's a maniac. High most of the time. Crazy bastard. I shouldn't have him around."

As if to prove the point, he took a halfhearted but solid shot at the downed man's head with his sneaker and then draped his arm around Bill's shoulders. "I'm real sorry. Come on up, all of you. I gotta make this up."

Bill paused long enough to stoop and retrieve the paper bag. After he and their host had turned their backs to address the staircase in the cramped entryway, Sam picked up the bearded man's abandoned gun, sticking it discreetly into her waistband at the small of her back. Just before she fell into step behind

Bill, who was following Bob upstairs, she leaned in close to Manuel, who started slightly in surprise, and murmured, "If I yell go, you go. No questions."

"Les, update, goddammit." Joe had seen the flash of the lamp being broken over the doorman's head, without knowing the details.

Spinney hesitated, still squinting through a pair of binoculars from his position closer by. "Sorry, boss. Had to figure it out first. I'm still not sure, but Sa— shit—Gatekeeper may have thrown a lamp at somebody, maybe the guy who met them at the door. I saw some shadows when the light flashed. Looked like she was still standing."

"What're they doing now?"

"It's quiet. I can see movement at the windows upstairs, but all the shades are drawn."

Gunther swore silently to himself. This whole operation was falling apart. He should never have let her do this.

"Call for backup, Les. Have them stand by at first, but let's you and me get ready to move. I don't like this at all."

Sounding like a herd of cattle, they all stomped up the narrow wooden stairs, each person's eyes on the heels of the one before him. Except for Sam, who was trying her best to peer around the bulk of the big man leading the parade who was still talking in a loud voice about how hard it was to get good help.

His voice was too loud, she thought, and his mood too falsely upbeat given what had just transpired. And she didn't like the fact that while they were climbing under a single light high above, the top of the stairs and the landing doubling back above them were cloaked in darkness.

Surreptitiously, she reached back and wrapped her hand around the gun butt.

Which is when she heard a small metallic click—as with a safety being released—above and over her right shoulder, where the landing gave way to a shadowed door on the second floor. She spun around, her gun out, just in time to see the glimmer of the overhead light on the black metal of a semiautomatic.

There was an enormous flash as the shooter fired at her, thrown off by her sudden move. She fired back, heard a yell, and spun around to snatch the paper bag from Bill Dancer's hand as everyone began shouting at once.

"Go, go, go, go," she screamed at Manuel, pushing at him and kicking him to get him going back down the stairs. Another shot rang out and a piece of plaster snapped next to her head. She paused a moment, fired four times wildly overhead, and heard several people diving for cover.

She and Manuel stumbled, jumped, and half fell down the staircase as more gunshots flashed like lightning, punctuated by a bedlam of voices.

Incredulous they were still alive and unhurt, Sam propelled Manuel out the door, yelling, "To the car, to the car," just as she saw Lester Spinney dive out of sight behind a bush near the front walkway.

But Manuel was too stunned to notice much of anything. He staggered toward Bill's car as instructed, looking over his shoulder at her and the house beyond, clearly expecting a small army to burst out in hot pursuit.

"Get in," she ordered, circling the hood to reach the driver's seat. She could hear sirens approaching in the distance, and as she slid behind the wheel, she caught a glimpse of Joe Gunther crouching behind a nearby parked car. Unseen by Manuel, she gave her boss a quick nod and a thumbs-up signal out the window.

She turned the key, fired up the engine, did a tight, wheel-squealing U-turn in the middle of the road, and retreated the way they'd come, heading for the interstate.

"Jesus," Manuel was saying. "What happened?"

"It was a setup. That idiot Bill set us up to get ripped off and killed. Probably bragged to the fat bastard that he had a fortune worth of dope to sell, or some damn fool thing. Guaranteed to get everyone good and greedy."

"Johnny's not going to like this."

Sam pulled over suddenly, killed the lights, and yanked Manuel down onto the bench seat with her. Two patrol cars went screaming past them, unaware the car wasn't empty. She straightened and resumed driving at normal speed, the car's peaceful progress at direct odds to the hammering of her heart. But not from fear, or even postaction nerves. It was excitement. Sam was

feeling on top of the world, as if she'd confronted the
lion of legend and bearded it thoroughly.

"Johnny's not going to know," she said confidently.

Manuel stared at her and pointed out the back window, his anger boiling over. "What the fuck you mean?
We almost got killed. I'm going to tell him you're a
fucking crazy bitch. What do you think?"

"I think," she said calmly, "that you can tell him
whatever you want, but not till we're done selling his
junk."

"Selling? Who the hell're you gonna sell to? You
gonna hang out a sign? Maybe the cops'll chip in."

"Nah," she told him, casting him a smile. "That
wouldn't work. Relax. Brattleboro may be blown for
tonight, but we'll get a few customers in Bellows Falls
and Springfield."

He stared at her in stunned silence as she hit the turn
signal and headed toward the northbound ramp.

"See what you can find on the radio."

She kept both her hands on the wheel, not daring to
show him how much she was shaking.

Chapter 12

You crazy piece of shit. What the hell do you think you're doing?"

Willy Kunkle was leaning over Joe's desk, one large hand planted on top of a pile of paperwork like a club.

"Sit down," Gunther told him.

"The hell I will. Answer me."

Gunther's voice didn't change, nor did he back away from the other man's glowering face. "Sit down."

There was a long, tense silence as the two men stared into one another's eyes, before Willy straightened and finally accepted the chair Joe had indicated.

"What's your problem?"

"As if you didn't know," Willy snapped back. "I expect everyone else to jerk me around. Par for the course. But you had me thinking you were a straight shooter."

Gunther didn't respond, refusing to rise to the bait.

"I'm talking about Sam, duh," Willy finally said in frustration. "What the hell did you think?"

"What about her?"

Willy stared at him and then jumped to his feet, knocking the chair over backward. He began storming around the small office, waving his good arm as he shouted, "What *about* her? You think I'm an idiot? She's gone undercover, for Christ's sake. You *put* her undercover, risking her life for a bunch of dope-sniffing losers and the sorry bastards that feed them." He froze and glared at his boss. "What the *fuck* were you thinking?"

"You were once one of those losers yourself, even if your drug was alcohol."

Willy's mouth dropped open. "You asshole," he finally said.

"Maybe. You saying she's not qualified?"

That put him in another box. His face darkened with fury. "I'm saying there's a good reason nobody sends a cop undercover in this state anymore. We can't give them the support they need."

"You may be right." Gunther pointed to the overturned chair. "You want to try using that again?"

Reluctantly, Willy complied, righting the chair and sitting in it.

"How'd you find out?" Gunther asked.

"I couldn't find her anywhere. Then I dropped by to see who they jailed last night from the OK Corral blowout and heard that prick Bill Dancer whining about how some bitch named Greta Novak had screwed him royal. I know we're tied into the drug task force. Rocket science it wasn't."

Gunther nodded. "She turned a bad situation completely around. Les and I were there, saw it go down. She was thrown a can of worms and she sorted it out."

"I heard nobody knows what the hell happened."

"That's what we told the papers. We do think Sam shot somebody in self-defense and that whoever it was has vanished, probably down to Massachusetts or New York to get patched up. But otherwise, we nailed everyone else for probation or weapons or drug charges. Your old pal Bob Ryan was at the top of the list, in case you missed that detail. And Sam not only made it happen, but she got out without being blown and even made points with her bad boy escort."

"Who is?"

Gunther shook his head. "Need to know, Willy, and you already know way more than you should."

Kunkle bristled at that. "Yeah, no shit. I'm the one guy who'd catch a bullet for her and I'm being kept in the dark. Fucking *Lester's* on the inside, for crying out loud. What the hell gives you the right to screw with people's lives?"

Joe smiled at that. "You think I put this together?"

Willy instantly grasped his meaning. "You could've stopped her. You can still stop her."

"How'd you react if you were me?"

Willy Kunkle seemed suddenly deflated by all the sparring. His shoulders slumped, and he stared at the floor for a few moments before conceding, "Crazy

174 ARCHER MAYOR

bitch. One of these days she'll get into a crack . . ." His voice trailed off.

Gunther took pity on him, now that it seemed safer to do so. Willy's ex-wife, Mary, had recently died in New York City. They hadn't kept in touch, but the guilt over how he'd treated her while they were married— and the fact that afterward she'd fallen on hard times— had propelled him to go AWOL in order to solve her death. He hadn't lost his job over it, although he'd come close, and he had been successful in his pursuit, but he'd been typically reckless and had almost cost Sam her life. The irony of that had been lost on none of them, and it had certainly done nothing to smooth Willy's rough edges. Life's lessons seemed as baffling and contradictory as ever to him.

"What she's doing isn't risk-free," Gunther admitted, "but we do have a good bunch watching her back."

"Why not me?" Willy suddenly asked, looking up at him hopefully.

"You know why," the older man said gently.

Kunkle might have blown up again at that, but he knew the ground rules, even if he so rarely followed them. With his personal attachment to Sam, neither he nor anyone else would know for sure how he might react in a crisis. Among cops, it was like not letting a surgeon operate on his own wife.

Joe watched him sympathetically for a while before saying, "I am sorry I kept you out of the loop. I tried calling you twice at home, but I couldn't find you. And I didn't want to leave a message."

Willy nodded wearily. "I know. I've been doing my

usual night crawling, keeping tabs on the scumballs."
He sighed and stood up quietly. "Could you give me an
update now and then? I mean, I'm guessing she's under
till the end, right?"

Gunther nodded. "I'll keep you informed." He
paused, rubbed his chin, and added, "But you keep out
of it, okay? I don't want to see you anywhere near this
operation. For Sam's sake."

Willy addressed the floor, his voice almost mournful. "Right."

Sam sat on one of Johnny Rivera's chairs, facing the
window, her feet propped up on its sill, staring out at
the clouds she could see floating by over the top of the
metal sheet blocking the rest of the view.

"You ever get out of here? This would drive me nuts.
Where do you actually live?"

Rivera ignored her, sitting at his worktable, counting
the money she'd brought in. Manuel was leaning
against the wall by the door, smoking a cigarette.

Sam got up, pulled her chair closer to the window,
and then stood on it to see over the top of the obstruc-
tion.

That caught Rivera's attention. He glanced up.
"What're you doing?"

She looked over her shoulder at him. "Admiring the
view. It's not half bad. All the missing buildings, you
can see pretty far. What's the town across the river?"

But Rivera was back to counting.

"Chicopee," Manuel answered quietly.

She smiled at him and he nodded, just barely. After escaping from the shoot-out in Brattleboro, they'd continued north, to Bellows Falls, Windsor, White River Junction, making phone calls and stops along the way, selling off the contents of the infamous paper bag in dark motel parking lots and back alleys. Unbeknownst to Manuel, all the buys had been rigged. But hidden from all of the buyers had been Sam's true identity. The task force had merely put the word out that a new operator was making a swing-through and that they'd appreciate all the help they could get in building a case. Confidential informants, "CIs" in the trade, cut both ways. Usually minor criminals who were working for the police to stay out of jail, they also maintained their ties to the underworld and could be trusted to spread the word of any new players. Thus the benefit to Sam's new image was doubled.

After the way the night had begun, it had almost become fun, and Sam had used the opportunity of their baptism of fire to get chatty with Manuel. It hadn't been entirely successful. He'd stayed reserved to the end, if no longer sullen, but at least the first impression she'd made of being a racist jerk had been removed, and by the time they'd arrived back in Holyoke, shortly after dawn, she was hoping the first flickers of a friendship had begun to catch hold.

Rivera finally sat back in his chair and rubbed his eyes. "Fifteen thou and change."

"I told you that when we walked in," she said, climbing down from her chair. "That's better than your highest hopes, right? Admit it."

"It's good."

"It's great. And four thousand of it's mine." She crossed the room with her hand out.

"Cute," Rivera said, but he was smiling. He already had the agreed-upon $3,000 in a separate pile, which he handed her.

She riffled through it happily, making a sound like a card against a bicycle wheel's spokes. "So I pass muster?"

"You did fine," Rivera conceded.

"Manuel give me good grades?"

He nodded. "He said you handled yourself okay. What about your boyfriend? What was that?"

"He's an asshole and he was never my boyfriend. I got what I needed out of him, which was a bunch of contacts. I hope he got his butt shot off."

"You were lucky," Rivera said, watching her.

"I was smart," she countered, jerking her thumb at Manuel. "Ask him. I knew damn well the bouncer wasn't acting on his own. That's not how it works. You smell a rat, you do something about it. I did."

"And you abandoned your friend. That might make me nervous."

"I cut out some dead weight you never liked in the first place. You unhappy we're rid of Dancer?"

"No," he admitted.

She put the money back onto the table and leaned toward him. "Then let's keep going. You got problems in Rutland, I'm a problem solver. You want to keep baby-sitting me with a partner? Fine. Manuel and I got along pretty good, but give me whoever floats your boat and let me have a shot at it." She got even closer, bending at the waist, fixing his eyes with hers. "I can make us a fortune up there, you know I can. To hell with the boy-girl, Latino-white shit. You broke the mold when you went independent and took turf away from Torres. Keep showing how smart you are by putting me to work."

She tapped the pile of money he'd given her with her fingertip. "I'll even invest in the business. Take two thousand back and buy some more product with it. I'll trust you to keep honest books."

He smiled and reached out to stroke her cheek. "You're quite the little firecracker, aren't you?"

But she straightened and pulled away. "Maybe, and maybe you'll get to find that out. But not now. This is business. We make a bundle, we can talk again." She smiled to cushion the rejection. "By then I might be up for a little R and R—on a sandy beach with no bullet-proof windows." She stuck out her hand. "Deal?"

He glanced at Manuel, if not for approval, then simple confirmation. Manuel stayed as he was, smoking his cigarette.

Rivera shook her hand. "Deal."

Not expecting more success than he'd had the last few times he'd tried, Joe dialed Gail's cell phone number.

"Hello?" Her voice sounded almost eager.

"Hi, it's me. I've been trying to find you—see if you were all right."

"I'm fine."

He was disappointed the eagerness had clearly not been for him. "I was just worried, given all you've been through. How's Laurie doing?"

"The same."

"Your sister come up yet to be with her?"

Gail's tone turned bitter. "Yeah. She carved out some time from her schedule. She'll be arriving this afternoon. God knows how long that'll last."

"She staying with you?"

"That's the plan. I don't know if it'll work out, given our past history."

"You can stay at my place if you want."

Her response came almost too quickly. "No, that's okay. You're sweet, but I ought to tough it out. Maybe if things fall apart."

There was an awkward pause, which Joe filled with, "Are you sure you're okay? You don't sound like yourself."

Her reaction surprised him with its hard edge. "Well, I wouldn't, would I? At least I hope not. It's not every day you have your niece lying in a coma because of your own inattention."

He was surprised she was still stuck there. And worried. "Gail, you know that's not the way it is."

She almost cut him off. "I know, I know—that's the same crap I tell people, too. Look, Joe, I appreciate the call, but I gotta go. I'll talk to you later, okay?"

The phone went dead before he could respond.

He and Gail had shared some rough roads and not just when she'd been the one in a jam. But he was starting to wonder about this one. He couldn't get his hands around it—it lacked a cause-and-effect lineage he could track, her concern with Laurie's condition notwithstanding. He sensed there was more at work here, perhaps an accumulation of past ghosts: the rape, the alienation between her and her sister, his and her peculiar relationship, at once solid but noncommittal. Even her restless pursuit of a variety of professions and causes through the years. Laurie Davis's influence on Gail's state of mind was real and profound, but he didn't think it told even half the story.

But he didn't know how to read the rest if Gail wouldn't share it with him. And he was saddened by her unwillingness to do so.

Gail snapped her cell phone closed and stared at it, aware of the hurt she'd just meted out. It was a truism that you routinely wound the ones you love—they are, after all, usually close enough to get caught in the crossfire. But there was also something about Joe specifically—much as she genuinely loved him, as she never had any other—that occasionally put her on edge. His stolid, dependable, trustworthy style, while great in a crisis, hardly made him the brightest star in the galaxy. Which wasn't a fault, of course. And most of the time, their contrasting styles were a perfect fit— she the type A careerist, ambitious and tough-minded; he no weaker of character, but less aggressive, a man more interested in being in the world than leading it. But there were times she felt like screaming at him to do more, be more, and to live up to his real potential. He had the brains, the ability, and the people skills to be the commissioner of Public Safety, for example, if he'd set his mind to it. But the thought never occurred to him.

She got up and started pacing, pulling away from the phone conversation and toward the real source of her frustration. With Debbie Holton's lack of response to her ministrations, Gail had begun questioning what she'd been hoping to achieve with the girl in the first place.

The phone rang again.

"Gail?" It was Debbie—tearful, weak, sounding very far away.

Gail instinctively bent over the phone, pressing it tighter to her ear to hear better. "Yes. What's wrong? Where are you?"

"Home. I messed up."

"Do you need an ambulance? Should I call for one?"

"No, no. I'm okay that way. I just . . . Can you come over?"

"I'll be right there."

All self-doubt gone, her energy back where she found it most comfortable, Gail grabbed her keys and headed for the garage.

Gail found Debbie curled up in a ball on the bare mattress, wadded into a tangle of blankets, smelling of body odor and vomit, her hair a knotted clot. Her eyes were red, her nose runny, and she looked up like a beaten child as Gail entered the room.

"Help me."

Gail went to her knees beside her, cradling her head as the young girl began crying more openly. "It's okay, it's okay. I'll take care of you. We'll get you better."

She looked around them at the stained walls and bare floor, the single grimy window filtering a dim shaft of daylight, and added, "For one thing, we're getting you out of here."

Debbie pulled her face from Gail's stomach and peered up at her, confused. "What do you mean?"

"You're coming to live with me for a while, kiddo."

Chapter 13

Susan and Lester Spinney were still up waiting for their son when he quietly slipped into the house through the kitchen door. They heard him lock the door behind him and open the fridge before walking into the darkened living room, where they sat side by side on the couch, having killed the TV when they'd heard him drive up.

As Dave was halfway to the staircase, Lester turned on the table light by his side.

Dave jumped and staggered backward, his eyes wide with surprise, almost dropping the soda in his hand. "Jesus. You scared me."

"Where have you been?" Lester asked.

Dave's eyebrows furrowed. "What? Out with friends."

"The Shermans?"

"Yeah—some."

"What were you doing with them?"

"Listening to music. Talking. What's going on?"

"We're worried about you," Susan said. "We don't want you making a mistake that could ruin your life."

Abandoning the soda on the side table, Dave approached them, his face blank. "What are you talking about? That thing at the Zoo? I told Dad nothing happened, and I haven't seen Craig or the others since, like I promised."

"I know you've been at the Sherman place, Dave," Lester said. "And I know the Shermans use weed like other people eat Twinkies."

Dave straightened as if he'd been slapped. "So that means I'm using it, too? You hang around criminals all the time. What's that make you?"

Lester stood up, taller and broader than his son by far. "We're not picking a fight with you, David. We both work goddamn hard to give you and your sister a fighting chance in a tough world. We just don't want you to screw that up."

"We're not accusing you of anything, honey," Susan added. "We just want to know what you're doing."

Dave turned away and retreated to the foot of the staircase. "Right. My whole life I live up to your expectations, doing everything right. First time I get caught—not even doing anything wrong—you guys think I'm like some junkie or something. Thanks a lot."

With that, he ran up the stairs. They heard him slam his bedroom door moments later.

Lester looked down at his wife. "That went pretty well, don't you think?"

Susan got up and kissed his cheek. "I'll go talk to him."

She went upstairs slowly, hearing her husband turning on the TV, and proceeded to David's door. She knocked briefly and walked in. He was lying on his bed, pretending to be reading a magazine.

"What?" he asked, not looking up.

She sat next to him and gently removed the magazine from his hands. He didn't fight her.

"I don't believe you guys," he said.

"Can you believe we love you very much?" she asked, resting her hand on his knee.

"I know that, but it's like I'm guilty with no questions asked. Child rapists get more respect than that. I mean, what happened to innocent till proven guilty?"

Susan smiled and shook her head. "Dave, nobody's comparing you to a child rapist. Don't blow this out of proportion. Your father and I see what drugs do to people every day. Can you blame us for not wanting any of that to touch the two people we love most in the world?"

"I'm not doing drugs," Dave said in a frustrated outburst. "Why is that so hard to believe?"

"It's not that we don't believe you, and we're not accusing you of anything . . ."

"That's not how Dad sounded."

"Sweetheart," she said, squeezing his leg, "think of what he does for a living."

"I *know* that."

"Do you? Really? If you did, I think you'd cut him some slack. He lives in a world of horrible people—people who act on the first impulse that enters their heads. It's not that he thinks you're like that, but he's worried what might happen if you get too close to them."

"The Shermans aren't horrible people."

She sighed. "I'm not saying they are . . ."

"He is."

"How would you deal with a son you were worried might be getting interested in drugs?"

He rolled his eyes. "I'm not, Mom."

"How would you deal with it?"

"I'd ask him, and then I'd believe him when he told me."

"Isn't that what your father did in the car when he picked you up at the police station?"

David hesitated. "Yeah."

"It shook him up when he saw you at the Sherman place, Dave," she explained. "Just like it shook him up when we heard you'd been picked up with those other boys. It's a scary world. He was concerned, and so am I. We'd be lousy parents if we weren't. Maybe we didn't do it just right tonight. If we hurt your feelings, we apologize. But can you see what made us do it?"

David made a face, as if tempted to argue the matter further, but then conceded, "I guess."

His mother leaned over and kissed him, as she had his father earlier. "I love you. We both do. Very much."

He kissed her back and gave her a grudging smile. "I

love you, too. But tell Dad to lighten up, okay? I know right from wrong."

Sammie Martens opened her eyes and looked around, trying to orient herself, only slowly remembering that she was still in Holyoke, in Johnny Rivera's urban fortress, behind the locked door of a bedroom she'd borrowed to catch a few hours sleep.

She threw off the dirty blanket covering her and sat on the edge of the bed—a sagging mattress resting on a tired, metal spring frame. Whatever success Rivera might already be enjoying was clearly not being spent on decor. Not that it ever would be. TV and the movies showed drug kingpins routinely enjoying hideaways worthy of Louis XIV, and from what Sam had heard, a few such places really did exist. But not in northern New England. It was true the money wasn't what could be generated in Miami or Colombia, or even Boston, for that matter, but still, the extravagance rarely went beyond owning some real estate and a few flashy cars. In a surreal parallel to the region's Puritan past, even the crooks seemed to tone down the excess.

Nevertheless, she thought as she got up to stretch and rearrange her rumpled clothing, a trip to the mall for a decent mattress wouldn't hurt.

She went into the bathroom, used the toilet, washed her face, and stripped to the waist to give herself a cold water bath at the sink, using some paper towels to dry off. This operation had been put into play so fast, she hadn't had time to set up an alternate apartment to her real one in Brattleboro and therefore had nowhere she could safely go for a shower and a change of clothes.

She knew undercover work would be dangerous. She hadn't thought about the lack of hygiene. You're back in the army now, she thought, replacing her clothes.

There was a knock on the door. She crossed the room, flipped the lock, and found Manuel standing in the hallway outside.

"Hey," she said. "Get some sleep?"

"Johnny wants you upstairs."

She tapped his chest with her fingertips as she walked past him. "Hello to you, too, tough guy."

Johnny Rivera was standing before a large wall map of Vermont, put up since her last visit to this room.

"Supervising your kingdom?" she asked as she entered.

He looked back at her, his entire attitude more open and friendly than during their previous encounters. "Yeah—the land of milk and honey, right?"

"If we do it right," she conceded, standing next to him and looking at the familiar terrain. It was a colorful topographical map, showing the spine of the Green Mountains running down the state's center in shades of brown, the blue of the Connecticut River on the right and Lake Champlain to the upper left. Seeing it like this stimulated a surprising pang of emotion inside her, as if she were about to enter into combat against this man for the preservation of her home. It looked so small up there, so insignificant—undeserving of this kind of malevolent attention.

"You said you could get Rutland going for me," Rivera continued. "How?"

"Run it like a business," Sam said simply. "Up to now, either mules or dealers drive up there with some product, unload it through a phone tree or a pager alert, and hightail it back for more, like we did last night. But most of the mules and dealers are users, too, so any profits go straight up their noses—or whatever. Business is good, demand is high, but that's where it stops. It's like sex without commitment—just a bunch of fast fucks."

Johnny burst out laughing. "God, girl. You do have a mouth. Tell me more."

"It's been catch-as-catch-can—a grab bag approach with no real organization. You want to change that, you have to do a few things different." She held up one finger. "First, be the sole supplier—besides a few free-lancers who you don't need to worry about. Put a business manager you can trust up there and either make deals with the local competition or force 'em out. Right now it's like you're shipping product without having a retail outlet to draw in customers. Crack houses work on that principle, which is why they're tough for the cops to bust—it's a controlled environment. I can set that up for you."

She held up another finger. "Second, the people you send up there stick out like sore thumbs—we already talked about that. They're junkie-city-flatlanders from a mile off, and they're unreliable to boot. They drop out of sight, they get busted, they die, or they rat you out to the cops. I can give you stability there. A lot of local people who aren't junkies will deal for us for old-fashioned cash. I can find them and put them on the payroll."

A third finger went up. "Last but not least, you don't know anyone up there who isn't either a customer or a buyer with customers—people in the business. By living in the community, I'll get to know more, including how the cops do what they do and who their snitches are. That was the mistake the gangs like Solidos made when they tried to move into Rutland way back when. They didn't pay attention to how the locals work, which is way different from city people."

"What about the money?" he asked. "How're you gonna handle that? I'm supposed to trust you with everything just 'cause you say so?"

She shook her head. "I told you that before, too. Pick out a banker for me. Like an accountant or a treasurer. Someone you trust. I don't care who it is. I can set up the business, he can run the books and the inventory. I don't care if I don't see the dope or the money." She smiled suddenly. "Well, I want to see the money, but at the far end, as part of the profits."

Johnny scratched his head, obviously a little overwhelmed. "Why so complicated?"

She stared at him wide-eyed. "What're you in this for?" She pointed at the barricaded windows. "You're risking your life here. Why did you piss off everybody grabbing this turf?"

His eyes narrowed, as if confronting a trick question. "The money?"

She rewarded him with a laugh. "Right." She

slapped the map with her palm. "We're talking Rutland now, 'cause that's what's hot and that's where you need help, but remember those freelancers I talked about? The ones you don't have to worry about yet? Well, them and Torres and the Canadians and some upstate New Yorkers are selling in Barre and Burlington and around St. Johnsbury and a dozen other places. We want to know who they all are. We want to either work with them or take them over, or just knock them off. Look at that map, Johnny. We do this right, maybe you can get hundreds of thousands out of Rutland every year—maybe. We do the same thing to the whole damn state, and we're talking millions. You can move out of this dump and live like a real man—make the rest of these so-called Holyoke bigwigs look like losers.

"But," she added, dropping her voice, "if you want to do that, you're gonna have to think big. Maybe it sounds complicated now, but you need a good foundation to make a business work."

He looked back at the map, shaking his head as if he were seeing it for the first time, which in a way he was. "Sounds good."

Sam went in for the clincher. "It'll make you a man to respect."

They stood next to each other for half a minute or so, gazing at their separate destinies, Sam hoping she'd just given another quarter turn to this man's cell door lock, and Rivera wondering if and how he'd ever get this woman into bed.

*   *   *

Joe waited patiently, listening to reports about the Hollowell/Lapierre double homicide, mostly from Chick Wilson, Rutland's deputy police chief. For these meetings in which Sammie Martens's activities might be discussed, only Joe, prosecutor Mara Coven, task force leader Rick McCall, Chick, and Peter Bullis of the local drug unit were invited.

"Long story short," Chick was concluding mournfully, "we still don't have much to go on. Usually, these people spill the beans pretty quick, but either the ones we've been squeezing really are clueless or somebody's got 'em more scared than we do. Sure as hell, if Hollowell was killed as a warning, nothing we can do will compete."

He turned to Joe. "Any hints from Sam about that?"

"Just the implication that Hollowell was part of Rivera's operation, but that's still iffy. She's on the inside now, ready to move in as Rivera's Rutland lieutenant, but as of our last phone chat, she still doesn't feel she can ask those kinds of questions yet."

"How is she going to set up here?" Bullis asked, curious about this complication on his home turf.

"Be best if we could find a rental property on the west side of town," Gunther explained. "Something a dealer would find appropriate, and we could rig for sound and video. Is that a possibility?"

"Assuming we can get a search warrant," McCall cautioned.

Joe rubbed his forehead. "Right. I forgot about that." A few years earlier, Vermont law was changed, requiring the police to get a so-called wire search warrant anytime they wanted to covertly record a conversation. "That going to be a problem?"

McCall shook his head. "I doubt it. I'll go after it the way I usually do. They're used to me by now. You gonna use your own equipment or ours?"

Gunther laughed. "All ours, Rick—that was the deal. The trick'll be to get into the house and rig it before they come shopping, and then steer them to the right place."

Rick looked at Bullis. "What do you think?"

"I don't see a problem," he said. "One of my CIs should be good for the second part of that. I just wish I had a better handle on how the street dealers are sorting themselves out in this supposed switchover. Right now it's hard figuring out who's with Rivera and who's not."

"That'll be part of Sam's job," Joe said, "but it does bring up another question: You've given us a pretty good idea of the players in the Rutland drug world, and I've passed that along to her, but a lot of it may be old news to Rivera. Is there any way we can make Sam look like a hotshot—as if she had the insider knowledge she's pretending to have?"

Bullis thought for a moment. "We know a lot of stuff we can't move on," he admitted finally, "mostly because we don't have enough evidence or time or manpower. I just . . ." He stopped in midsentence and smiled. "I have an idea," he resumed. "There may be someone we've never much bothered with, mostly because he's small potatoes and a little out of our area of interest. But he might be a great source. Let me work on that. I'll do it fast. Promise."

"I have a question about Sam," Mara Coven then said, having largely kept silent up to now. "How is she going to be the local lieutenant and avoid making drug sales?"

"She may not be able to at first," Joe explained. "We'll have her sell to informants first, to establish credibility. After that, she can claim executive privilege or whatever and hand it over to a flunky—probably Manuel. I've been told they'll be setting this up along business lines, with different people doing different jobs, so that should give her some wiggle room.

"But that's another reason I think a video record will help," he went on. "Not just to capture what happens, but for what doesn't as well. If somebody in court later claims Sam sold them dope direct, we can ask for a time and date and show them the transaction—at least that's the perfect-world scenario."

"Hell," Mara said, "the perfect-world scenario would be that we tell them we have it all on tape, and they don't even ask to see it, 'cause you're not going to tell me every deal is going to happen in front of a camera."

Gunther shrugged. "That's what I am hoping for. This'll be a retail store of sorts, like a traditional crack house. You want some dope, you get vetted by one of Rivera's people, who escorts you to the house, where bingo, you get on *Candid Camera*. The artifice of the vetting will explain why the cops can't get inside and shut the place down. These are not Ph.D. candidates we're talking about, after all."

Mara merely nodded, prompting Joe to add, "Nothing's guaranteed here. This is brand-new for us, and it's moved at amazing speed. Sam fell into this at exactly the right time, what with the Hollowell killing having upset Rivera's applecart. But the trade-off is we're driving without headlights. I think we better assume that some mistakes are going to happen."

"Little mistakes I can live with," McCall said gloomily, not bothering to spell out the one disaster they weren't mentioning.

"Okay," Wilson said with artificial brightness. "Let's find a house they can rent."

Chapter 14

Gail braced herself for the inevitable. Her sister, Rachel, hadn't been in the house for five minutes, and already the familiar patterns had begun to surface. The two of them were standing together in the small study off Gail's living room.

"What is that girl doing here?" Rachel demanded in a whispered hiss.

After moving her in and cleaning her up, including a change of clothes, Gail had settled Debbie Holton on the living room couch opposite the TV set, surrounded by pillows, blankets, and an ignored plate of fruit.

"She's my guest, like you," Gail answered levelly, knowing it would only cause a fight.

Rachel's face reddened. "You're comparing us? My God, Gail. You are so perverse. That girl—"

"Debbie," Gail interjected.

"—probably *sold* heroin to Laurie. What were you thinking, putting us in the same house? I can't believe you'd be that thoughtless, so typically confrontational. Did you think I'd benefit from some epiphany here?"

"I didn't think of you at all, Rachel. I reacted to a human being in trouble."

Rachel rolled her eyes. "Oh—right. You forget that I know you, Gail. So, it was pure coincidence that this particular human being was also the same one doing drugs with Laurie? I really believe that." She shook her head. "You've really outdone yourself this time, I must say. Subtle as a fucking crutch."

Gail crossed to the window and looked out onto the lawn. "Have you been by the hospital yet?" she asked, not turning around.

Rachel's long silence substituted for the shocked expression Gail knew from experience she'd be wearing.

"I'm going there now," was the frosty reply. "I thought I'd settle in first, see my sister, find out how she was doing. What a great idea. You'd think I'd wake up."

Gail turned and faced her, repressing a knee-jerk reaction before saying formally, "I'm sorry. You're tired and upset. I should have been more sensitive. Go see Laurie. Stay there as long as you want. I've got all sorts of food I can warm up in no time for dinner whenever you get back."

They stared at each other for a few moments, leaving things where they were, choosing Gail's starchy politeness as a way out. Rachel merely muttered, "Okay," and left through the side door into the hall, avoiding the living room.

Gail stood alone for a while, hearing the muffled TV through the closed door, then her sister's oversized SUV starting up in the driveway. They were Mutt and Jeff, she and Rachel. Gail was the elder, the more relied upon by their parents, historically the built-in baby-sitter for a sister eight years her junior, and in return, the substitute punching bag for when Rachel wanted to lash out at her parents while maintaining her angelic reputation. Spoiled, lousy at school, lucky in a marriage to an upwardly mobile furniture chain scion, Rachel had been allowed to believe that trendiness mattered, that social status was proof of Darwin's theory, and that motherhood could be done by proxy through nannies, summer camps, and prep schools. She reminded Gail of a Rhode Island yacht—sleek, beautiful, very expensive, and perpetually moored for all to see in a safe harbor.

With a small sigh, Gail opened the door to the living room and walked in on Debbie, who was randomly pushing buttons on the remote.

"You feeling better?" Gail asked, sitting at the far end of the couch.

"I feel like shit," Debbie answered, not looking at her. "And your sister hates my guts."

"She doesn't even know you. You're just a symbol to her."

"Thanks. That sounds great."

"You're like a neon sign of her own poor parenting. At least that's how she sees it."

"It's not my fault Laurie's in a coma." Debbie's voice was petulant.

Gail rubbed her forehead, wondering if this conversation was going to be as taxing as its predecessor. "Nobody's saying it is."

Debbie looked at her, her expression curiously vulnerable. "But you're still going to throw me out, right?"

Suddenly understanding, Gail rose and crossed over to her, crouching by her side and taking up her hand. "No, I'm not. You're safe here, Debbie, and welcome to stay for as long as you like."

Debbie glanced at the TV and hit the Off button on the remote. In the abrupt silence, her next words sounded all the more fragile. "Why didn't your sister come up before?"

"To see Laurie? She was busy—had a lot of commitments she felt she couldn't break. My sister's very practical in her way. She knew Laurie was in a coma, she knew I was here in case something came up. She's always managed things like that well."

"Like her own daughter was a pet or something—maybe not even."

"No," Gail admitted. "Rachel loves Laurie, but I think maybe she was waiting for Laurie to get older so the two of them could have a really good time together."

"Fat chance of that now."

"You never know," Gail countered, trying to sound hopeful.

Debbie didn't respond, staring out the double glass

doors that led onto the broad deck with the huge maple tree growing through its middle. Gail allowed for the silence to prompt whatever might come next.

"My mom would've been drunk," Debbie finally said.

"When?"

"If I'd been in a coma," the girl explained.

Gail didn't argue the point. Chances were too good Debbie was right. "What about your father?" she asked instead. "Where's he?"

"In Florida. He's married to somebody else. I don't see him."

"Any brothers or sisters?"

"Yeah—a few. We don't get along. Different dads and stuff. You got anything good to eat?"

Gail smiled at the abrupt change of topic. "You want to order some pizza?"

Sam got out of the car with Manuel and surveyed the building before them critically. They'd been at this for several hours already, looking at houses, duplexes, and apartments as potential bases of operation. In each case, she'd found things to object to—proximity to neighbors, not enough or too many exits, poor floor lay-out for clandestine activities and/or self-protection if things went wrong. Manuel had been reasonable throughout, even agreeable at times. Sam had been sur-prised at how mellow he'd become, despite the lean, al-most feline sense of quiet menace he carried like a scent. The lethality was real—of that she had little doubt—but it almost seemed as if it was a reluctant burden to him, like a badge might be to a peace-loving lawman.

"So far, so good," she said, knowing full well this was the house Gunther and the task force had already filled with eavesdropping equipment. "I like the way it sits back from the street."

As usual, Manuel stayed quiet, looking around, standing slightly to her rear, like a bodyguard. The traditional mannerisms of macho dominance appeared lacking.

A round, bearded man in a spattered work shirt emerged from the house and clattered down from the front porch using a noisy set of stairs. "You the people looking to rent?"

Sam shook his beefy hand and then wiped her own against her jeans. "Yeah. You Mr. Badamo?"

"Julius Badamo. That's right. Rutland born and bred." He eyed Manuel suspiciously. "You from around here?"

"Our money is," Sam answered shortly. "You want to show us around?"

Badamo considered this for a moment before saying, "I suppose I could do that."

Gunther had told Sam in one of their scheduled furtive phone calls that the landlord had no idea what was afoot. The surveillance equipment had been installed during a phony municipal inspection conducted by a team led by Lester Spinney.

"House was built in the 1860s," Badamo was saying, leading the way. "As if you give a damn about that.

It's got five bedrooms and two and a half baths. The building code people just gave it a clean bill of health a couple of days ago, in case you're thinking of burning the place down and then blaming me."

He led them inside and toured them around. Above and beyond being wired by the police, the place had its own built-in appeal, Sam thought, and was perfectly suited to their needs. And her colleagues had done a good job. She saw not one sign of their visit—or of the toys they'd left behind. Several times, still pretending to be critical, she cast a look over her shoulder at Manuel, who also nodded his approval. They were in if the landlord didn't turn thumbs down, and given their first exchange, she began worrying that might happen, if only to prove that Murphy's Law was alive and well.

Badamo finally threw open a kitchen door to reveal a large garage, one wall of which was lined with an oversized fluorescent green rendering of a lumbering giant in torn clothing, his teeth bared and fists clenched.

"The Incredible Hulk," Manuel said in astonishment, speaking for the first time since their arrival.

Badamo turned and looked at him. "It speaks," he said, but Manuel's outburst had obviously pleased him. "You a fan?"

"Oh, sure," Manuel admitted, approaching the huge drawing. It was more like a set piece, old and stained and battered around the edges, crudely painted on plywood. "I loved all the Marvel and DC characters."

Badamo laughed. "Look behind it."

Sam watched, amazed, as Manuel's aloof and chilly

manner melted into something closer to that of an enthusiastic kid coming face-to-face with an old friend. He tilted the painted panel toward him and craned to look behind it.

"Oh my God: It's Thor. These are wonderful." Manuel shifted the Hulk aside to reveal a blond-haired, muscular Viking carrying a massive hammer in one hand. "Why are they here?"

"Old souvenirs," Badamo explained. "From years back. We have an annual parade in Rutland—every Halloween. In the old days, writers and artists from Marvel and DC would come up from New York dressed in costume to ride the floats we put together. Those things were part of it."

"Why?" Sam asked, incredulous.

"For fun. There was a guy named Tom Fagan who worked for the paper who also knew Stan Lee and a couple of other comic bigwigs. He invited them up and I guess they thought it was loopy enough to accept. They did it for years. Basically, just a way for a lot of people to get drunk and stoned, but it got to be quite the tradition. The parade was even mentioned in a few of the comic books, along with Fagan himself."

Manuel was shaking his head. "Wow. I learned to read from these things. My uncle used to have them by the hundreds. I couldn't get enough of them."

Sam watched them looking at one another like long-lost cousins, wondering at life's odd twists.

Julius Badamo waved a hand toward the house behind them. "So, you interested?"

Manuel glanced at Sam, who'd been so picky all

day. She smiled and said, "Who can argue with the Incredible Hulk? Works for us if it works for you."

Badamo looked a little rueful. "You said your money's good. You got it."

After they'd sealed the deal with both a security deposit and a down payment in cash, which Badamo did a poor job of pretending to take in stride, Sam and Manuel retired to their car.

"A comic book fan?" she asked him before starting the engine.

He was staring straight ahead. "How soon do we start operations?"

"A comic book fan?" she repeated, laughing now.

His face reddened. "I was a kid once. Drive."

She still didn't turn the key. "Where did you grow up?"

"In an apartment."

"In Holyoke?"

He hesitated. "Nobody grows up in Holyoke. I was born in the Bronx."

"Holyoke's got to be better than that."

He tilted his head equivocally, his eyes still fixed ahead, as if this entire conversation were taking place inside his head. "Better," he conceded. "That's still not saying much."

"You're upwardly mobile," she argued. "If Johnny pulls this off, you'll be sitting pretty."

He didn't answer.

She watched him a moment before asking, "You don't think?"

For the first time since they'd entered the car, he looked at her. "I hope so."

She waited expectantly, but that was it. The next thing he said was, "Drive."

Joe pulled into the gas station parking lot off the immaculate and picturesque village common of Rochester, Vermont, roughly halfway between Rutland and Waterbury—the agreed-upon meeting place that he'd set up with Bill Allard on the phone an hour earlier.

Neither one of them bothered leaving their cars. Old-time cops both, they'd instinctively parked door-to-door and simply rolled down their windows to have a comfortable and private talk.

"Too restless to use a phone?" Joe asked his boss, smiling.

"Yeah—a little. Good day for a drive," Allard answered. "I didn't want anyone hearing this, either, even if it is total horseshit."

"Sounds political."

Allard let out a short, mirthless laugh. "Yeah. You could say that. Governor Reynolds is getting twitchy about seeing results."

Gunther raised his eyebrows. "Twitchy? When was the last time we put together an operation this fast, much less one involving an undercover?"

Allard was sympathetic. "He's running for office,

Joe. You know how they get. He wants a headline he can claim credit for."

Gunther repressed his irritation. "Can't give him one. Not yet."

Allard tried a more general approach. "Where do we stand overall, starting with Sam?"

"She's in place, and all the surveillance equipment is working fine, although audio ain't the best—too much echo. Usable, though. But nothing much has happened yet. She and Manuel are still setting up shop, scoping out the neighborhood, getting a feel for the competition. They don't want to start selling until they know the ground. Hollowell's murder is still a fresh memory."

"Anything new on that?"

"You mean, anything new on who killed Lapierre?" Joe countered. "Not a whole lot. Sam finally got Manuel to admit that Hollowell was their guy in town, so I guess that means Rivera didn't kill him."

"What was Hollowell's job?"

"Rutland BCI is running that. I have access to their reports and can sit in on their briefings, but I don't know what's being kicked around in the squad room. Last take I heard is that Torres or one of his Holyoke buddies did in Hollowell to shut down Rivera before he got started. But that doesn't explain Sharon Lapierre. If she just happened to be in Hollowell's motel room when he was hit, why the rigmarole with the tourniquet and the syringe? Why not just make it look like Hollowell killed her? Or, for that matter, why care about her at all? They probably didn't know her grand-father was connected to the governor."

"What's the less obvious take, then?" Allard prompted.

"Still no clue about Lapierre," Gunther continued. "But an alternate theory for Hollowell might be that it had nothing to do with the Holyoke crowd. All these people are screwed up enough to eat their young for lunch. And Christ knows, Torres, Rivera, and the others are just the ones we happen to know about. There're a ton of freelancers out there, too. Hollowell may have just pissed off the wrong guy."

Allard didn't look happy. "What about forensics. They find anything?"

Joe shook his head. "The motel room was a hole-in-the-wall—had more prints, hair samples, and body flu-ids than a bus depot bathroom. They gathered stuff, as usual, but nobody I talked to thinks it'll come to any-thing. The best hope is the interviews they're conduct-ing with Sharon's friends and contacts, and so far, all of them are playing dumb. Murder makes them skittish."

"Go figure," Allard muttered to himself.

"By the way," Gunther added, "we ever going to get to the part where you explain why we're meeting out here other than the pretty-day-for-a-drive line? I know it's not because we're dumping on the governor—everybody does that. The people downstairs upset with us again?"

The tiny VBI offices in Waterbury were on the top floor of a building largely filled with the Vermont State Police.

"They're not too thrilled," Allard admitted. "There's some bitching that we went around the outside and slipped in the back door."

"They don't know about Sam, do they?" Joe asked in alarm. "I figured McCall for better than that."

"No, no," Allard assured him. "That's not where this is coming from. McCall seems perfectly happy, as does the Rutland chief. This is just the brass chasing its tail while the field troops are getting the job done. Sam's safe and I think you guys are secure in the task force. But people are grumbling, and unless I can get the governor calmed down, they might find a way to his ear. If that happens, anything's possible. Reynolds is already unhappy I made him downgrade his 'end of drugs in Vermont' spiel."

"Christ," Gunther said softly.

"Don't worry about it, Joe," his boss reassured him. "This is all pure FYI material. Ignorance ain't bliss when the lions are circling the compound, but at least it only counts if they find a way in. I'll do everything I can to stop that from happening. Okay?"

"All right."

"More to the point," Allard went on, "how's Sam doing emotionally?"

"So far, so good, as far as I can tell. She's charged up about the job, feels she has a handle on the players, and is settling in with the man Rivera partnered her up with."

"Tell me about him," Allard requested.

Gunther recited what he'd gleaned from the computer search they'd conducted on Manuel as soon as

Sam had forwarded his name. "Manuel Ruiz, age twenty-seven, born in the Bronx of Puerto Rican parents. High school dropout, ex–gang member in New York, list of petty crimes as a juvenile, ramping up to assault, weapons charges, drug possession, et cetera. He's also suspected of having been the bad guy in a fatal knifing down there. The feeling is he moved to Holyoke to get out of the heat. The NYPD was interested to hear we were asking about him."

"But they don't have a case?"

"Right."

"You comfortable with him being with her?"

"She is, and that's all I can go by. I mean, Christ, Bill, none of these guys are virgins. They shoot each other in cold blood in Holyoke, right on the street in the middle of the afternoon. Sam tells me Ruiz is a comic book fan. I think she likes him."

Allard stared at him. "Likes him? What the hell's that mean?"

Gunther laughed, in part to discharge the tension. "Just what I said. The woman sleeps with Willy Kunkle, for crying out loud. You surprised she'd take a shine to a loony with a knife who reads comics? Get real."

Bill smiled despite himself. "Sorry. Still . . ."

"I know," Gunther admitted, getting serious again. "To be honest, I'm not too thrilled about Ruiz myself. I think he's dangerous as hell. But she does have to work with them—all of them—and that means getting friendly. It's a risk of the job."

He held his hand up to stop Allard before he responded

to that. "I'm not saying she's falling for him. Stop reading into this. I'm suggesting we have to let her act it out as she sees fit. She knows what she can and can't do legally. She knows the line that'll be drawn in court. The rest is up to her. We have to trust her here."

"She is pretty levelheaded," Allard commented, as if to comfort himself.

"Right," Gunther reinforced him. But, in fact, he wasn't being entirely truthful. Sammie Martens was reliable, loyal, dedicated, and as true to her job as a bloodhound to a scent, but "levelheaded" implied something she was not. She could work up a passion bordering on zealotry sometimes—and he'd seen it affect her judgment.

Were he to be absolutely honest, he just hoped he wouldn't be questioning his own in the end.

Chapter 15

George Backer stood by the tree in deep shadow for a slow count of thirty, eyeing the dark house before him, listening for any sounds that would turn him back. The driveway at least was perfect—long enough to allow for a slight curve that hid the house from the road behind a row of bushes.

Satisfied, his heart pumping with the comforting high of this part of his routine, he walked quickly from the tree up the short flight of steps leading to the kitchen door, tried the knob, found it locked, and instantly punched out the small window right above it—his hand protected by the extended sleeve of his sweatshirt. He reached in, turned the lock, and entered.

As always, he wasn't positive the place was empty. That was part of the rush. He didn't stake a house out for long. He did the obvious things—checked for cars, signs of life, any dogs, circled the whole building—but mostly, he tried to get a feel for it, kind of like a Zen thing, or what he thought was a Zen thing.

He walked quickly through the kitchen into the living room beyond, his hands by his side. "You touch it, you take it" was one of his rules. He didn't use gloves. Took away from the fun. He had quite a few rules—no jewelry, no silverware, no art, nothing too heavy, nothing too high end, no super rich houses, no white houses. They tended to be owned by wealthy people, and wealthy people owned alarms. But he didn't much care about doorknobs. Someone had told him once that the cops never dusted doorknobs, because everybody used them. Made sense to him.

Backer glanced around, seeing by moonlight, a flashlight at the ready in case he needed it. He saw an open closet—clothes, shoes, a rifle in the corner. Forget that. Don't steal firearms. People took that seriously in this state. On the shelf above were hats, a few boxes. He moved on.

He ignored the TV, the radio, the expensive phone, paused at the bedroom door, knowing this was the make-or-break point concerning anyone being at home. Then he turned the knob and stepped inside, quiet as a ghost.

It was empty.

He crossed to the dresser, seeing the glint of glass in the dim light. Sure enough, there was a large jar, half full of spare change—a habit so common, he'd come to expect it. He weighed the jar carefully in his hand, found it acceptable, and dropped it into his backpack.

Feeling better now, he checked his watch. One minute down. His own two-minute rule half done. Moving faster, he checked the closet here, saw nothing immediately interesting, dropped to his knees, shined his flashlight under the bed, got up empty-handed, and finally returned to the kitchen. He wasn't distressed. He knew people's habits—especially people like these. It might be a wash except for the change jar, but he had one last standard place to check.

He opened the freezer door, shoved aside the usual items and chuckled at his own prowess. Reaching in, he extracted a frost-covered baggie and held it up to the light at the window, just seeing a fair amount of its flourlike contents.

"Bingo," he said softly, and checked his watch one last time. A hair over two minutes. Not bad.

He circumvented the broken glass at the door, stepped out onto the small landing, and was halfway down the four steps when he was suddenly caught in the crossbeams of several powerful flashlights.

"Don't move, George," came the authoritative but almost friendly voice of Peter Bullis. "You are officially busted. Keep your hands where we can see them."

Sammie Martens stumbled and dropped the bag of fast food she was carrying next to the trash can by the edge of the parking lot. Swearing audibly, she stooped to retrieve it, collected a small cell phone from behind the can as well—deposited there minutes earlier by

Lester Spinney—and hid it in her palm. She then moved to her car, slid in behind the wheel, pretended to reach into her jacket pocket, and flipped the cell open.

It was the same make and model as the one she regularly carried, and the one both Rivera and Manuel knew she used to make business calls. Except that since it was a different phone altogether, there would be no record of the call she was about to make.

Gunther picked up on the first ring.

"It's me," she said.

"Who's this?" was all he said, which was their code for her to confirm she was safe and alone.

"Gatekeeper."

"How're you doing, Sam?" His voice was concerned but relaxed. This was one of their scheduled calls, attempted daily unless circumstances ruled otherwise.

"Good. Our first shipment'll arrive in a few hours. The driveway camera should catch the couriers in case they don't come inside, but I'll try to be the affable hostess. Won't be much—a bundle or two. Rivera's making it a test run. They're optimistic, though. Manuel's digging a cache in the cellar so we can build a stockpile and streamline the supply-and-demand surges. That'll probably be our maximal way to knock out the competition."

Joe smiled at the terminology. She was so much in character, she wasn't distinguishing between him and the people she was conning. He wondered if someone who was truly in legitimate sales wouldn't laugh at her jargon.

No matter—it only needed to work on a select few.

"Too bad we didn't put a camera down there," he said.

She was nonchalant. "That's why you have me. Too dark, anyhow."

"You having any luck identifying who's playing what side of the fence in the Rutland trade?" Gunther asked.

Here she was more equivocal. "Some. Manuel owned up to Hollowell being more than just a local rep—he was their main man, meaning his death caused more damage than I thought. Rivera's so full of bluster, I figured he had a deeper network locally, like he has elsewhere. Still, I'm keying in on some of the obvious movers. Everyone's lying low right now—lot of hinkiness left over from the murder, nobody knowing who did it. Should make our entrance into the market good, though, since that also means people're hungry. Still, bullshitting Rivera and making this happen as advertised might be tough."

"Maybe not," Joe told her. "Peter Bullis just busted a kid—George Backer, calls himself the Schemer, like out of a Batman movie. He's a B-and-E expert—has probably knocked off a couple of hundred homes—but he claims he only goes after bad guys, or at least people who won't report they've been ripped off. Bullis caught him last night with some coke he'd lifted from somebody's freezer in less time than it would take you to unload groceries. The thing is, he's supposedly a walking telephone book—names, addresses. Knows who's buying what from whom, where, and when, all so he can rip them off when they're not at home. Bullis busted him to see if he could help you out. The kid's not especially into heroin—Ecstasy floats his boat—but he trades and sells everything he doesn't use himself. Anyhow, we thought you'd like his mental black book, since he seems so keen to cooperate."

"The Schemer, huh?" Sam reacted. "Sounds like that's what we should call Peter from now on. Tell him thanks from me."

"Will do. I'll get something to you as soon as we strike a deal and he coughs it up. How're you getting along with Manuel?"

"So far, so good."

Gunther paused, a warning to watch herself there on the tip of his tongue, but then he thought better of it. "All right. Good luck tonight."

"Roger that, boss," she said, and hung up, snapping the cell phone closed. She then ate her hamburger, put the phone into the crumpled bag, walked back to the trash can, and dropped the wadded ball not into, but next to, the can, as if missing by mistake.

Sliding in behind the wheel again, all her cautions notwithstanding, she was caught totally by surprise. As her hand touched the ignition key, a voice from the back seat ordered, "Don't do it, Sam."

She jumped as if electrified but kept staring straight ahead. "Willy, what the hell're you doing here? You'll blow my cover."

"Not likely," he sneered. "Your cover's so pathetic, there's nothing left to blow."

"What's that mean?" she asked, feeling suddenly hotter than was comfortable.

"I'm here, aren't I?"

Her tension eased a notch. "That's not proof of anything. You know who Greta Novak is, for Christ's sake, and you know who all the cops are. You probably tailed Spinney here and saw him drop off the cell."

He ignored her. "You're in danger, Sam. This was set up too fast and without enough safeties in place. One wrong twitch by anybody and you're dead."

"What kind of twitch?" she asked, trying not to move her lips in case anyone was watching. "Like some idiot crawling into my back seat just to see the mess he can put me in? Get out of the car, Willy, and get out of Rutland. You're the one who's going to screw me up here."

"You need to quit this," he said again, but they both understood there was nothing he could do that wouldn't also jeopardize her career, something for which he knew she'd never forgive him.

"Get out. Now."

Without a word further, he slipped out the door facing the battered shrubbery alongside the car, closing it behind him with barely a click.

Sam took a deep breath, turned the key, and drove back to the house, parking in the garage beside the Hulk. As she emerged from the car, she saw Manuel standing in the doorway leading to the kitchen.

"What took you?" he asked.

She held up another bag with a burger in it. "I got hungry, so I ate mine in the parking lot."

He took the bag from her and peered at its contents

as they entered the house. "This stuff is shit. We're not going to do this forever, right?"

She cut him a quick look, her Greta Novak character back in place more slowly than usual after her encounter with Willy. "I'm not cooking, if that's what you mean."

But he stopped her. "I'll do the cooking. We just need some groceries."

She stared at him. "You're a cook? What? Mac and cheese? This crap at least has meat in it." She pointed at the bag in his hand.

He laughed. "No. Not mac and cheese. Maybe *chicharrones de pollo* or *habichuelas rositas*. You like beans and rice? Good for the system."

"I like tuna from a can."

He shook his head and reached inside the bag, removing the wrapped burger and gazing at it a moment as though it were a fallen meteorite, which in a day it would probably resemble.

"You don't want it, I'll eat it," she offered.

He shifted it beyond her reach, although she'd made no move for it. "I don't like it, but I gotta live. Besides, you already had yours. My God, you eat a lot for a little one."

She'd bolted her meal right out of the bag in the car, as she tended to in any case, but Manuel rummaged around the kitchen cabinets—the place had come furnished after a fashion, including some bulletproof china—and found a plate onto which he almost delicately arranged his burger before moving it and himself to the battered wooden table by the window.

Sam sat opposite him, caught up in the ritual, thinking of how little she knew about this careful, quiet, dangerous man.

"Where'd you learn to cook?" she asked him.

He studied the burger before taking a bite, pausing to swallow before answering her. "My *mamá*." He put the emphasis on the last syllable, although she'd noticed that he spoke English better than most of her colleagues.

"Big family?" Sam guessed.

"Five kids."

"You had to be the youngest."

"Why do you think that?"

She shrugged, but she chose her words cautiously, not wanting to offend. "I was thinking maybe the youngest might see his mom cooking for a lot of people—get interested in it."

He nodded, chewing again, before finally saying, "You sound like a cop."

That came as a surprise. She laughed. "Right. Next I'll sound like a priest. Just as likely."

But he stayed relaxed, smiling back at her. "No. I meant that was right out of a TV show or something— detective thinking, you know? You're right. I was the youngest."

"Sounds nice—family meals."

Neither his expression nor his voice changed as he asked, "You ever see any home movies?"

She hesitated a moment, wondering where he was going. "You mean like videos? Family-at-the-beach things? Sure, everyone's seen those. Awful."

"But happy, right? Everybody smiling, waving at the camera."

He seemed to be awaiting a response. "Yeah," she finally said.

"Yeah," he repeated meditatively. "Always happy, and always called home movies."

She got the point. "So maybe your family meals weren't all that great, or learning to cook from your mom."

He smiled wistfully before admitting, "Right."

She watched him chewing slowly, and thought of them both sitting here, thrown together in an illegal enterprise, from totally different worlds, neither one of them knowing the slightest thing about the other. She knew what her role was, and she knew of her own duplicity. What about him, aside from the criminal record Joe had told her about? What was he, truly? Certainly more than any run-of-the-mill deadbeat thug.

A pair of headlights flashed against the window. Smoothly, quickly, and without a sound, Manuel was on his feet, heading toward the door to the garage, the half-eaten meal abandoned on its plate. "Meet them at the front," was all he said.

His speed and sudden sense of purpose caught her unaware, reminding her abruptly of the man who was no longer the philosophical youngest of five, learning to cook at his mother's side, but instead someone with a distinctly practical view of the value of life and death.

She walked to the entryway and opened the front door, turning on the porch light so the camera could better pick out the license plate of the two men walking toward her from the car in the driveway.

"Hey," one of the men called out. "Kill the lights, bitch."

She waited a couple of seconds before complying. "Up yours, asshole. I wanna see who I'm dealing with."

The second man laughed. "Dealing with. That's good. Real funny. Where's Manuel?"

"Behind you," came a quiet voice from the darkness.

Both men swung around, their hands diving under their clothes for weapons.

Manuel emerged into the light coming from the window. "Don't bother. You'd both be dead."

"Jesus, man. What the fuck you doin'?"

Manuel gestured to both of them to go into the house ahead of him. "Protecting myself. You got the stuff?"

"Sure."

Sam stepped back to let them in, studying their faces as they passed by. One of them she recognized from Holyoke as a man nicknamed Flaco. The other was new to her.

"How're you doin'?" she asked. "I'm Greta."

Flaco, the one with the mouth, stared at her contemptuously. "We know who you are, bitch."

Without pause, she slapped him across the face, causing his hands to fly up, and then kneed him in the groin, dropping him flat to the ground, where he rolled around swearing. By the time he reached for his gun, barely two seconds later, Sam had already yanked it from his belt and was pointing it at his head.

"Say my name," she ordered him.

His companion was frozen in place, scared and confused, his eyes wide with surprise. Manuel was leaning against the wall, smiling, keeping everyone in view.

"Say my name," Sam repeated.

"What the hell?" complained Flaco. "Shit."

She stepped on his knee, making him cry out.

"You that stupid?" she asked.

"Greta. Damn."

Sam twirled the gun around and dropped it in Flaco's lap, making him jump one last time. "Just 'Greta' is fine."

He stared at her, amazed, the gun now in his hand, but not pointed at her, fully aware of Manuel's presence and realizing the encounter was over whether he liked it or not. "You are one crazy fucker, you know that?"

She smiled down at him. "Yeah, and now you do, too. You got the stuff?"

Wincing, Flaco pulled himself into a sitting position, his back against the wall. He tucked the gun away and removed a large, flat, plastic bag from under his oversized shirt, where he'd taped it to his bare chest. Almost reluctantly, he extended it to her.

Sam didn't move. Flaco looked at her, confused, until Manuel stepped forward, slowly bent over, and took it from him. *"Gracias."*

The two mules didn't stay the night, although Sam extended the offer. Still limping, Flaco said he'd sooner sleep in the street than under the same roof with her—

something about Sam strangling him as he slept for the hell of it. It was an image she was happy to have reported back to Holyoke.

"Was that fun?" Manuel asked later as they were burying the bulk of the shipment in the basement.

"What? Knocking him around? I didn't hurt him."

"That's not what I asked."

She was sitting on a cardboard box, her back against the wall, as he smoothed over the hiding spot so that it blended with the rest of the dirt floor. "I don't like it when people talk to me like that. If I deserve it, I don't mind so much, but that asshole doesn't even know me."

Manuel straightened and dusted off his hands against one another. "He does now. That was part of the point, right?"

As before at the kitchen table, she was caught off guard by his insight. "Can't hurt. I'm trying to build something here. I can't do that unless I get respect. Being a woman is hardly my strong suit with guys like that."

He extended his hands to her, which she instinctively grasped. He pulled her gently to a standing position so close to him, they were almost touching.

"It is to someone like me, though," he said softly.

She looked up at him, enjoying him, thinking back to her angry run-in with Willy earlier. Greta would do this, she thought. Hell, she'd jump at the chance. And Sam wasn't sure she'd fault her.

Manuel placed his hands on her waist, moving them slowly up her sides. She couldn't resist doing the same, and found the heat and hardness of him under his thin shirt amazingly stimulating.

Their faces were only inches apart.

"I don't know," she murmured, hanging on by a thread.

Which seemed to be all he needed. "Then we shouldn't do this. Not yet."

He hadn't moved, but she tilted her head back to better focus on him, as surprised at his comment as by her own disappointment. "We shouldn't?" she blurted out.

"Not if you have doubts."

She laughed and placed her forehead against his chest. Christ, did she have doubts. "You're a disgrace to the stereotype," she said.

He kissed the top of her head. "Thank you."

Later that night, lying in bed alone, staring at the ceiling, Sam couldn't believe what she'd almost done—probably would have done, if not for Manuel. What the hell had that been all about?

There were paradoxical assumptions among cops concerning undercover work. It was death on marriages and relationships; half your support team wasted no time believing you were dirty; it was dangerous and frightening and lonely and made you paranoid. It was also a constant question in every cop's mind—what would it be like? As one of the high-mark achievements in the profession, akin to the gold shield or the special weapons teams, it also stood apart from them, teasing like a dangerous double dare—a knife edge between destruction and the ultimate high.

Except for moments like this.

Longing for sleep, unable to nod off, Sam began wondering if the real peril of undercover work lay less in the danger and deceit, and more in the subtle corrosiveness of believing you could take on two separate personalities.

Having almost gone to bed with Manuel Ruiz was bad enough. Wondering when she might face such a choice again—perhaps a more lethal one—and knowing now that she could make the wrong decision, that was truly destabilizing.

She was going to have to watch Greta as never before.

Chapter 16

George Backer sat comfortably at the metal table in the interrogation room, an amused expression on his face, as if he were listening to a friend's long-winded tall tale after a satisfying meal. Instead, sitting opposite him, were Peter Bullis and Lester Spinney.

Bullis was doing the talking. "George, you do understand these rights as I've explained them to you, right? If you talk to us, it's by your own free will."

"Sure," George said. "Like I said, I'd sooner deal with you direct. But I am gonna get a deal. I mean, that's the understanding. I want that part straight."

"You'll get a deal," Bullis said vaguely.

"A 'get out of jail free card'?" George asked, smiling.

"What do you think?"

He laughed. "Well, doesn't hurt to ask. You could've lied just then."

"We're professionals, George, you and me. That deserves some respect."

George looked satisfied. "Cool." He pointed casually at the mirrored window overlooking the room. "Then maybe the lawyer standing behind that thing can come in here and tell me exactly what we're talking about, 'cause, professional or not, I know you guys don't call the shots, and you'll lie your asses off to make me think different."

"You been watching too much TV, Schemer," Peter told him, flattering him with the use of his nickname. "We don't have the time or the money to have a prosecutor stare at you being a wiseass."

"I thought we were getting along so good, too," the young man responded. "Guess I'll have to clam up, then."

"I wonder, George," Lester Spinney said. "What cards do you think you're holding right now? Just out of curiosity."

Backer made an equivocal face. "I've got a lot to offer. I told you that. Now, we're sitting here, one of me and two of you. You're not a local, like Detective Bullis here, or I'd know you. Maybe you're federal, maybe not, but you're fancy somehow. That means you want to deal. Also means you carry weight."

Spinney glanced at Bullis, who shrugged. "Yeah, I do," he admitted. "What charges do you think you're looking at?"

Backer paused a moment. "B-and-E?"

Spinney nodded. "Yup. That and possession of stolen property, possession of a controlled substance, possession with intent to distribute, and probably conspiracy to commit, based on how you usually work with others on these deals. We can turn this into a federal rap on the quantity of drugs alone. Not to mention we got you locked into a few dozen other break-ins."

George Backer's eyes narrowed, his poise disturbed. "You can't make all that stick. Half of it's bullshit."

Lester looked unconvinced. "I don't know. You're the one who said I carry weight. You realize I have my very own prosecutor? And we have an amazing relationship with a whole bunch of judges. We could send you up for years. I would personally make a project out of it—maybe to make a point that not everybody gets off light in Vermont."

Backer pressed his lips together, feeling less sure of himself. "Why all the heat? I told you I'd deal."

"Because," Bullis spoke up again, pointing at Lester, "while you may not know him, I do know you, George, and I know how you play the odds. That's been okay in the past—we all know the game. But this is outside the game. You need to realize that. I want you to fully understand that if you hold anything back, if you create any little fiction, the consequences will be very hard. Remember you commenting that this gentleman might be federal? The feds ain't Vermont, and when they send you up, it won't be to one of the sandlots around here."

Backer crossed his arms and slumped in his chair. "This is nuts. I told you I'd deal."

Lester Spinney gave him a wide smile. "Then let's get started."

*   *   *

Gail Zigman woke with a start, her body tense, her eyes wide, trying against common sense to see through the darkness surrounding her. Out of habit, after years of similar paranoid awakenings, she simultaneously reached under the bed for the handgun Joe had taught her to use and glanced at the security control panel mounted next to her bed. One red light was silently blinking on and off, indicating a breach. Somewhere a door or window was open.

There'd been a time when both the hardware and her reliance on it would have seemed an absurdity. One of the appeals of the area was its sense of serenity. She knew people in Vermont who had no idea where their front door keys were—hadn't used them in years.

But the rape had taught her otherwise. Late at night, in the presumed safety of her own home, she'd been reeducated. Now she had a gun, multiple locks, powerful motion detection lights outside, and a high-end security system connecting her directly to the police.

Except that ever since Debbie moved in, Gail hadn't turned all of it on. The girl had complained that the system made her feel like she was in prison, that Gail obviously didn't trust her enough to let her come and go at will.

Against her better judgment, Gail had acceded to the young woman's demands.

She now lay very still in bed, listening, wondering what it was that had bolted her from sleep.

She heard nothing. Only she and Debbie were in the house. Rachel had announced earlier she'd be sleeping at the hospital. And Gail couldn't swear to Debbie's whereabouts.

She slipped out from under the covers, pulled on a pair of jeans and a T-shirt, and, gun in hand, stepped out into the carpeted hallway.

Her bedroom was on the second story, the main staircase to the left at the end of the hall. She moved slowly, keeping next to the wall, hoping the floor wouldn't squeak there.

At the top of the stairs, she stopped to catch her breath, shifted the gun from one hand to the other, and wiped her sweaty palm against her leg. Before her, the staircase fell away like a plunge into a well. She started down.

At the bottom, she finally heard something, not much more than the soft hissing of an object being pulled along a polished hardwood floor.

Only then did she think about calling 911. Why she hadn't earlier confused her at first, until she acknowledged what her subconscious had apparently already suspected—that this might have something to do with her recently adopted ward.

Taking slim comfort in that possibility, she put the gun into her back pocket, happy to be rid of it, and continued very quietly toward the source of the muted noise, still fighting the panic inside her.

From the living room door, she saw two shadows outlined against the open doors to the deck, each at one end of a large, square black void they were struggling to push across the floor. She could hear them breathing with the effort.

She also recognized one of the shadows.

Anger replacing fright, she hit the wall switch beside her, freezing Debbie Holton and her boyfriend, Nelson, with Gail's large TV set between them.

Gail didn't say a word.

Debbie's eyes were as big as quarters. "Hi, Gail. This doesn't look too good, does it?"

Gail had to think about that for a moment, caught up as she was in a swirl of emotions. She tried to keep her voice level. "No. Were you hoping to sell that?"

As she spoke, she glanced around and found a number of things already missing.

"I'm sorry," Debbie said, straightening and putting on an anguished face. "I just had to get some more stuff. I'm hurtin'."

Gail stared at her. "You look pretty good to me. If you were really hurting, you wouldn't be moving furniture around. I'm guessing Mr. Idiot here has already given you a fix. How much of my stuff have you already moved out?"

Nelson straightened and stuck his thin chest out. "Hey, lady. The name is Kicker."

"The name," Gail retorted, dragging out the last word, "is Nelson, asshole, and you keep quiet."

Nelson's mouth dropped open. Gail addressed Debbie, suddenly feeling lighter in some way, as if a migraine had been lifted after days of turmoil. "This was the plan from the start, right? Let the crazy rich woman work out her guilt over Laurie and then rip her off?"

Debbie's expression turned sour. "You came on to

me, remember? You never even bothered finding out what I wanted. You just assumed I was some stupid junkie who needed all the help she could get. You used me for your guilt trip. Why shouldn't I use you, too?" She waved her hand around in a sweeping gesture. "You live all alone in a huge house with all this junk. What do you need it for? To show it off to your friends? Sit around drinking French wine and talk about how you're going to help the poor. You people are so full of shit. You have no clue."

Nelson had taken the opportunity during this speech to collect himself, and now took a few steps in Gail's direction. "Yeah," he said. "You rich bitches are all the same—fancied up and looking good. Fuckin' useless." He paused, getting closer, and added with a cartoonish leer, "Or maybe just good enough for that, if nothing else. You got nuthin' on under that T-shirt, do you?"

Gail straightened as if stung, the sudden change of subject giving her stomach a lurch. She began to feel dizzy, as if being pulled into a hothouse of repressed memories. Watching this boy approach, pulling a knife out of his pocket, she didn't hear Debbie ask, "What're you doin', Nelson? Cut the shit." Instead, she saw his face change shape and appearance and become the man who'd assaulted her with another knife so many years ago.

Nelson was close enough now that he could reach out with his knife and barely touch her left breast with the tip of it. "What d'you think? Want to give it a try? Debbie can keep us company."

Her heartbeat pounding in her temples, Gail removed the gun from her back pocket, shoved the barrel into Nelson's nostril, and pulled back the hammer.

Speaking in a whisper through her almost closed throat, she told him, "I don't think so. Drop the knife or die."

He dropped the knife.

"Ohmygod," Debbie said, shifting from foot to foot, waving her hands. "Please, Gail, don't do it. We'll put everything back. I'm real sorry. We just wanted the money. I didn't know he'd do this. He's just stupid is all. He didn't mean it."

Gail ignored her, her eyes fixed on his. "Get on your knees."

"Oh, no," he half sobbed, beginning to comply. "Don't kill me. I was just kidding."

That line cleared her head a little. She gave him a shove with the gun, jerking his head back and throwing him off balance. He staggered and fell over onto the floor. As he went down, she followed him, so she was kneeling by his head when he landed. He was bleeding from the nose, so she poked the gun under his chin, forcing him to extend his neck.

"That's not a smart thing to say to a woman, Nelson. We don't consider rape a joke."

"Rape?" he squealed. "I was just making an offer."

Gail reached for the cordless phone on a small table by the sofa. "Yeah, well, you can try that on the police. Guess who they'll believe."

"Oh, shit," Debbie exclaimed. "You're not calling the cops? Come on, Gail. We'll make it up to you."

Gail looked at her, her face hard and intense. "That

you will. But not him. He's mine. Now, get the hell out of here."

Debbie hesitated, caught off guard.

"*Now,*" Gail shouted at her.

Debbie turned on her heel and fled out the open door. Gail watched the dark rectangle through which the girl had just vanished, took a deep breath, and glanced down at Nelson, whose Adam's apple was working furiously in its exposed position.

"How're you doing?" she asked him.

"Good, good. Fine."

"Excellent," she said quietly, and dialed 911.

The Rutland fairgrounds are huge. They cover twenty acres of prime real estate in the middle of the city, just off the west side of heavily commercial Route 7, and except for a few days out of every year, they stay empty and unused, locked up behind thousands of feet of chain-link fence. A throwback to a rural heritage, they were created in the mid-1800s to attract farmers from miles around, offering them a place to show off their produce and livestock, have a little fun, and help make Rutland the agricultural center it became before the marble quarries and the railroads stole the show.

Not that any of that was of much relevance lately. The Rutland County Fair has become a pale shadow of its prior self, but is held nevertheless because of a wonderful bit of quirkiness. The Rutland County Agricultural Society's 1846 charter dictates that a county fair is to be held for at least one day every year, or the land will revert to the heirs of the property's original owners. Suggestions have been made to move the whole operation out into the sticks, but so far, by merely holding their annual fair, the society's members have literally been able to hold their ground.

And so it sits, a Realtor's black hole—among the most valuable patches of turf in Vermont—beside the garish, crowded, traffic-clogged, but highly profitable snarl of Route 7, resistant so far to all attempts to change its status.

This striking disparity between urban glut and total emptiness is most noticeable at night, of course, which is why Joe arranged to meet Sam in the fairgrounds' center field, having had one of the gates discreetly unlocked for the purpose. For the field was not just vast and unpopulated—it was also an ideal spot to see anyone approaching from a distance without being seen in the surrounding gloom.

Sammie Martens took her standard precautions against being tailed or observed by chance, parking far away, walking in a pattern that didn't betray her destination and allowed her to double back several times to check for tails.

After a half hour of this, she finally reached the gate and slipped inside. The contrast was immediately striking. Although she'd entered from a dark and quiet street, the pitch black enormity facing her felt almost like the sea at night, with the distant city's traffic appearing as fishing boats hugging the shore. She stepped free of the buildings lining the fence and walked forward tentatively, almost expecting to get wet. What she felt underfoot was just grass, however, and the farther out she got, the more liberated she began to feel, as if she'd left behind her complications in exchange for temporary solace.

She met Joe standing in the middle of the huge field, solid and still.

"Hi, Sam. Any trouble getting here?"

"No, boss. Good to see you." They didn't touch, although for a brief moment, she fought the urge to give him a hug.

"Nice night, huh?" he commented, tilting his head back.

She did the same, and took in the half sphere of stars overhead, usually muted by Rutland's own nightly glow. "That why you chose this as a meeting place?" she asked.

"Didn't think it would hurt. How're you holding up?"

"Fine. Things haven't really cranked up yet. We got our first shipment. You probably saw that. I'm supposed to be rounding up customers now."

"You're covered," Joe told her. "I have Peter Bullis steering some of his CIs over there to make buys, all claiming you sent them. As for helping you dig up the competition, I think we hit a gold mine with this young B-and-E maverick of Peter's."

"The Schemer?" she asked.

"The one and only. He was as good as advertised." Gunther handed her a sheet of paper, which she could only make out as a pale rectangle.

"It's a list," he explained. "Names and addresses, or

at least locations. I wrote it by hand with a pencil to make it look like the kid did it himself. You can claim to Manuel that's how you got it, if he asks, since we're putting George Backer on ice for a while. Peter's checked everything out, of course. He vouches for it all."

She folded the page up and put it in her back pocket. "How many names are there?"

"Eight. Only major players. He has dozens more, all filed in his head. Kid's amazing. He has dates, the ways the houses were laid out, exactly what he stole. Lester said it was like listening to a chess champion of theft. Incredibly engaging, too. Bullis had already warned us—said we'd probably want to take him home after meeting him. Almost right, from what I saw."

Sam was understandably skeptical. "What's Lester's take on him?"

"Told me he feels like the real McCoy. That list is supposedly only those people who actually deal on a significant level, whether they import the stuff themselves or just handle it once it hits town. Spinney and Bullis are still extracting more background information—what Backer can tell them about supply lines, way stations, and anything else." Gunther pointed at her pocket. "The names with an 'H' next to them are people the kid thought had been contacted by or were already working with Hollowell before he was killed."

"Any red flags?"

"Not that we've found so far. You'll have to play it by ear in any case. They aren't all skanky dopers living in dumps. Some of them are businesspeople in town—respectable citizens, so called."

"You have paper on them?" she asked.

"If you want that. I thought ignorance might be bliss in this case, though, since you'll be approaching them as a competitor. Might look suspicious if you knew their rap sheets."

She nodded. "Good point."

"You getting on with Manuel?" Joe asked after a pause.

She looked up at his darkly shadowed face, wishing she could read his expression. This was the second time he'd asked that. "Yeah. He's an interesting guy. Surprising."

Joe nodded, pondering the possible meanings of the word.

Sam then dropped her small bombshell. "Willy came by to tell me to bail out."

"When?"

"Last night. Right after I ditched the phone."

"You think anyone saw him?" Joe was clearly perturbed, and Sam wondered why she'd even brought it up. Willy was going to get a serious thrashing for this one.

"Unlikely. You know how he can come and go when he wants. One moment he was in the back seat of the car, the next he was gone. Joe, do me a favor, will you?"

"What?"

"Don't go after him for this. He's feeling left out is all. He wouldn't blow my cover. You nail him, and it's only going to cause me grief down the road. I only mentioned it because I felt I had to."

Joe was immediately conciliatory. "No, no. I see what you're saying. I'd like to rip his head off, though."

She laughed, grateful for the opportunity. "Yeah, well, join the crowd. Just find another excuse and leave me out of it."

"You got it." He looked around at the distant ring of lights. "I guess we better wrap this up. You sure you're all right?"

"I'm fine, boss."

"Okay, then." He almost sounded disappointed. He quickly looped his arm across her shoulders and gave her a hug. "You better scat."

She smiled at that, as if he were releasing her to the playground. "See ya, Joe."

Gunther watched her vanish into the surrounding gloom with mixed feelings. If he'd ever had a daughter, he could've done far worse than Sam, which was why his concerns for her played more to his paternalistic side than the supervisory one. She could be impulsive and headstrong, of course, but many good cops were. It was more her emotional welfare that worried him. She'd matured over the years. That was true. And maybe it was just his having known her for so long that made him uncertain now. But he always sensed with her an undercurrent of longing to be someone else, and with it a certain fatalism that she was stuck on a course she could do nothing about.

They'd never discussed this in detail, not along those lines, at least. It had never seemed appropriate.

But it did keep him wondering.

Letting out a small sigh, he turned on his heel and began crossing the ghostly fairgrounds to where he'd parked his car.

He was halfway there when he felt his cell phone vibrate on his belt.

"Hello?"

"Joe? It's me. Gail."

He stopped in his tracks. He could tell from her voice something was wrong. "What happened? You okay?"

"Yeah . . . Well, not really. I mean, I'm not hurt or anything. I just had a bad experience."

"Tell me."

"It's stupid. I am such a fool. I almost didn't call you because I didn't want to admit it. Even my sister saw it coming."

He stayed silent, giving her time to get to where she was going. He was happy enough they were finally talking—the topic seemed almost secondary.

"It's Debbie Holton. I caught her and her boyfriend robbing my home. They were wrestling with the big TV set in the living room when I walked in on them, for Christ's sake. It must weigh a ton."

"They broke in?" he asked.

She sounded mournful. "No. She was staying with

me. I took her in. It was just a con they cooked up to rip me off. I feel like such a jerk."

"You were hurting. They took advantage. That's not being a jerk."

There was a long silence he let pass before finally saying matter-of-factly, "There's more."

"I used that gun you gave me."

Something in his chest collapsed. "You shot someone?"

"No. Almost. I shoved it up the boyfriend's nose and pushed him off his feet."

He burst out laughing with relief. "Jesus, Gail. Nice job."

But she didn't join him. "He had a knife on me, Joe. I thought it was going to happen all over again. He even touched me with its point, just like before."

He held his other hand up to his forehead. "Ah, shit. I am so sorry. You have anyone to talk to?"

"Yeah. I have friends here right now. I just ducked out 'cause I wanted you to know."

"I'd like to come see you, if that's all right."

"I was hoping you would."

He was relieved by her acceptance. Years back, that hadn't been the case. It had taken a long time for her to take him back into her life.

"I'll be there in a little over an hour."

Chapter 17

Lester Spinney killed the lawn mower motor, wiped his face with a rag from his jeans pocket, and walked to the open door of the garage to admire his handiwork. It wasn't much of a yard but still looked good. He'd taken his time putting in flower beds, pruning the two small trees, and tending to the grass obsessively enough that he could claim in all honesty that it was the most attractive lawn at this end of Summer Street, and maybe for several blocks around. He had to ruefully concede the qualifiers, however. As with most of Springfield, Summer Street was nothing if not inconsistent. To the west, closer to downtown, there was a string of nineteenth-century mansions. There was no competing with their lawns. Immediately around him, however, were blocks where an abandoned car in the front yard fit in like a birdbath would elsewhere. Spinney's pride, therefore, was rightfully constrained to as far as his eye could see.

Susan would have nothing to do with it. To her, anything that was covered by snow half the year didn't deserve that much attention. But she understood its therapeutic value, and so allowed him his excesses with fertilizer, grass seed, bug killer, and whatever other paraphernalia he deemed crucial to his pet's survival.

He reached over to a workbench near the door and retrieved a can of soda he'd perched there earlier. It was still faintly cool and certainly felt good going down.

"Dad?"

He glanced to his side to see his eleven-year-old daughter looking up at him.

"Hi, sweetie. What's up? You still cleaning your room?"

"I was. I found this." Wendy held up a short brown cylindrical object. Her voice betrayed that she already had a pretty good idea what it was. "It kind of looks like a dog poop."

He took the fat joint from her, actually a cigar emptied out and stuffed with marijuana, called a blunt in the street. "Looks like it's seen better days," he replied, keeping his voice light. "Where'd you find it?"

"On top of that box thing that's over the curtain rod. Above my window, you know?"

He smiled down at her. "Wow. You were cleaning up there?"

"I was going to surprise Mom with my thoroughness."

He laughed and tousled her blond hair. "Thorough hardly touches it, Wendy. I should have you clean this garage."

"*Dad.*"

He dropped the blunt into his T-shirt pocket. "All right. Don't worry about this, okay? It's probably been there for years. I'll get rid of it."

But her face betrayed a continuing concern. "That's not the only one."

His smile faded as her full meaning sank in. "Ah."

"And I've seen him smoke them, too."

He crouched down to get on her level. "So you weren't just dusting."

She looked at the concrete floor. "No. I don't want him to do it anymore. They told us in school what it does."

He gave her a hug. "I don't want him to do it anymore, either, sweetie. But don't worry about giving me this, okay? You're a good daughter, and even better, a really good sister. This proves you love Dave a whole lot."

He straightened up. "You better show me where the others are, though. Where is he, by the way?"

Wendy began walking toward the door connecting the garage to the kitchen. "He went camping, Dad. Don't you remember? He left after Mom went to work this morning. He'll be gone for a few days."

Sam sat in her car for a while, reconnoitering the layout. It was a good place for this kind of business, really—a body shop and used car parts store with lots of people coming and going, some regulars, others unknown. And the place was a tangle of odd pieces of equipment, offering more hiding spots than a Chinese puzzle box, all just lying about.

She glanced down at the sheet Joe had given her. Ralph Meiner had both an "H" and a star next to his name, which Sam assumed put him higher on the list than most. Joe hadn't mentioned anything about stars, but there were three names so adorned. And as for Meiner's, all she had to do was look above the front door opposite to see it repeated with "Proprietor" written next to it.

She got out of her car and checked for traffic before crossing the street, thinking how pleasant it would be when she could stop wearing Greta's tight clothing and painful shoes.

"Hey," she addressed the first person she came to, a filthy man carrying a hammer and covered with a splattering of paint, grease, and just plain dirt. "You tell me where Ralph is?"

He stared at her as if she'd dropped from a cloud. "Ralph?"

"The boss."

He rubbed his nose with the back of his hand. "Out back."

He swiveled on his heel as she walked past, his eyes glued to her.

She went through an open gate alongside the garage and traveled the length of the building, ending up in a large enclosed area to the rear, so cluttered with old cars, either in whole or in parts, it made the front of the establishment look pristine. She stood there looking around, waiting for some sound or movement to direct her.

"I help you?"

She stared straight ahead of her and finally discerned a man standing next to a pile of rusty, twisted metal, his bearded face and stained overalls making him blend almost perfectly into his environment.

"You Ralph?"

"Who's asking?"

"Greta Novak. I was a friend of Jimmy Hollowell's."

"That makes one of us."

"You didn't like Jimmy?"

"Did you?"

"Not especially."

Meiner separated himself from his camouflage and walked toward her, wiping his palms across the voluminous belly of his overalls. "I'm Ralph. What're you after?"

"A business proposition."

The closer he got, the worse she thought he looked. His eyes bloodshot and dark-rimmed, his chest under the tangled beard lined and hollowed out, despite the unhealthy bulk of his body. Ralph Meiner was apparently a man who took life straight in the teeth.

He smiled thinly as he stopped about four feet from her. "Being a friend of Jimmy's, I can guess what kind of business it is. Why come to me?"

"You're a big operator in this town."

He laughed and looked around. "Damn. I'll have to let my banker know about that. Who would've guessed?"

She gave him a sour expression. "Cute. You want to screw around, I better go someplace else."

"Like where?"

She recalled another name from George Backer's list. "Stu Nichols."

He raised his eyebrows. "You think Stuey's in my league?"

"I think Stuey and me combined could bury you."

He laughed again and shook his head. "That is some way to talk. We don't even know each other, you and me."

"I'm standing here," she countered.

He watched her quietly for a moment before nodding approvingly. "So you are. You wanna take a load off?"

He turned and headed back toward where he'd come from, leading her down a narrow canyon formed of opposing piles of scrap metal. At the end of it, there was a small wooden cabin, looking as if it had been flown in from some Louisiana backwater. She half expected an alligator to be tied to a chain on its narrow front porch.

"Real homey," she commented, impressed at what a dump it was.

He looked over his shoulder. "Ain't it? Built it myself. Good place to get away from it all."

She glanced about, thinking it was an even better target for an avalanche.

"Come on in."

She walked up to the threshold and stopped, trying to adjust to the darkness inside.

"Have a seat."

Slowly, she made out a small room with a table, two armchairs, a couple of filing cabinets, and some shelves laden with odds and ends, from magazines and catalogs to unrecognizable engine parts. There were piles of debris in every corner, and a pungent odor of stale human being.

She looked very carefully at the seat of the armchair she'd been offered before sitting down.

"It's okay," he said. "That's the guest chair. It doesn't get used much."

She didn't comment.

"So," he continued, settling down comfortably, "what's on your mind?"

"A merger, a partnership, if you want."

"I don't want. Why should I?"

"More money, more drugs, better security, a guaranteed revenue source, and a chance to expand beyond anything you've dreamed of."

He looked surprised. "Drugs? I thought we were talking the car business here."

She pushed herself back out of the chair and looked down at him, disappointed. "I knew this would be a waste of time. It's been a real treat getting a glimpse of the good life."

He waved at her to sit back down. "Jeez. That's some short fuse you got. Is it going to kill you to take a little time here? We just met and you're talking building a drug empire or something. Give a guy a chance."

She sat back down. "We don't have to be buddies. I want to get this thing going."

"Fine, fine," he agreed. "We'll talk. How 'bout something to loosen up, first? I got some good shit here." He reached over to the nearest filing cabinet and pulled open the bottom drawer.

She shook her head. "Maybe later. I don't want to do this with a buzz on."

He closed the drawer and gave her an enigmatic smile. "Right. I didn't think so. Why don't you give me your sales pitch, then?"

A small tingle of concern flickered in the back of her brain. "Like I said, it's a merger, or whatever you want to call it—a way to get us all organized so we can stabilize the market, streamline our supply sources, and work together to keep the cops off our backs. You gotta admit, things could be better."

"Everything in life could be better," Meiner agreed. "Doesn't mean it will be. Sometimes the cost is too high."

She leaned forward in her chair. "But that's the beauty here. Your costs will go down. Only the profits'll go higher."

"Isn't that wonderful? And all because I'm such a nice guy."

"I don't care if you're a flaming asshole," she said. "I just want you as part of the solution here, not part of the problem."

"And you would be the queen of the solution? The boss?"

She shook her head vehemently. "No. There'd be a council. We could structure that any way we wanted, once we all got together. The key, though, is to get everything out on the table, eliminate wasteful competition, and build a structure with some element of security."

"Right now I want security, I take care of it myself."

"Exactly, and so does Stuey and so did Jimmy and everybody else. What's the point? What I'm saying here is just Business 101. It's not like sending a rocket to the moon. People in this line of work only think from day to day. This is a really simple concept. It'll work."

"What would I have to give up?"

"Aside from this fancy lifestyle? Nothing."

"Don't shit on my lifestyle, lady. I'm my own man here. I'm not so sure what you're selling would be an improvement there."

She sat back, crossed her legs, made her voice slightly less friendly. "Ralph. In the long run, it may not be a choice. You know how Wal-Mart does it?"

"Yeah, yeah—the big fish eat the little fish. You know, this is just a wonderful idea, assuming I had any knowledge of the drug business, which, of course, I don't. But, speaking of big fish, what would you do about the ones upstream? There're a few people in Holyoke that might not like your screwing around in their business. You wouldn't look much like Wal-Mart to them. Think how Jimmy ended up."

Sam went out on a limb. "Jimmy was dumb. He tried

pushing his weight around here before he had things lined up down south. Me, I'm talking for those same people, like a representative."

Ralph Meiner was caught off guard. "You work for Torres?"

She tried not to show her own surprise. "I work for Rivera. He took the business away from Torres. Where've you been?"

"I never heard of Rivera."

She recalled the scuttlebutt about how many of the dealers had pulled in their horns following Hollowell's death, waiting for new players to show themselves. Meiner's ignorance may have been a sign of his lying low. "You will soon enough, unless you get in on it now."

Meiner pushed his lips out thoughtfully. "All right. I'll think about it. Now, how 'bout a little something to seal the deal?"

She stood up. "When we seal it, we'll see. Right now I got other people to talk to."

Meiner didn't move. "You a vegetarian, too?"

She looked at him. "What's that mean?"

"It means I feel like a meatpacker who's just been pitched by a vegetarian. Why do I get the feeling you're not so hot on the product?"

Sam felt her frustration growing. She'd been almost out the door. "I told you, I don't want a buzz on when I'm doing business."

Almost nonchalantly, he removed a pistol from his pocket and laid it on his lap. Its barrel was pointed vaguely at her knees. "Which is exactly the kind of excuse a cop would use."

The tingle she'd experienced earlier spread like an electric current. She feigned astonishment. "A cop? You think I'm a cop? What the fuck's that? Did I try to sell you anything, or buy anything? Cops don't talk about making a drug business work better. Jesus, Ralph. That's why I don't do any shit when I'm working. It scrambles your head."

"Sit down," he said, his expression grim.

"Why the hell should I?"

He lifted the gun so it was pointing at her. "Call it a show of faith. We do a little dope together, my faith in you improves."

She sat back down. "This is a pretty piss poor way of beginning a partnership."

Keeping the gun on her, he reached out and opened the filing cabinet again. "I don't think so. Name your poison."

She rolled her eyes in exasperation. "Fine. Give me some weed. I could do with a little mellowing out, if the others're all going to be like you."

He pulled out a shoe box full of pill bottles, small boxes, twists of aluminum, and small pale blue baggies. "Fresh out," he said, not even looking. "What's your number two choice?"

Sam had no time to hesitate, and knew she couldn't stall. His refusal to give her marijuana showed that he wanted her to commit to something weightier. Narcotics officers face this choice commonly enough—it was both the druggie's equivalent of sharing a beer with a pal and a way for them to separate the undercovers from the real users.

Except that it wasn't foolproof. The courts had held that if an officer took drugs under threat of mortal danger, such a transgression was allowable.

Ralph's gun certainly helped there.

All that was left was for Sam to make a choice she hoped she could live with. Or she could just pretend to take one of his offerings, assuming he left her a split second loophole. The latter possibility encouraged her to choose a pill. "Got any E?"

He smiled. "That I do, although I would've pegged you for a cokehead."

"Used to be. I had a bad experience."

He was rummaging around in his box. "Not that I'm complaining. I like a little E myself when I'm feeling frisky. I might even join you. Maybe we'll get something going."

She gave him a warning look. "I wouldn't count on it. I'm a one-guy girl, and right now that guy is just across town, complete with bad attitude."

"What he don't know won't kill him."

She raised an eyebrow and he laughed in response. "Right," he said. "What a waste. Anyhow—here we go."

She held out her hand to receive the brightly colored pill, about the size of a large aspirin, but Meiner shook his head. "Open your mouth."

She scowled at him. "What? And close my eyes? I don't think so. Give me the damn pill."

He watched her carefully. "Listen, missy. You do

this my way or we don't deal, okay? Call me finicky, but I don't like my gifts to be wasted. Open your mouth. I don't care what you do with your eyes."

Reluctantly, unsure of what she'd exposed herself to, Sam did as ordered and felt the Ecstasy tablet drop onto her tongue. From the taste, it was no breath mint.

"Here," he said. "Wash it down with this." He handed her a half-empty bottle of Scotch.

Feeling the pill dissolving already, she took a swig and swallowed hard, trying to remember what the side effects of Ecstasy were supposed to be. She knew it was the rave drug of choice, supposed to flood the brain with serotonin and release inhibitions. She also knew most such claims for illegal drugs didn't tell the whole story.

She returned the bottle. "Thanks. You wouldn't have a few more for down the line, would you?"

"Not so reluctant all of a sudden?"

She frowned. "Look, Ralph. We all got baggage to carry, okay? I try to do one thing at a time, and do it right. I know how messed up I can get. This deal means a lot to me—it's kind of like my one shot, as I see it, and I don't want to screw it up. I've done that enough times already."

She got up and walked to the grimy window and looked out on the narrow canyon of junk outside. "You're a guy. You can take what you want in life. Me, it's always been the shit end of the stick. I want a change."

She turned and looked at him. He'd just finished taking a pill himself and washing it down. The gun was no longer in view, and he'd put three more pills on the arm of her chair.

"You said part of your plan was to streamline our supply sources. I think that's the words you used. What did that mean?"

She was struck by the change of subject. Had her ingestion of a single Ecstasy tablet turned the tables? "Just what it sounded like," she answered him, pocketing the extra pills. "Right now it's catch-as-catch-can. You got a bunch of competing bigwigs in Holyoke, a few more out of upper New York State, some from Canada, a shit-load of one-shot wonders working street corners—"

"I know one who deals right out of her vagina," Ralph interrupted. "Little wet bags of the stuff. You ever do that?"

She ignored him. "There's no control. Everyone looks at this as a really ripe market, 'cause the prices are so good compared to Massachusetts or New York, but that misses the point. It's short-term thinking. If we set up a dependable, consistent pipeline, and enforce it to keep everyone else out, think how that would change the business."

He looked skeptical. "That works both ways, though. You're saying we should do all this through Rivera. What's to stop him from jacking our prices up? Right now we can shop around for the best deal."

Her heart gave a triple beat for no reason, and she felt an odd wave of warmth run through her. She sat back down, brushing it aside in the interests of making her point. "It's a monopoly, Ralph. You pass the costs along."

"Meaning we're right back where we started, at the same profit margin."

She was shaking her head. "Wrong. You forgot the consistency advantage. You got more product and more clients as a result. Even if Rivera doubles his price, forcing you to do the same, you'll still be selling to four times more people, if you do this right. Plus, we plan to go outside Rutland and push this till it covers the state. There is an element of the top dog winning out, but that's you already, right? You're one of the top dogs in town."

Unsurprisingly, that last comment proved the most effective. Ralph smiled broadly and settled back into his mildewy armchair. "You could say that. Sure you don't want to fool around?"

Sam was feeling hot, her heart was beating more rapidly than made sense. The drug was kicking in and making her nervous, even slightly paranoid. But she also had energy to spare all of a sudden, and a strong desire to get things done.

She stood up. "Sorry, Ralph. Not in the mood. And I gotta get crackin'. You in or not?"

"I'm not in or out. I want to think about it."

She opened the door and looked back at him. "Okay, but the clock's ticking."

"I got a question for you," he said unexpectedly. "What happens if Torres and the others don't take kindly to this?"

"They've been dealt with. I told you."

He gave her an enigmatic look, his face washed by the anemic light slipping in through the open door. "I like you. Otherwise, I wouldn't waste my time. But Jimmy Hollowell thought the same thing. Maybe you should ask yourself what happened to him."

Chapter 18

Sammie kept trying to concentrate. She knew she'd heard something important while talking with Ralph Meiner, but she couldn't get hold of it. Instead, she was distracted by everything she saw passing by the windows of her car—lights, trees, endless rows of buildings. Although slightly blurred and a little stuttery, as in an old silent movie, it all took on an intensity, a beauty, and a mysterious serenity that she'd never before noticed. She found herself unexpectedly walking across a broad stretch of park, out of the car, not remembering having left it, totally attuned to the smells and sensations around her. She felt happy, even euphoric, tingling with sensuality. She dropped to her knees and placed her hands on the ground, curling her fingers through the grass as if it were a lover's hair, grinding her teeth with the passion, before finally stretching out to feel the resonance of the earth against her body. In an unexpected shift, however, that same sensation led her back in time to when, as a child, she'd press her ear against a wall to distinguish the muted murmurings on the other side. Now, as back then, she was confronted with messages she couldn't decipher—except that this time it was a dilemma she found pleasantly seductive, even sexually stimulating.

By the time the effects of the Ecstasy wore off, she was tired, dirty, disoriented, and let down. It was late and dark, and it took her half an hour to locate her car at the park's edge. As for the overall experience, she was caught between worrying about any long-range consequences and the strong, lingering memory of having tasted something unimaginably appealing. She realized with a shock that had she been on the drug the night before, when standing so close to Manuel in the basement, she wouldn't have hesitated entering his embrace—a thought that troubled her beyond anything else.

"I was stupid."

Joe reached out and took Gail's hand in his own. "You were trying to make amends for something you shouldn't have felt guilty about in the first place. It still doesn't mean it wasn't worth the attempt."

"She took me for a patsy, and she was right. I played right into it."

"I'm glad you didn't shoot her boyfriend," he said, half as an aside.

Gail thought about that for a couple of beats. "I didn't even see him. All I saw was the other guy's face."

The other guy—to Joe's knowledge, she hadn't spoken her rapist's actual name in years.

"But you stayed in control. You did what you thought was right, realized you were being had, and you corrected the situation. Take that for what it is, Gail. You were not stupid."

She smiled thinly. They were in her living room, her more pawnable possessions still gathered near the double doors where either Debbie and Nelson had piled them up or the cops had placed them after cataloging and removing them from Nelson's rust bucket of a van.

"You say the nicest things," she said with irony. "I just wish it made me feel better."

"How's Laurie doing?" he asked.

"The same. I called Rachel a while ago." She'd been staring at the floor but now fixed him with a direct look. "Joe, I'm sorry I shut you out."

"You had a lot on your mind."

She shook her head. "I'm not sure I did. I think I had only one thing on my mind—to turn back the clock somehow. You know, the funny thing is that I never much liked Laurie. The little time I spent with her, all she did was complain about her life, which for my money was pampered and privileged and overindulged. And yet she whined about how bored she was and how terrible her parents were. I didn't know what she was doing in Brattleboro because I took no interest. I had a Post-it note on my computer—'call Laurie.' I saw it

every day until I finally threw it out. Never called her
once."

"You think anything would've changed if you had?"
he asked gently.

He gave her credit. Someone else might have flared
at that. Gail merely nodded acceptingly. "Probably not.
I still wouldn't have liked her. And she never saw me
as anything other than her mother's sister, anyhow."

"That may not be true," he countered. "She ever say
that?"

"No," she admitted. "We never had that long a conversation."

Joe sensed they were past the worst of Gail's self-
recrimination, certainly far enough for him to ask, "So
why did you go after Debbie so hard, if Laurie meant that
little?"

He'd overplayed his hand a bit. She looked at him
sharply. "We didn't have much in common—but I still
loved her. Love her."

But he didn't back down. The question floated between them.

"All right," she conceded. "I've been feeling out of
sorts lately. Not sure that what I'm doing is what I
really want out of life. It's thrown me off and made me
doubt a lot of things—my job, my goals, even the two
of us sometimes."

"Oh?"

Her hand remained in his but lay there unmoving.
"Well, not that much, but still . . . Somehow, seeing
Laurie in the hospital kind of pulled the rug out from
under me. It wasn't just that I felt guilty. It was also the

waste of it all—the stupidity. I mean, what the hell is going on? It's crazy. Laurie from the lap of luxury; Debbie from a home not fit for a dog. And they end up in the same jam. Nobody's doing enough, Joe. This war on drugs is a total crock."

He kept silent. They didn't discuss politics much. Too many potential land mines. But he had his own reasons for agreeing with what she'd said. Virtually every drug cop he knew only worked the assignment for the juice or the promotion potential connected to it—not because any of them believed it would actually make a difference. Being a drug cop was a feather in one's professional cap, a chance to get out of the spit and polish, and allowed for an occasional stretching of the rules unavailable elsewhere on the job.

He was considering how to respond when she continued on her own. "Of all the therapists and counselors I know who deal with this, there are some things they all seem to agree about. One is that this whole thing about kids getting into trouble because they're bored is baloney. Kids have more available to them than ever before. So, I have some serious doubts about skateboard parks and more rec centers being the solution. And another thing is that with a huge percentage of young substance abusers, there's always a parental figure who sets the course—teenage drinkers and druggers are the children of drinkers and druggers. The numbers are like a neon sign. Getting more cops on the road and building more prison cells is not going to do one damn thing about that."

Gunther nodded sympathetically. Again, he didn't

disagree with her. He'd seen the stats himself. But he was as shy about cutting back on law enforcement as he was about turning the country into a military state. Joe tended to the middle ground on topics like this, which generally meant he kept his mouth shut—a habit he'd learned after being hammered from both sides in the past, and something he shared with a great many police officers.

"We need to go deeper," she was saying as if he were no longer in the room. "We need for our leaders to stop going for the headline and the next vote and take responsibility for the future—to start acting not for themselves, but for future generations. Right now they all talk that line, but they do jack shit to back it up—all this 'three strikes and you're out' crap isn't doing fuck-all."

He laughed gently at that. "It was a perfect election speech till that last line. Is that where you're headed?"

She blinked and focused on him. "It's crossed my mind," she admitted slowly.

"For what office?"

She got up and walked to the double doors to gaze out upon the moonlit lawn, its canvas of lush green grass and verdant trees rendered a deep blue-gray in the lunar glow. Without actually seeing them, she watched the feeble flickerings of a few lightning bugs pirouetting in the near-darkness.

"I haven't decided yet, but I think it's time."

He rolled that over in his mind. She was an ambitious woman, and one used to success. He had no doubt she'd follow through on this. What he was less sure about was how it might affect them. But he took a more roundabout way to broach the subject.

"Gail, this thing with Debbie. I mean, I understand what you just said. To be honest, it's kind of surprised me you haven't run for office before—except for the selectboard, of course—so you know I wish you the best. But I just want to make sure that what happened here"—he waved his hand toward the pile of possessions by the door—"isn't left behind in the process. This was serious. You were hit pretty hard. And it had nothing to do with the fate of your youth or the merits of 'three strikes and you're out.' "

She turned back from the night and faced him, her expression cast in shadow from the lamplight directly beside her. "I'm not so sure," she answered quietly, thoughtfully. "After I was raped, I didn't know what might happen to me. Intellectually, I knew what to expect, and I had you and my friends and my family backing me up. I had things to occupy my brain— going back to law school, becoming a prosecutor for a while, then the lobbying job. On the outside, I knew I was doing okay—even better than okay. The paranoia lessened, my uneasiness being around men."

She moved to a straight-back chair by the wall and sat on its edge, her hands in her lap. "But on the inside—deep inside—I still had that fear, you know? Not just that some man might try again, but a larger fear about what I had left to deal with. You know what they say about the foundation of the Brooklyn Bridge?"

"No," he answered.

"That while the original plan was to dig deep

enough to put the footings on granite bedrock, deep underwater, they could never reach it, so they finally gave up. The whole bridge sits on sand—all these years later."

"And you're feeling the same way?"

She leaned forward, her elbows on her knees. "I don't know anymore. I did when I was dealing with Debbie and fighting with my sister—I wondered if I was losing it all over again. But in the end—when that little twerp started waving that knife around in front of me—I suddenly found a chance to test myself. And when I shoved that gun up his nose and knocked him on his ass, all I felt was determination. It was like a rebirth in a flash of light. I know you try to stick to the realities you can hold in your hand, Joe, but this was almost that real to me. There was an element to it of being given a second chance."

"Is that why you let Debbie go before you called 911?"

She rose and crossed over to sit next to him on the couch again. "I know. Probably still makes me look like a patsy to you."

"Maybe a little," he answered truthfully.

"But she wasn't the one responsible anymore. She may have even cooked up the idea to rip me off, but *he* was the ghost I needed to defeat. Involving her felt like missing the point. I'll deal with her later if I feel like it, or maybe he'll rat her out and I'll have to admit what I did, but that's a trade-off I can live with. Does any of that make sense?"

"Sure it does," he said supportively, and kissed her.

But in the back of his mind, he still wondered where it might lead.

Sam pulled into the driveway and killed the engine, still feeling the aftereffects of the drug Ralph Meiner had given her. More lucid now, she actually had no idea if it had been Ecstasy or something else, since her experience in that line had been purely academic until now. The real source of interest to her, however, was how enjoyable it had been. All her professional life, she'd viewed dopers as weak-minded losers, hell-bent on escaping reality. She was not disposed to change this view, of course, but she was surprised at herself for not having realized that part of a drug's attraction might be the pleasure it offered. It was a revelation so simple, she felt stupid even thinking of it.

The saving grace was that this discovery carried no yearning for a second exposure. Sam's nature was nothing if not self-denying, at least when it came to pleasant indulgences, and she was already looking back at this epiphany with a stern distaste.

She sat in the car and watched the house for a while, seeing shadows playing across the drawn shades as Manuel conducted business with Peter Bullis's crew of slowly escalating CIs and undercover cops, all posing as word-of-mouth, walk-in customers.

It was an odd moment for her, especially given what she'd just gone through. Sitting in this car, those memories still as fresh as the dried sweat on her skin, and thinking of Manuel doing business under a battery of hidden cameras, she felt a lack of definition—half crook and half cop—and couldn't help but link it to her life as a whole. Because for Sam, almost everything about her felt in limbo. She was no longer a kid, but still couldn't compare to an adult like her mentor, Joe Gunther. She was no longer a municipal cop, but part of an elite unit that still had to negotiate its way into almost every investigation. And she wasn't single, in the sense of being alone, but was involved with a maniac and now felt drawn to a criminal.

The whole package made her feel as if where she'd come from was long gone, and where she was headed was out of reach.

In that way, if in no other, she had to envy Greta Novak.

She left the car after seeing the two buyers slip out of the house and disappear into the bushes lining the driveway. She walked up to the front door, rang the bell in the coded tattoo that she and Manuel had agreed upon, and then used her key in the lock.

As she closed the door behind her, she more sensed than saw Manuel standing just around the corner, watchful and waiting.

"Honey, I'm home," she announced to the empty entryway.

He appeared silently, tucking a pistol away under his shirt, a smile on his face. "Yes, darling. And supper's almost ready." His eyes narrowed as he took her in more fully. "What happened to you? You okay?"

She was struck by the genuine concern in his voice. "Yeah. Long story with no damage. I just fell down and got messed up. Hooked an ally, though. At least I think so. If I play him a little more, it might mean a big jump in business."

But he didn't seem to be listening. He'd approached her and now cupped her chin in his hand, raising her face to the light to better see it. "You been doing more than falling down."

She gently removed his hand. "I had to do some dope with him to prove I wasn't a cop. It was a bit of the bad old days I could've lived without."

"What'd he give you?"

"Said it was Ecstasy, but who knows? Anyhow, it made him happy and I'm okay. Might've been worse with coke—that's where I had a problem. We have any beer?"

They went to the kitchen together, where, to her surprise, dinner was in fact simmering on the stove, something in a pot that smelled very rich and very good. When on her own, Sam subsisted on any variety of boring food, so long as it came in either a can or a box, but she had to admit she'd always been fond of home-cooked meals.

"Wow. That looks delicious," she said, glancing at the stove while removing a beer from the fridge.

"Garbanzos con chorizos," he said. "Nothing fancy. Beans and sausage, with attitude. Should be ready in another half hour."

She opened the bottle and took a deep swallow, enjoying the cold beer washing straight down into her stomach. She wiped her lips with her wrist and sighed.

"That and a hot shower and I'll be ready to eat like a horse."

"Take your time," he said, picking up a long spoon with which to stir the pot.

She went upstairs, taking the beer with her, pondering the domesticity of it all. Narcotics and home cooking—American capitalism, alive and well. Was this what advocates of legalized drug dealing saw as the future? And who on which side of the debate was under the biggest delusion? The futility of it all made her happy she was just a line soldier, following orders—and all the more eager for that soul-cleansing shower.

After dinner, already late in the evening, Sam and Manuel prepared for the high-volume part of the day, a standard in a business that tended toward the nocturnal. While he got ready to sell his assortment, she, refreshed and fed, set out to duplicate her earlier visit to Ralph by tracking down Stuey Nichols, from George Backer's list, someone Ralph clearly considered a competitor.

Nichols lived in a section of Rutland nicknamed the Gut. In the industrial days of seventy-five years earlier, the Gut was an ethnic, working-class neighborhood, initially made up of Italians, Irish, and others, but finally consisting of Italians overall, after the Irish contingent had pulled up stakes and moved elsewhere in town. The handle is actually a misnomer, since it conjures up images of Upton Sinclair's steaming, fetid slaughterhouses of old Chicago. In fact, although the

Gut is located on the far side of the railroad tracks, it is a bland residential area of neat, straight avenues, old, expansive trees, and weathered, modest homes so small and so lacking in traditional New England detail that the neighborhood is also known, if less generally, as Nebraska.

It is a poor section—and host to a large affordable housing complex—but again not as crime-infested as the name implies. For that matter, when the hunt was on to find a suitable location for Sam and Manuel, the logic was to go where some of the city's bigger flare-ups with bikers and gangs had already occurred. That turned out to be north of the Gut's upper boundary of West Street, around Baxter and Maple.

That having been said, however, when Sam found out where Stuey lived, it didn't come as a surprise. Hard times had visited Rutland for long enough that only a few neighborhoods remained immune from Stuey's form of self-employment, and the Gut was certainly not among them. In fact, one of the latest of Rutland's heroin overdoses had occurred right here.

She found the house with relative ease off of South Street, surrounded by darkness and quiet. At this time of night, the rest of Rutland, with its traffic and bright lights, seemed very far away.

Stu Nichols was clearly not into home maintenance. By the feeble glow of a distant streetlamp, Sam picked her way carefully through an odd and inexplicable assortment of holes, cinder blocks, and heaved-up chunks of stony earth, along with a scattering of seriously used children's toys. The house itself looked perfectly suited to its battlefield yard.

Sam made it to the weather-beaten front porch, illuminated by a harsh yellow bulb hanging overhead from a wire, a corona of interested night bugs circling its orbit in tight, continuous flight. The front door was wide open, and she could see through the screen door a living room rigged like a stage set for a war movie. Seeing no buzzer and hearing children crying and adults shouting somewhere in the back, she pounded on the door frame hard enough to break it.

"Who the fuck's that?" an angry male voice demanded.

"Greta Novak," she shouted, figuring the female voice alone would draw him out.

She wasn't wrong. A skinny, balding man in his forties stumbled into the room, squinting to see through the screening. "Who're you?" he asked, wiping his mouth on the back of his hand, no doubt to make himself doubly attractive.

"Are you Stuey Nichols?"

"That any of your business?"

"I'm a friend of Jimmy Hollowell's, picking up where he left off," she said. "I thought we should maybe talk, since Ralph Meiner called you a pissant when I told him that you and I combined could put him out of business."

Nichols straightened. "He called me a pissant? That little prick?"

There was an outburst of renewed crying from inside the house. Nichols swore, turned on his heel, and vanished from view. Moments later, Sam heard him screaming obscenities at the top of his lungs, the slamming of a door, and then silence.

Stuey reappeared, showing his yellow teeth in a welcoming smile. "Come on in, lady," he said, swinging open the door on squealing hinges. "What'd you say your name was?"

"Greta Novak."

He stared at her in surprise, studying her face as if she'd sprouted a horn. "No shit," he said after a pause. "You a foreigner?"

"My parents saw too many old movies."

He gave her a blank expression. "Right. You want a drink?"

Sam stood in the middle of the room, wondering if anything might jump out and bite her ankle. "I'm all set. You got a lot of kids?"

He spat on the floor, to little effect. "Little bastards. You can have 'em if you want. I'll even wrap 'em up. So you're next in line to Jimmy, huh? That mean you're gonna get strung up, too?" He laughed uproariously before turning on his heel and beckoning to her to follow him. "Let's go to my office if we're gonna talk business."

She picked her way through the debris, noticing the smell of diapers and rotting food increasing the deeper she entered the building, making her feel she was progressing through the innards of some beast. Stuey Nichols turned left down a short hallway, proceeded through a door at its end, and stopped to usher her through before closing it behind her.

"Have a chair," he offered, pointing to a half-deflated beanbag propped against the wall.

She glanced around for something a little less absorbing. "That's okay."

He looked offended. "What? Not cushy enough? You don't want to catch somethin'? Nice start. You came to me, lady. I'm being polite here. Don't need to put on airs."

Sam shook her head and sat—actually half collapsed—into the low-slung beanbag, feeling like her butt had just been grabbed by mud. "Jesus, Stuey. Don't make a federal case out of it, okay?"

Nichols himself perched on the edge of a debris-strewn table nearby, one leg up, the other still planted on the floor, all offense vaporized. "How'd you know Jimmy?"

"An ex-boyfriend and him were friends."

"Long time ago?"

She tilted her head slightly, looking up at him. "This twenty questions time?"

"Yeah. You got a problem with that?"

"No. About four years."

"Where?"

"Where what?" she asked. "Where did I meet Jimmy? Springfield. We were living there then. He came by to sell some stuff to the boyfriend."

"What was the boyfriend's name?"

"You wouldn't know. He was a flatlander-bum-jerk-off named Nicky Meadows. We split up and he went back to New York."

"How'd you meet him?"

"Nicky? What do you care?"

"Humor me," Nichols persisted.

"I work winters at Tucker Peak. You meet a lot of people in a place like that."

Stuey laughed. "And do a lot of dope. That what wet your whistle to get into the business?"

"That's where it started, yeah."

"So how'd you make the leap from meeting Jimmy to taking over after he got whacked? That's a big gap."

"Jimmy worked for Rivera. Now I do."

Stuey shook his head as if confused. "Rivera . . . Johnny Rivera? He's a Holyoke nobody."

"He took over Torres's Vermont run."

"You hook up with him through Jimmy?"

Sam had hoped to avoid this part. "No. Bill Dancer from Bratt led me to Torres. That's how we found out about Rivera. Just my luck we walked in right after Jimmy died."

Stuey smiled sympathetically. "No shit. You sound like one lucky girl. A lot luckier than Dancer, from what I heard."

He held her gaze a little longer than was comfortable. Sam became even more aware of being wrapped in Styrofoam beams. "That supposed to mean something?"

He slid off the table and pretended to stretch, exposing his pale, soft, hairy stomach. "Well, you know . . . the boyfriend disappears where no one will find him, Jimmy dies right on cue, Dancer gets busted as soon as you meet Rivera. Almost too good to be true."

He lowered his arms, shifted his feet slightly, and

stood facing her silently like a boxer, ready to start. Sam knew not only that she was in trouble but that she'd been there from the start. The beanbag was a trap. If she'd had a gun, she couldn't have reached it, and in any case, she was hard-pressed to move without real effort.

Nothing left to lose.

She pitched violently to her left, spilling out of the bag and scrambling to gain her footing. Simultaneously, Stuey Nichols snatched a baseball bat off the table beside him, swung neatly around on his heel in a windup, and came up like a golfer, hitting her in the upswing, right across the abdomen as she was still on all fours. The blow lifted her off the floor and sent her rolling against the wall, doubled over with pain.

She opened her eyes just enough to see him standing over her, the smile gone and the bat held ready. "Who do you think you're shitting, lady? Think I'm a fucking moron? You're a Brattleboro cop. I know you. You busted me five years ago, for Christ's sake. You must take me for a fucking idiot."

"I do," said a male voice behind him.

Nichols swung around. Sam saw Willy Kunkle smack the other man across the head with a heavy metal flashlight, dropping him like a cement bag at Sam's feet.

Willy knelt down next to her. "You okay?"

"Don't know yet," she said weakly. "He dead?"

Willy barely glanced at Nichols. "He's breathing.

What the hell were you thinking? That he wouldn't recognize you?"

She rolled her eyes. "I didn't recognize him, for crying out loud. How did you know?"

He smiled slightly. "I been tailing you, just in case. Soon as I saw him through the screen door, I pegged him. I just couldn't figure out what your plan was. Pretty clever, getting yourself almost killed. Good way to gain his confidence."

"Up yours."

Willy sat back on his heels. "You must be feeling better. You want to try moving?"

He held out his hand to help her. Slowly, she straightened her legs, getting her stomach to relax, and palpated her abdomen. Other than feeling tender and nauseous, however, she sensed nothing vital was broken. Slowly, groaning with discomfort, she rolled onto her knees and used the wall to help her stand, Willy's strong right hand on her elbow for support.

She stood there a moment, the room spinning around, her throat constricted and her stomach in turmoil.

"You gonna puke?" Willy asked, the sensitive nursemaid.

She spoke through clenched teeth. "If I do, I'll make sure I hit you."

He didn't laugh as he might have normally, but steered her over to a nearby legitimate chair. "Sit. Looks like you'll live."

He returned to Nichols and checked his pulse. Apparently satisfied, he glanced down the hallway to make sure it was still empty and then sat on a small side table opposite Sam. "So what the hell went wrong?"

She gave him an exasperated glare. "I don't have your encyclopedia brain, Sherlock. Nothing triggered when I saw him."

Willy shook his head. "Well," he conceded, "he used to have a lot of hair and a mustache. Still . . . What about our flawless boss? Didn't he tell you the guy had a Brattleboro rap sheet? That might've been vaguely helpful."

Given all that Gunther had done over the years to ensure Willy's employment as a cop, Sam could never believe the latter's constant lack of gratitude. "Give it a rest. It was a screwup. Everyone survived."

"This time," Willy said disgustedly, and stood up again. He began looking around the room. "But I knew this would happen. This whole thing's been half-cocked from the start. He never should've okayed it."

"I forced him to. I'd already signed on with Rivera before I told him."

He turned to face her. "That's not how it works, and you know it, Sam. He's the top guy. He calls the shots. He was playing politics and you were helping him. That's not police work. It's . . . I don't know . . . bullshit."

She watched his face, its intensity showing more concern than anger, and she realized once more how oblique he could be in showing affection. Christ almighty—she could pick them.

"What do we do now?" she asked, to change the

subject. "This jerk's punching-bag girlfriend isn't going to stay in her corner forever."

Willy was back in motion, poking around, searching for something. "Yeah, yeah. I'm working on that."

He finally lifted up a pale blue baggie, filled with the familiar dusting of white powder. "Bingo. Okay. You call your pals on the task force, tell 'em you got burned and you need a cover team to pretend to bust this guy for this." He waved the baggie back and forth. "That'll legitimize their crashing in here and tossing the place and making it look good for tomorrow's paper. After that, they can put him under guard in the hospital or shoot him in the head. Anywhere he can't flap his gums."

He handed her his cell phone so she could make the call.

But Sam was looking at the baggie in his hand, the memory of what she'd been trying to recall earlier, just before the Ecstasy took over, coming back to her.

"That's Torres's stuff," she said.

Willy glanced at it. "So?"

"I saw his lieutenant packing it when I was in Holyoke. Same pale blue baggies. It's a signature, like the panther stamp Rivera uses on his. You ever see any like that before?"

"No. Maybe he just got a good deal on them."

"Maybe, but Rivera's supposed to have taken over the run. And, like I said, he uses regular bags and his own stamp."

"Yeah, but he took over just recently, right?" Willy

countered. "Couldn't this be a leftover from the Torres days?"

Sam wasn't convinced. Something wasn't right.

Stuey Nichols let out a small groan from the floor. "Make the call, Sam. We gotta get going."

Chapter 19

Spinney kept trying to slow down, control his breathing, keep at the speed limit. He was driving from Rutland back to Springfield on Route 103, fresh from another session with Peter Bullis and young George Backer. They'd been grilling the kid for his knowledge of Rutland's peripheral drug traffic—Bellows Falls, Fair Haven, Castleton, Springfield, and elsewhere—when the name Sherman came up.

"Sherman?" Spinney had asked, sitting up.

"Yeah," Backer had confirmed. "He's been operating out of Springfield for a long time—years and years."

"Moving heroin?"

The Schemer had shrugged. "Not always. It's just what I heard lately."

"You know this guy?" Bullis had asked Lester.

"Yeah. But never connected to heroin."

Spinney passed another car on a curve, causing an angry blast of the man's horn. That had been the extent of Backer's knowledge—a vague rumor, really. Except that given the young man's accuracy so far, even a rumor carried weight.

It certainly did with Lester, who'd begged off attending the afternoon session for some emergency personal time off.

He had yet to speak with Dave about the blunts Wendy had found in her bedroom—his son was still supposedly on a camping trip. As a result, the growing anxiety about that inevitable confrontation had combined with hearing Sherman's name linked to heroin like a match with a fuse. Simple surveillance was no longer the issue. Now Spinney was acting as a firefighter might, running into a burning building with the sinking sensation that it was already too little, too late.

And the stimulus wasn't restricted to a father's love. There was guilt, as well, for not having acted sooner, for having put harmony over honesty and experience. After all, who better than a cop to know how, statistically, marijuana leads to harder drugs? And how a parent is always the last one to admit there's trouble?

Spinney entered Springfield from the west, sped through the intersection near the Zoo, and burned the red light downtown, cutting off several cars in the process. All self-restraint gone by now, the only thing he could see in his mind's eye was putting his hands around Sherman's neck.

He hit the South Street hill hard, only a small part of

his brain wondering how he'd react if he was pulled over right now, and proceeded to where Sherman had his half-hearted garage business not far from the high school.

He came skidding to a halt before the open garage door, launched himself out of the car, and strode into the service bay. A pair of legs was sticking out from under a car with its hood up.

"Sherman?" he shouted.

"What?" came the startled reply. "You almost gave me a heart attack."

Not answering, Spinney grabbed both the man's ankles and pulled him out as if he were yanking a tablecloth from under a plate. Lying on a small, wheeled creeper, Sherman went shooting across the floor and crashed against a tall metal tool cabinet.

He rolled off the creeper, both hands wrapped around his left knee. "Jesus Christ," he moaned. "You son of a bitch. Damn, that hurts. What the hell's your problem?"

Spinney dropped down next to him and grabbed his collar to pin him to the ground. His face was inches from Sherman's. "My problem is what you're doing to my son, you asshole, not to mention god knows how many other kids. You know who I am?"

Natty Sherman was not a street smart bad guy, big on attitude and striking a mean pose. In outlook, at least, he was like the hippies of yesteryear—peace-loving, self-indulgent, careless of the rules, and generally aimless. Confronted with this kind of rage, he was not one to fight back.

"Sure I do," he answered, his eyes wide with fear. "You're Spinney's dad—the cop. What're you doing? What did I do?"

Lester bore down, making Natty squirm with pain against the hard concrete floor. "You're breaking the law, you're fucking up people's brains, and worst of all, you're messing with my family."

The other man was now red in the face, gasping for air, and could only just get out, "I just blow a little weed."

That made Spinney even angrier. "Don't you get it? We're not on the record here. I'm one inch away from breaking your neck, and I'll do it to save my kid. Don't give me the 'blow a little weed' crap. You're pushing heroin, and you will go down for it."

Sherman was flopping around by now, his feet flailing and his hands pulling at Spinney's forearm. "No heroin . . . It isn't me."

Spinney loosened his hold slightly, and Natty gasped for air like a man breaking free of deep water.

"I swear to god," he continued, "I wouldn't do that. Heroin kills people. It's not like weed. Ask anybody. They'll tell you. I wouldn't allow it in the house. It's weed only. Never anything else. I make sure my kids know that. That they spread the word. I don't even let 'em smoke cigarettes."

Lester Spinney stared at him for a moment and then released him. "Where're your kids now?"

Sherman blinked. "My kids? What? . . . Hold it."

Lester grabbed him again. "Focus, Natty. Answ—— the question, for both our sakes."

Natty's eyes widened. "Andy's at home. Jeff's . . . I don't know. He said he went camping."

Spinney let go again and pounded his fist against the cabinet just above Sherman's head, making the latter wince. "Shit," Lester yelled in frustration, and then took hold of Natty's face. "That's the line Dave gave me. Now, think about this: Is that likely? Is it likely the two of them would go camping together?"

Sherman tried shaking his head. "No. I was happy when he told me because it's not something he's ever done before. I was surprised. And he didn't mention Dave."

"Who did he mention?"

"Nobody. He just said 'with friends.' "

Lester pulled Natty up to a sitting position and propped him against the cabinet. The mechanic moved his neck around and felt the back of his head for any damage.

Spinney leaned in close to him once more, crowding him. "Natty, you better be flying straight here. You see where I'm going with this?"

"You think Jeff's been doing heroin."

"Maybe, maybe not. What I know is that a grade A source just told me someone named Sherman had been dealing the stuff lately. I'd like to think Andy's too young. You claim it's not you. That leaves Jeff. Look me straight in the eye and tell me that's impossible— that there's no way in hell he would do that."

Natty Sherman dropped Lester's gaze. His voice was a monotone. "He might."

Spinney backed off and sat on the dirty floor next to

Sherman. They looked like exhausted runners after a marathon.

"So, if they didn't go camping, where are they?" Lester asked tiredly.

Natty rubbed his forehead, leaving a dirty smear. "Christ. I don't know."

"Think of Jeff's friends. If it's possible he's doing this, then you can probably think of the people he hangs out with you wish he didn't."

"There's Craig Steidle."

Lester closed his eyes briefly. "Right," he murmured. Steidle was the young hood driving the car the night Dave was picked up at the Zoo—the one Dave had claimed he wasn't seeing anymore.

"That sounds right," Lester said. "You know where he lives?"

Westview is one of Springfield's poorer neighborhoods. Developed in the early forties to house the overflow of factory personnel needed for the war effort, it was once probably considered pretty upscale, or at least solidly middle class. It was that no longer. Its dominant feature—a large affordable housing development—had become a regular stop for police and probation officers alike, along with a steady flow of welfare, social, and drug rehab workers.

Typical of an impressively topsy-turvy town, Westview was placed on top of a steep hill, accessible only from a single road connecting it to Springfield's downtown artery, and as shielded from the rest of the world as a distant suburbia. The comparison was apt. In what was becoming a signature of modern affordable housing, the Westview development at first glance looked for all the world like a trendy Connecticut condominium village. Spread along a pleasant tangle of short, winding streets essentially leading nowhere, these plastic-sided, two-story, beige-colored apartment buildings looked as perfect as a planning committee's proposal—and as tidy on the outside as the lives within them were not.

"It's up this way, I think," Natty said, half to himself, craning forward to better see the buildings gliding by.

Spinney slowed to a crawl. "You know the address?"

"I know Steidle's car," he said, predictably enough. "I worked on it enough times."

"You know him well?"

Natty grunted equivocally. "He comes by a lot, but I can't say I know him. He's Jeff's friend."

"Is he why you thought Jeff might be dealing?"

The other man sighed. "I don't like him. Never have. But you can't tell your kids who to hang out with."

Spinney didn't argue the point.

"Steidle has a record, leads a wild life. Jeff looks up to him for that, I guess. I hoped I was setting an example for a better way."

Spinney couldn't stop himself. "By smoking weed with him and his pals? You're famous all over town for that. I told my kid to stay away from your place."

Natty didn't take it personally. "Yeah. I heard that.

People get so bent out of shape. If they just legalized the stuff, everyone would see it's just like beer."

"And that's better? Drinking with underage kids?"

Sherman looked at him, appalled. "Oh, come on. Get real. You think they're not doing that already? I thought you guys knew what was going on. I should lay down the law at home so they'll go off and drink and get high Christ knows where? I'm as protective as any parent. I want them where I can see them. You play ball with your son, I bet—go fishing with him. What's blowing a little weed except more bonding?"

"We're looking for Jeff right now because he's suspected of dealing heroin, Natty. What does that tell you?"

Natty shook his head at Spinney's denseness and went back to looking out the window. A minute later, he pointed to the right side of the street. "There it is." He was looking at a Firebird with more miles than flash left on it. "And that's the house, too. I'm sure of it. I been here once or twice. Didn't know if I'd remember it. They all look the same."

Lester didn't need convincing. His son's bicycle was leaning against the wall. He pulled over across the street. "You stay here."

"What're you gonna do?"

"I just want to get Dave."

"What about Jeff?"

"I don't care about him, Natty. He's your problem."

Spinney got out, checked for traffic, and took in a few people loitering up and down the block, several of whom were watching him closely, knowing his profession from experience. He crossed the street, climbed the porch steps, and knocked on the door.

The man who opened up was a familiar type, even if unknown to Spinney personally. It seemed that no matter their social status, humans veered toward uniformity. From skinheads to millionaires, we find comfort in cloning one another. This guy was dressed in boots, jeans, tight black Harley T-shirt, long hair, and the requisite tattoos.

"You Craig Steidle?"

"Who wants to know?"

"I'm looking for my son, David Spinney."

Steidle smiled lazily. "You're the cop. He's not here."

"His bike is."

"I wouldn't know about that. People leave their junk around all the time."

"Mind if I come in?"

"Sure I mind. You got a warrant?"

Spinney forced a smile. "Look, Mr. Steidle, I'm not shopping here, not looking to cause any trouble. I just want my son. I have absolutely no bone to pick with you or anyone else inside."

Steidle leaned against the doorjamb and crossed his arms. "Got that right, 'cause you're not comin' in."

"He's underage, Mr. Steidle."

"Tough. He's here of his own free will."

Spinney laughed. "God, you guys are stupid. You just admitted he was here. I'm his father. You don't give me access, that's custodial interference. Get out of the way."

"Fuck you," Steidle said, stepped backward, and started slamming the door.

Spinney threw his shoulder against it and barreled across the threshold, sending Steidle stumbling in the process.

"Dave?" Spinney shouted into the house. "Get down here. Now."

"I don't think so," Steidle said menacingly, and pulled a switchblade from his boot top.

Spinney didn't hesitate. He spun on one heel and buried his foot in Steidle's stomach, doubling the man up and making the knife skitter along the floor. He then unholstered his gun and aimed it at him. "You're totally nuts, right? Dropped on your head when you were a kid? Get your face on the floor, asshole, and put your hands behind your back."

Groaning, Steidle did as he'd been told. Spinney retrieved and folded the knife, put it in his pocket, and snapped a pair of handcuffs on Steidle's wrists.

"You move, you'll be in worse shit than you are already," he warned him, and headed upstairs.

He didn't call out his son's name again. From the loud music pulsing behind a door at the end of the hallway, he figured it would be a waste of time. Instead, still holding his weapon, he walked the length of the house and paused at the door, listening for more than just the raucous music.

Hearing nothing else, he placed his hand on the knob, gently turned it to see if it was unlocked, and then threw open the door, entering simultaneously in a crouch, his gun covering the room before him.

He saw his son, Dave, a joint falling from his open mouth, holding a small packet of aluminum foil that Jeff Sherman had just handed him.

"Dad."

"Nobody move," Spinney ordered.

Jeff said softly, "Holy shit."

"Who else is in the house?"

"Dad," Dave began.

"Answer the question."

"Craig," Jeff answered.

"That it?"

"Unless someone came in after us. The rest of them went off somewhere."

Spinney holstered his gun and straightened up. He tilted his chin at the shiny packet they were still holding between them. "What is that?"

"Crack," Jeff answered immediately.

"You're doing heroin, too." It wasn't a question.

"Yes, sir."

"Collect it all, put it in a bag or something. If there's more outside this room, get that, too. I want it all."

Dave was watching him carefully. "Dad, what're you doing?"

"Later," Spinney ordered. "Do it. And crush out that joint you dropped."

Quietly, fearfully, Dave set to work collecting bags and bottles and joints from various corners of the room, as Jeff squeezed by Spinney to do the same elsewhere in the house.

About halfway through his labors, Dave found the

courage to address his silent father again. "What's going to happen?"

"You and I are going home. Jeff's father is waiting downstairs. I'll have one of the local cops pick up Steidle."

Dave kept working. "What about Jeff and me?"

"I'll try to keep you out of it."

His son stopped and stared at him.

"I can't promise anything," Spinney continued. "If Steidle talks too much, you might get sucked into it. We'll just have to deal with that if it happens."

"Couldn't you get in trouble for this?"

Spinney hesitated a moment, mulling over just how true that was. He was risking his job certainly, and maybe more.

"Yeah," he conceded.

Chapter 20

Sammie opened her eyes at the sound of the doorknob turning. Joe stepped inside the hospital room and quietly closed the door.

"Hey, Sam. How're you doing?"

She smiled lopsidedly. "A little sore. My pride took it worse."

He crossed the room, sat down on the edge of the bed, and placed his hand on hers. "Yeah. Your fairy godfather told me."

"Really? I thought he'd stay in the woodwork."

Gunther laughed. "Willy? And spare reaming me a new asshole? I don't think so."

"I am sorry," she said.

"Those things happen, Sam, and he was right. I should've dug into those names deeper—found out where everyone had been busted and who by."

"Nothing went off in my head, Joe. Not even Stuey's name. I hate to think—if Willy hadn't showed up."

Gunther squeezed her hand. "His full name's Allan Steward Nichols. He was calling himself Al when we knew him. I checked. 'Stuey' is part of his new, cool image. Should serve him well in jail. And even Willy conceded he'd changed his appearance."

"Is my cover still good?" she asked.

"Sure. Nichols is under wraps, in isolation for as long as we can get away with it, and you're in here under an alias. The doc said he had one more test coming back and that if it clears, he'll kick you loose in half an hour. You think you'll have a problem with Manuel?"

She shook her head. "Don't see why. I'll come up with something. If they're doing a blood test, by the way, it'll probably come up dirty. I had to take something when I interviewed Ralph Meiner. He said it was Ecstasy, but I don't know for sure. I kept a few extra for analysis. He held a gun on me and put the damn thing in my mouth himself. I couldn't get out of it. I was going to tell you at our next check-in."

"You do all right with it?" he asked, concerned.

"It was weird. I hope I don't have to do it again."

"Bad, huh?"

"No," she admitted. "Too good, I mean, it's not my taste, but I could see what people get out of it."

He gazed at the floor. "Yeah—that's the irony, isn't it? It's like telling a bunch of kids they shouldn't eat ice cream 'cause it'll kill them."

A meditative silence fell between them, after which

Sam confessed, "I think something's a little screwy with this case."

He looked at her carefully. "What?"

"I told Willy about it last night. It's the pale blue bags the heroin's being packed in. I saw ones just like it when we visited the Torres headquarters in Holyoke. First time I've ever seen colored baggies. I knew they weren't Rivera's, so I called the Holyoke PD's drug unit an hour ago to find out what they knew about it. It's Torres's trademark, like I thought. He calls it Blue Heaven."

"And that's what Nichols had?"

"And Meiner," she added. "Willy thought maybe they were leftovers from when Torres dominated the route, but heroin has a short shelf life—sold within a couple of days of arrival. I mean, I know Manuel and I are stocking it in quantity, but that's supposed to be revolutionary for around here. Otherwise, it's first come, first served, bim-bam and you're out of town for more."

Gunther scratched his cheek thoughtfully. "What do you think?"

"I don't know. I can't figure it out. And there's another thing: After Meiner thought I'd passed his undercover test by taking the Ecstasy, he asked me what I thought Torres would do if he found out we were setting up shop here. I was surprised, 'cause despite Jimmy Hollowell getting killed, Rivera had told me he now owned the route, at least for the moment."

"I remember," Joe commented.

"Well, Meiner said that Hollowell had thought the

same thing and that I should ask myself what had happened to him."

Gunther scowled. "We figured he was a combat casualty, that there might even be more. Do you have any idea who else Rivera has in place? I know he wouldn't tell you because you had to pass muster, but it seems now would be the right time to bring everybody together."

"I could go down there and rattle his cage," Sam agreed. "Be a reasonable question to ask. I might as well do it now, so I can tell Manuel that was the plan when I disappeared last night."

Joe glanced at her stomach. "You up for that?"

She flipped the cover off and swung her legs off the far side of the bed, looking like a kid in her hospital johnny. "It's sore," she said, moving around, touching her toes, "but if the doc clears me, I think I'm good to go. What'll you be doing in the meantime?"

Gunther stood up and moved toward the door. "I think I'll drop by the Rutland BCI unit. Find out where they are on the Hollowell case."

Sam looked up sharply and saw him smiling at her. "Thanks, Joe. And thanks for not being ticked off."

Lester had called his wife at work from his cell phone, so by the time he and David reached home, she was only ten more minutes from joining them.

They were sitting in stony silence at the kitchen table when she entered, wearing her usual nurse's uniform and a concerned expression on her face.

"Is everything all right?" she asked. "Where's Wendy?"

"She's fine," Lester said. "I sent her over to Louise's for a while." He pulled out a seat facing the third side of the table, between his son and himself. "Sit down, Susan. David's got something to say."

Tentatively, she joined them, looking at Dave as if he might break apart before her eyes. Dave stayed silent and withdrawn, staring at his clasped hands.

"Dave?" she asked fearfully. "What's up?"

"Dad found me at Craig Steidle's house."

Susan glanced at her husband, the name meaning nothing to her.

"The guy he was picked up with that night at the Zoo. The one we told him to stay away from. There's more."

"What else?" she asked her son, touching his hand with her fingertips.

He moved his hand away. "There were drugs."

She covered her mouth. "Oh my God. Were you taking any?"

"You bet," Lester said.

Dave looked up quickly. "It was only weed. I wasn't doing anything else."

"Only weed?" his father burst out. "What the hell were you holding when I walked in—after I cuffed the guy downstairs for coming at me with a knife?"

Susan's mouth dropped open.

"Jeff was showing me what he had, Dad. I wasn't doing anything."

"What was it?" Susan asked in a small voice.

"Cocaine," Lester said.

"Oh, sweetheart. What were you thinking?" She looked at her husband again. "And someone came at you with a knife? Were you hurt?"

"Not physically. I don't know about professionally."

She turned her head from one to the other of them, as if they were lobbing a ball back and forth. "What do you mean?"

"Ask Dave."

Their son sighed, still watching his hands. "Dad covered for me."

"Les," she exclaimed, "what've you done?"

"I had them collect all the dope, and I dropped it in a Dumpster near the town offices. That way, Steidle will have to stand for assaulting a police officer, probably with mitigating circumstances, but the cops can't nail him on the drugs. Not this time, anyway."

"But why?" she asked, dumbfounded.

Dave broke in harshly, "It was a deal, Mom. He let Craig off the hook so he wouldn't tell the cops Jeff and me were handling dope."

She put her hand on her forehead. "Jesus. So, what's going to happen?"

"Don't know," Lester answered her. "Time will tell. I told Steidle our story was that I came looking for Dave because I'd heard he might be at Steidle's from Natty Sherman, who was with me to get Jeff. Steidle denied Dave was there—despite his bike being outside—so we got into an argument, he pulled a knife, and I brought him down. Which is pretty much the truth, as far as it goes."

"But what about the drugs? What happens to them? Couldn't someone else end up with them?"

Here her husband looked shamefaced. "An anonymous phone call was made to the PD fifteen minutes ago, telling them where to find them. When we were pulling in, we heard on the scanner that they picked them up."

"That was taking a big chance, wasn't it?" she pushed.

His expression darkened. "That's hardly what's important here, is it?"

A strained silence filled the room.

"Why, honey?" she finally asked David. "Did we do something wrong?"

"No," he said reluctantly.

"We must've," Lester stated flatly. "Otherwise, why slap us in the face?"

Dave looked up. "I didn't."

"The hell you didn't. What the fuck do you think just happened?"

"Les," Susan said sharply.

But Lester paid her no attention. "We both bust our humps to feed you, clothe you, send you places on vacation. You got a computer, a new camera, CDs up the wazoo—"

"Thank you very much," Dave shouted at him, his face red and contorted. "And I make the beds and shovel snow and do the laundry. I'm the only kid I know who does the whole family's laundry, for Christ's sake. And why? Because I'm the only one who lives here most of the time."

"Your sister—" Lester began, but his wife stopped him with her hand.

"Wait. Hang on. This is important. Dave, is that really how you feel? Like you're living alone?"

Dave rolled his eyes. "Jesus, Mom, look around."

Spinney stiffened at his son's tone, but Susan grabbed his wrist to keep him quiet. "Go on."

"Dad and you are never here. Yeah, you feed us and send us on vacations and all the rest, but when was the last time we did anything together?"

"That's what you want?" Lester asked incredulously. "For us to go on vacation together?"

David looked like he'd been caught in a trap. "No. I mean . . . No, not to Disney World or anything dumb. I just meant . . . I don't know. Nothing. Stupid idea."

"I don't think so," Susan said quietly. "I know you wouldn't want to go to Disney World, but a family meal now and then wouldn't be so bad, would it? Or a trip to the movies?"

"You wouldn't like the movies I like."

Lester could see what was happening, even through his anger, disappointment, and fear. Wasn't that why he'd just put his job on the line? He swallowed hard and commented, "How do you know?"

Sam drove into Holyoke late in the afternoon, marveling once again at the contrast between this stained and beaten pile of asphalt and brick, and the green hills and sun-dappled waterways she'd just left in Vermont. It wasn't a fair comparison. It wasn't meant to be.

Vermont had its blighted areas, just as Massachusetts had the Berkshires. But imagining her home as a pristine counterpoint to an urban combat zone helped in the attitudinal shift she needed to get herself back into Greta.

She parked in front of Johnny Rivera's large, shuttered apartment building, watched as always by the several men loitering near the entrance.

"Hey, boys," she said, recognizing two of them. She slammed her car door and crossed the sidewalk toward them. "Watch my car, okay? Unless one of you wants to wash it or something. There might be a bonus in it for you."

Most of them stared at her sullenly, but one of them actually laughed and said, "I don't think so, *muchacha*. I heard what a good time you gave Flaco. He's still walking with a limp."

"He deserved it," she said, stepping inside.

She took her time wending through the building's maze of staircases and corridors, still uncertain of the way. By now, she'd made the trip several times, but, as intended, it was still not easy, and slow going in any case, given the many holes in the walls she had to step through carefully.

She finally found herself in Rivera's outer sanctum, the windowless room with the armed guards, where she waited as usual as one of them announced her.

Rivera immediately appeared at the door beaming and waved her inside. "Good to see you. What a surprise. Everything's okay, right?"

He shut the door behind her and ushered her toward the couch. She took the chair next to his desk.

He laughed and sat where he'd been herding her. "Still playing with me, eh? Time will come. Nothing wrong up north?"

"No. Everything's fine. Manuel been complaining?"

Rivera shook his head forcefully. "No, no. He thinks you're great. You're not buying his vote somehow, are you?"

Christ, she thought. Give it a rest. "Just a blow job now and then."

He laughed a little too forcefully. "That is bad. You shouldn't do that to me. You want a drink?"

"No thanks. What I want is some cooperation, now that you're so happy with me."

He knit his eyebrows. "Cooperation? What d'you mean?"

"Things're getting going in Rutland. Manuel's moving product, I'm working on the local dealers. It's time you hand over your contact list so we can work on an overall strategy."

"So fast?" he said, smiling. "You haven't been there long. You must still have lots to do. We move too fast, we could lose everything."

"Meaning you don't trust me?"

He laughed. "Don't trust you? I'm sending you the goods, no? I'm paying you a bunch of money. Of course I trust you. But I'm not stupid, either. You have a business plan—very big, very impressive. But you're not the only one with brains. I think things are just great the way they are."

She frowned at him. "Torres is still moving product up there."

Rivera shrugged. "He's not the only one. I didn't put him out of business all the way. You have to be careful with a man's pride—something you wouldn't understand. Guys like him should be allowed to work a little. Otherwise they get mad, try to get even, and now you got a fight instead of dollars coming in. Dumb idea."

"Why did Hollowell get killed, then?"

"Why does anybody? You know who did that? I don't. People are saying Torres, but I don't see it that way. That's narrow thinking. Doesn't do any good. Till I'm told otherwise, he got killed 'cause he pissed somebody off. That's all."

"So, you're not going to give me those names? You're going to force me to duplicate our efforts, waste time and money, risk exposure to the cops, and maybe let the wrong people get in behind us, all because you claim you have brains? Get out and smell the roses, Johnny. When was the last time you left this building? You're like a rat in a steel box in here. You have no clue what's going on."

His face darkened during this outburst, and his eyes hardened. "Careful, girlie," he said threateningly, accentuating the second word. "You work for me. That means I do this"—he snapped his fingers—"and you're dead. That's all you need to know till I decide to tell you more."

He stood up, all pretense of pleasantry gone. "Now, you can get the hell back to Vermont and do your job, or I can hand you over to the men outside this door.

They're not too crazy about you, after what you did to Flaco. They wouldn't mind paying you back their own way."

She rose also, but kept her voice contrite, realizing she'd overplayed her hand. "Johnny, I'm sorry. I really am. I know you're the boss. I've been waiting for this for so long, I get carried away sometimes. It's like I can almost grab it—everything we've talked about—and it sort of takes me over. I'm sorry I said those things. I didn't mean any disrespect."

He looked at her in silence, clearly pondering his choices. She could tell the temptation was great to feed her to the wolves, either from wounded pride or from just the pleasure of being able to do so. But for some reason—and it finally dawned on her possibly why—he demurred.

He put his hand on the doorknob and said, "Go back. You'll get everything you want, but in time. Leave the thinking to me."

She had nothing more to gain here. In fact, she was pretty sure she'd been wasting her time from the day she'd met him, which weighed more heavily on her now than any threat he could have made. For, aside from her own ambition, her loyalty was to Joe, and at that moment, she was feeling she'd completely let him down.

"You got it, Johnny," she said tiredly, and then added with more sincerity than he could have possibly known, "I just got carried away—makes me stupid sometimes."

                    *   *   *

Detective Sergeant Heather Hall paused on the threshold and looked at the older man staring down at the conference table before him, its surface covered from one end to the other with crime scene photos and sketches, case reports, forensics documents, and autopsy results. He had his hands in his pockets, his chin tucked in, and for all the world looked like he'd fallen fast asleep on his feet.

This was the famous Joe Gunther, she thought. All in all, a pretty forgettable figure, really. Nothing particularly outstanding about him, except maybe his eyes, which could shift from fatherly to intense in a flash. But he didn't seem all that brilliant, had nothing about him that attracted attention, wasn't charismatic the way some of her peers were, who could enter a room and make everyone take notice.

She liked him, though. He was quiet and kind and thoughtful. He'd asked her for her opinions with genuine interest. He was a really nice guy.

Which meant something to her. Squarely built, with short hair and blunt features, Heather Hall had been a beat cop for seven years before anyone had paid her the slightest attention, and then it was only because another female officer had filed suit against the town for gender discrimination. That case was still tangled up in the legal system—had been for two years—but in the meantime, Heather had found herself quickly courted and then promoted to the Rutland detective squad, the so-called BCI.

She wasn't ungrateful. She liked the new job, not to mention wearing nice clothes and not having to lug around a heavy belt loaded with gear. But it had also made her suspicious of what might come next. She'd started this job thinking she'd advance on her own merits. Now she had no clue.

"Any luck?" she asked, placing a coffee cup on the table before him.

He looked up at her and smiled. "Thanks. I appreciate it." He picked up the coffee and sipped from it thoughtfully, surveying the field of paperwork once more.

"Amazing things, these cases," he said eventually. "They start out so simply—a man and a woman found dead—but the more you dig, the harder they get to figure out. You know darn well no genius killed them—that it was probably a cause-and-effect kind of scenario. But there are so many variables to the one correct answer. It's like finding a needle in a haystack, just like they say." He pretended to hold a needle up between his thumb and index finger. "When you get there, you can only shrug and say, 'Jeez, it's just a needle.'" He paused and dropped his hand. "Fascinating process."

She nodded, figuring it was better to just let him ramble. "So I'm guessing no needle yet."

He laughed. "Right." He leaned forward and extracted a single photograph from a stack of autopsy shots. "There is this, though."

She moved closer to peer at it. It was a picture of James Hollowell's left hand. Along the back of it, crossing the knuckles and smearing the web of skin at the base of his thumb, was a dark smudge—like an oily stain.

"Not the cleanest guy I ever saw," she commented. "His motel room smelled like a sewer. And look at his fingernails. Gross. God only knows what's under them."

Gunther smiled. "If God doesn't, I know who might." He pointed at the phone. "How do I get an outside line?"

Chief Medical Examiner Beverly Hillstrom picked up the phone. It hadn't been a great day so far, and she suspected no great news from this. "Dr. Hillstrom."

"Doctor, it's Joe Gunther."

She was wrong. Few people in the world made her feel better just by being there, and Joe Gunther was one of them. It hadn't always been thus, not surprisingly given her general view of the world—which also explained the way she routinely approached newcomers. Gunther had entered her autopsy room years ago, uninvited and unannounced, and had asked her to dig deeper into a case she'd already processed. That had not been an auspicious beginning. Except that he'd been right, as he had been several times since. The man was a digger, more given to hard work than to flashes of inspiration, although she didn't doubt he had those, too. But he didn't rely on them, and didn't show off in any case. All of which made him someone she could like.

Not that she'd relaxed her professional standards as

a result. Beverly Hillstrom came from the old school, where respect was earned, but courtesy was a given. Despite her admiration for the man and his doggedness, she brooked no diminution of her own rules of engagement. She forever referred to Gunther by his title, and expected no less of him. These were ground rules she proffered to everyone, excepting her family and personal friends. And it didn't hurt her kind feelings toward him that he'd instinctively understood that from the start, without the instructions she gave to virtually everyone else. And which, quite unfairly, had given her a reputation among law enforcement as an ice queen.

"Agent Gunther," she therefore said, the pleasure palpable in her voice. "To what do I owe this privilege?"

Joe, for his part, was considerably less doctrinaire. He'd tried to get her to at least call him "Mister," since the "Agent" handle still made him feel like an impostor, but it was clearly of no use. On the other hand, the respect was mutual. Never before had he met someone with such a mind for detail and such an instinct to pursue it. Even if she didn't know what she was looking at, chances were that Dr. Hillstrom would take a sample. Just in case.

"I'm on another fishing expedition, I'm afraid," he admitted. "Exactly what you probably don't want to hear."

"Nonsense," she countered. "Right now some fishing would be right up there with a bowl of ice cream."

"Doctor," he said with mock surprise, "I had no idea. Any particular flavor?"

"Never mind," she said, embarrassed not only that she'd admitted to a pleasure but that she felt awkward about her embarrassment. "What do you have for me?"

"James Hollowell, date of birth—"

"I remember Mr. Hollowell," she interrupted briskly. "Any problem with my findings?"

"None. Actually, this is a real long shot. No reason for you to have noticed. But I'm in a bind for ideas."

"Stop dancing around, Agent Gunther."

"Hollowell had a greasy smear on his left hand, along the back. Do you remember that?"

She nodded at the phone. "I do. Let me put you on hold while I get his file."

A minute later, she returned. "I have a photo of it before me."

"All right. Here's the long shot: any idea what it is?"

"None whatsoever," she stated flatly.

After a telling hesitation, he said, "Okay. Well . . ."

"But I kept a sample," she added.

He laughed. "Nice. Break my heart, then bring me back around. Cruel."

"It's been that kind of day. Sorry. I couldn't resist."

"No, no. That's fine. Any way you could have it analyzed?"

"I'll have it delivered to forensics today."

They exchanged a couple of more pleasantries before Joe hung up the phone, still smiling.

Heather Hall was watching him. "What did she say?"

"She kept a sample. The crime lab'll get it later today."

Hall nodded, still not sure why this had any bearing. "What do you think they'll find?"

"Something to do with a car engine," he said brightly. "And if we all keep our fingers crossed, it'll be something traceable."

Chapter 21

Sam, where the hell have you been? You were supposed to call yesterday. I thought Rivera had you. I was about to call in the cavalry."

Her voice on the other end sounded down and exhausted. "Sorry, Joe. I had to check something out. I've blown it big time."

"What do you mean? Where are you?"

"I'm at a pay phone. This whole thing's been a fraud from the start, Joe. I led us all down the wrong road."

Joe rubbed his forehead, trying to make sense of what she was saying. "We need to meet, Sam. Get off the phone and hook up with me at . . . Shit, I don't know . . . Are you in town?"

She hesitated. "I can meet you in an hour."

His hand tightened on the phone. There was something about the way she was speaking. "Things've changed since you dropped out of sight, Sam. In fact, I'm thinking we ought to pull you out. Come straight to the PD."

"What? Why?"

"I was going over the Hollowell case, like I said I would. Couldn't find a thing. Kept going around and around. Finally, I noticed a photo of a greasy smear on one of his hands, and a shot someone took on the bridge where he was hanged of a puddle of something oily on the road. I had Hillstrom compare the sample she collected with the one they got from the bridge, and just heard back they were both power-steering fluid— from the same source."

Sam didn't respond. He wasn't sure if that was because she was listening or had simply walked away, leaving the phone dangling. From the anxious tone of her voice, the latter wouldn't have surprised him.

"Sam?"

"I'm here."

"We got lucky. Most cars use standard power-steering fluid. Hondas don't, and that's what we found. I cross-checked everyone we have on our radar right now with the cars they own, and I got one hit. Lucky the bad guys don't think much of fuel efficient imports. It was Manuel Ruiz, Sam. That's why I think we ought to shut down."

"Manuel killed Hollowell?" She sounded stunned.

"Looks that way. We have a lot more homework to do. But, come in, all right? It's getting too screwy and it's not worth the risk anymore."

"You don't know the half of it," she said in her monotone.

"What?"

"Rivera doesn't have an organization. He's got a bunch of goons with guns in that building of his, but that's it. Until you just said that about Manuel, I thought he was Rivera's only operative. Now it looks like I was wrong about that, too."

It was Joe's turn to fall silent.

"You there?" she asked.

"Yeah. Sorry, but I thought it was Torres who pointed you toward Rivera in the first place."

"It was. Specifically, it was one of his lieutenants named Ricky. But I was conned from the start and let my ambition screw up the rest. Christ, Joe, even Bill Dancer pegged Rivera as a punk from the start, but was I going to listen to a loser like Bill? Hell no. I had to prove him wrong. I overestimated Rivera and underestimated Torres, and led us all down the wrong path as a result. I am so sorry. I'm thinking I should resign."

"Sam, this is crazy. Come on in."

"I will. I'm on my way—one hour."

The phone went dead in Joe's hand.

Sam walked up to the house, gave the signal, and unlocked the door. "It's me," she announced to no one, knowing that as usual Manuel would be lurking.

He was. He appeared from around the corner looking as lithe and trim as ever. "Where you been?" he asked, his voice guarded.

She looked at him for a moment, her head slightly tilted. Purposefully, she hadn't planned this, preferring to play it spontaneously, keeping inside Greta as much as possible. As such, on impulse, she walked up to him, took his face in her hands, and gave him a long, deep kiss. He responded, but only with his mouth, with which he smiled as she finally broke away. But his eyes were still watchful.

"*Hola.* Welcome home. Was it my cooking?"

She walked past him into the living room and sat in one of its worn armchairs. "No," she said. "I was in Holyoke, seeing Johnny."

Manuel perched cautiously on the arm of the couch. "Oh? Problems?"

"You could say that. I found out you were playing me for a putz."

"Sorry?"

"A jerk. You been funnin' with me. Fucking with my head."

He didn't respond.

She stared at him. "What was the point? What did I ever do to you? It couldn't have been that stupid comment I made when we first met. You're not that thin-skinned. Plus, I saved your butt a few hours later. I was good. My heart and head were in the right place. I was going to make us rich. Why did you lie to me?"

"What did Rivera say?"

She shook her head. "Right. Get your stories straight. Well, sorry, but he didn't say squat. That's the whole deal. That's what woke me up. I went down there to ask for his contact list so I could combine it with what I've been building. Reasonable request, I thought. But only if you're being straight with your partner. Dummy me. He puts on an attitude, says I haven't proven myself yet. I have to wonder why. I mean, I already know Torres hasn't been cut out of the Vermont business—I'm running into his Blue Heaven shit everywhere I turn. So I started asking around, calling my sources, traveling the whole Holyoke, Brattleboro, Rutland corridor. That's where I've been all this time. And guess what I find? Rivera has nobody out there. You've been running a scam. Using me and my strategy to build something you could only dream about."

"Why would we do that?" he asked.

She looked at him sourly. "Spare me. If I'd known you were just a load of hot air, I would've gone someplace else. I was like a gift from God to you guys. Manna from heaven."

He gave a short laugh. "Whoa. I wouldn't go crazy with that."

She glared at him, pulling her anger from the very flip side of her argument—that she'd tried to pull a scam on them, and had been as let down as they'd been in the end. "You saying you didn't snap me up when I came through the door?"

"All right, all right. But so what? What's the big deal? You're here now, things're going great. Who cares if we didn't have a network? We got one growing right now. We'll just start over—everything out on the table." He shook his head with a bewildered expression. "Greta, why'd you kiss me if you don't think this'll work? It's a crazy business. Nobody trusts any-body. We could've done a lot worse."

"Like kill Jimmy Hollowell?"

He remained looking faintly amused, but she could tell that had surprised him. An almost imperceptible cloak of stillness draped over him.

"Sure," he said affably, after just a hair too long of a pause. "Like that. At least we aren't killing people."

"The day we met, Johnny said that's what you do. Remember? He said you didn't have his management skills—that you just killed people."

"He was making me look mean."

Sam slowly felt the blood fill her face as she sud-denly saw her way clearly at last. "Like Miguel Torres does."

"What?"

"You heard me. You know, it's sometimes handy to talk out loud like this. It helps get the thoughts out of your head so you can hold them up and look at them. You work for Torres, don't you? I mean, I know you used to, like Rivera did, but you still do. You always have."

"Did you have another one of those pills?"

"You wish. You know a guy named Ricky? Works for Torres?"

"No."

"You shouldn't have said that. You were busted with him last year. See, that's another thing I did after I left Rivera's. I stuck around town, asking questions. That's how I found you in the first place, after all. So I just did the same thing in reverse. I got curious. If Rivera was just living in a dreamworld, then why did the Torres people—specifically, Ricky—send me over to Rivera, claiming he'd stolen Torres's route? What was in it for them? The answer was they wanted their mole— you—to see what I had to offer. I came out of nowhere, thinking I would be good for Johnny, but in fact—stupid me—I was actually perfect for you and Ricky and Torres's whole bunch."

That was all pretty accurate, except that she hadn't discovered it in the street. She'd dropped by the Holyoke PD and consulted their computers and their drug unit.

"That doesn't make any sense. Maybe you're drunk," he said, but she could tell he wasn't putting any effort into it anymore.

She was actually getting excited telling her story, seeing it in sharp detail at last, ignoring the danger looming ahead. She leaned forward in her chair. "No, hear me out. It was perfect. You were Torres's mole. You'd just killed Hollowell—Rivera's only man up here—and you were probably working on a way to get to Johnny next, if you could lure him outside of his fortress, when all of a sudden Bill Dancer and I walk in. Very quick thinking on your part. Well, Ricky's part, since the guy we'd talked to first, Carlos, was clueless. Carlos had just heard that Rivera had made a play and was now considered a bad guy, but he didn't have any details, and he sure didn't know you were involved. Bill and I, on the other hand, thought Ricky was just the doorman—Don Juan with the fast hands. *He* fed me all I needed to go to Johnny, and he was perfect. How would I know he was just taking a break downstairs, that he's in fact number two in the Torres organization? Right up there with a consigliere in the Mafia? He must've figured what the hell? Send this broad and her big ideas over to Rivera. She might draw him outside somehow. And if not, maybe she'll do what she says she will and create something from nothing—a crackerjack organization that you can inherit after Johnny's met his maker. You two must've killed yourself laughing when he called you to say I was heading over."

But there was still something wrong, something escaping her. She got up and began pacing the room.

"It could make an okay movie," Manuel humored her. "A TV movie, maybe, since it doesn't make sense, but some people might like it."

"What's wrong with it?" she challenged him, hoping to draw him out.

"Why hang Hollowell? If I was making an example of him, who was I making it to? You say Rivera had nobody to impress—he had nobody out here except Hollowell."

She burst out laughing, the last piece falling into place. "Exactly. You were making a point to *Torres's* people. Hollowell worked for Torres once, too, like you all did." She slapped her forehead. "So dumb."

"Greta. You can't just change your mind to make it fit. This whole story is make-believe." His face suddenly got serious. "Are you okay?"

She waved that off. "Spare me. Hollowell worked for Torres. That should be easy to find out. But he must've gone over to Rivera—for real. Johnny's got all those gunmen on his side, after all. It's not like he's a total loony—just guilty of false advertising with me. But he wanted to get this done, and until you killed Hollowell, Hollowell was the means. That's why you hanged him. It was a double message. I mean, yeah, it made a point with Rivera, but it really hit home with the boys in the 'hood, right? 'This is what happens to traitors.' Why the hell didn't I get it sooner? What a moron."

Manuel straightened, ran his hand through his hair, and then stood to his full height. "You shouldn't be so hard on yourself."

She froze in her pacing. "I'm right?"

"Very good." He took one step away from the couch, in her direction.

"Why did you kill the girl?" Furtively, Sam began looking around, thinking tactically, knowing things were about to get dangerous.

He furrowed his eyebrows momentarily, as if trying to remember. "She was in the way. I didn't know she'd be there."

"But you made it look like a drug overdose."

"I didn't need two murders." He stopped and studied her closely. "How did you know it wasn't an overdose? That wasn't in the news."

She opened her mouth, but nothing came out. It was like having cold water thrown in her face—the startling revelation that she'd made a crucial mistake.

"I heard it somewhere."

His hand shifted to the small of his back, where he kept his gun.

Sam ran at him, head down, taking him totally by surprise. He staggered back, tried pulling his gun, but she collided into him before he could, sending them both sprawling backward over the couch behind him, and onto the floor in a tangled, thrashing embrace. She grappled blindly at his arms, swatted his face, did all she could to keep him on the defensive until she could control the gun.

But he was fast and not easily distracted, and he eventually threw her off, pushing at her with his feet. He rolled away, came up in a crouch, and aimed the gun between her eyes, all in one fluid movement.

In the distance, approaching fast, sirens were wailing.

"I'm a cop," she said breathlessly, still crumpled on the floor. "This whole place is rigged with video. That's why they're coming now. Everything's being recorded."

He rose slowly, the gun steady, not reacting to her outburst. "You slipped, saying the girl didn't overdose."

"Give it up, Manuel. You can make a deal. Shut down Torres, maybe more. Witness protection, even."

He smiled, but there was a lover's betrayal in his eyes. The sirens were almost on top of them, filling the room.

"I don't think that's how it would turn out. I am sorry, though," he added sadly. "I liked Greta Novak. I would have enjoyed cooking for her more."

He paused for a split moment, as they exchanged a

lingering glance, no words left, before turning quickly and vanishing from the room.

She scrambled to her feet, blue lights already reflecting off the ceiling, and followed him outside into a swirl of strobes, dust, the sound of cars skidding to a halt.

"Stop where you are. Put your hands in the air."

"The guy with the gun," she shouted, bathed in a crosshatch of headlights. "Did you see the guy running out of here?"

Nobody had.

Chapter 22

Nice job on the Rutland case," Gail said.

Joe merely shook his head. They were in his car on Canal Street. He'd just picked her up from the hospital. His voice was almost bitter when he spoke. "I shouldn't complain, since we ducked a bullet, but this was nothing to brag about. When you get down to it, we were pulled in to make the governor look good, and screwed it up. He made it happen anyhow, of course. Instead of presenting somebody's head to Roger Lapierre for Sharon Lapierre's murder as planned, Reynolds substituted the surveillance video of Manuel Ruiz admitting to it, just before he got away. And it worked. Apparently, Lapierre was satisfied with the promise that 'we'—whoever that is—will nail the guy in the long run. Makes you wonder why we bothered."

"You shut down a couple of drug rings," she countered. "That's what the paper said this morning: 'Rutland Drug Lords Stopped in their Tracks.'"

He let out a short laugh. "Pure spin. There were no lords and no tracks, for that matter. We busted a few guys. Mouse fart in a high wind. Given our high hopes, the resources expended, and the risks to Sam, the whole thing was a wash. I doubt the people we arrested had even been fingerprinted before their successors were already setting up deals. I'm happy to leave that entire drug merry-go-round to the task force. Not my cup of tea."

"Did Sam do a good job?" Gail's voice was more tentative against this unusual dourness.

Here his tone lightened. "Oh, hell. If she'd been a crook and Rivera had been honest with her, they would've made an amazing team. She was great. Totally convincing. The only hitch was that he couldn't organize a drug ring any more than we could stop one. Talk about ironies. Of course," he confessed, addressing her question, "Sam won't accept any of that. She just sees the end result and blames herself. So she's a little bummed out at the moment."

Gail reflected that Sam was obviously not the only one. "Is there blame going around?"

He smiled again. "Everyone's tiptoeing away from this one, counting their lucky stars. Yours truly included. My gut instinct was to hold Sam back when she first discovered Rivera, but I went with the flow. Everyone got so excited about working an undercover, it never crossed our minds to check the horse we'd chosen to ride."

Joe pulled off Canal and stopped next to a gas pump at a convenience store. He swung out of the car, turned the unit on, and wedged the nozzle into his tank opening.

Gail leaned over in the front seat so she could see him through the open driver's window. "But you're all okay, aside from a little wounded pride, right? There's no long-range damage?"

He leaned his elbows on the windowsill. His expression was more philosophical now.

"I think so. Allard's happy we got off light. The governor's ratings are up. Sam's licking her wounds and Willy may or may not be helping her. God only knows there. Spinney's gone on vacation. He got into a fight with some scumball in Springfield who tried to stop him from retrieving his son from a friend's house. I don't know the details, but he's shrugging it off. He told me he was going to see a whole bunch of bad movies with the family, whatever that meant. I'm glad he's taking the time."

"Basically," he concluded, "all's well, if you label pure survival as success."

He stopped to gaze at Gail. "What about you, Mother Zigman? All this concern for others. How're you holding up?"

She smiled at him. "Fine. Guess it was something I just had to do. Pretty crazy, the way things catch up to you when you're not paying attention. But except for what happened to Laurie, I'm not unhappy about any of it. These lessons come in strange wrapping sometimes."

He nodded ruefully at that. "No kidding. I have to pay for the gas inside. Be right back."

He left the car and crossed the lot to the convenience store located in its middle like a customs house. The bell above the door tinkled as he entered. He handed his credit card to the young man at the counter. The store was empty. He leaned over the counter slightly as the clerk's back was turned and looked at the floor where Laurie's blood had once flowed from edge to edge. It was pristine now.

"Is Arnie in?" Joe asked, signing the receipt moments later.

"Yeah. He's in the back. Last door beyond the rest rooms. Says 'Employees Only,' but you can walk in."

"Thanks."

He made his way to the back, pushed open the door, and found himself in a narrow, cinder-block-walled room filled with piled boxes and crates, along with one steel desk and a fluorescent lamp. There were no windows, so the lighting made the man sitting at the desk look pasty and haggard.

Joe showed him his badge. "Arnie Weller?"

The man's voice was listless. "Yeah."

"Mind if I sit?"

"Free country."

Joe moved a few papers off the chair beside the desk and sat. "I'm Joe Gunther. I worked a little on the Laurie Davis case. Thought you'd like to hear how she was doing."

Weller's face transformed. His eyes widened with

hopefulness, giving him almost a plaintive air. "She better?"

"She is physically. Woke up this morning, talked to her parents. She's still very weak, but the docs're saying she should make it—that the coma was actually a good thing. Gave her time to heal on her own."

To Joe's surprise, tears welled up in Arnie's eyes, which he awkwardly wiped away with the back of his hand. "Oh, Christ, that's good news. I've had that girl's face in my head ever since it happened. I can't sleep, I don't have any appetite."

Joe leaned forward and patted the other man's shoulder. "You weren't the one who put a knife in her hand to start with. Remember that. She made her own choices, and she'll have a lot more still to make—her work's barely begun. You were just a step in that process—a lucky one, as it turns out." Joe reflected a moment before asking, "You still carry a gun, by the way?"

Weller cradled his forehead in his hand. "Shit no. I got robbed again two nights ago. I just stepped away from the register and let him take what he wanted. I'm getting out of this business. It's too much to take—almost killing someone, almost getting killed. It's not worth it."

He suddenly looked up and stared directly at Joe. "And you can't tell me it'll get any better, can you?"

Joe studied him for a moment, thinking back to what he and his team had just gone through, and the minimal results they'd gathered.

"Damned if I know."

More
Archer Mayor!

Please turn this page
for a preview of

THE SURROGATE
THIEF

available in hardcover.

Chapter 1

Dispatch to zero-thirty."

Officer Paul Kinney unhooked his radio mike and answered, "Zero-thirty."

"Domestic disturbance, Sixty-three Vista Estates. Neighbor called it in. Address listed to a Linda Purvis."

"Ten-four."

Kinney replaced the mike and pulled into a smattering of traffic. It was almost midnight, which was late even for a town of thirteen thousand like Brattleboro. This was still Vermont, where phoning people after nine and staying up past eleven was unusual, even slightly inappropriate, behavior.

Kinney was feeling good. It was summer, two

days ago he'd been released by his training officer to patrol on his own, and he was flush with self-confidence. To his thinking, all that remained was to learn the ropes thoroughly with the Bratt PD, establish a reputation, put out some feelers, and pick from a variety of plum federal jobs, from the FBI to Homeland Security to God knows what. He felt poised before a veritable trough of opportunities.

He headed down Route 9 into West Brattleboro, the main town's smaller offshoot. Given its less-urban makeup, West B played host to a range of trailer parks, from the seriously upscale—expansive, complete with paved roads, car parks, and garages—to the barely solvent, where the odds favored Mother Nature repossessing her own.

Not surprisingly, the loftily named Vista Estates fit the latter category.

Kinney wasn't concerned. He didn't know this address specifically, but he judged himself pretty adept at handling domestics. He'd studied his FTO's style—an old-timer who'd been a field training officer for too many years—and as a result, had mostly learned how not to behave. And even though he'd handled only a couple of domestics on his own, Kinney was convinced of the merits of his technique. People under stress didn't need a friendly ear. They were secretly yearning for the comfort of a little imposed discipline.

Vista Estates was to hell and gone, almost out of town, and proffering neither vistas nor estates. A trailer park whose assets were better known to the tax courts than to any Realtor, it was a threadbare clearing among some roughly opened woods, crisscrossed with narrow, root-tangled dirt lanes, and populated with as many empty lots as decaying trailers.

The one thing the park owners had bothered with, Kinney noted gratefully, was numbering the addresses. He found sixty-two, sixty-three, and sixty-four without much trouble, although he'd used his flashlight to better see out his side window. Vista Estates had clearly deemed street lamps a luxury.

Kinney drew abreast of the rough scratch in the dirt serving as a trifurcated driveway, told dispatch of his arrival, and pulled himself free of the car. Before him were two distant trailers and an empty space for a third. The home on the left was blazing with light, its neighbor all but dark, save for a single curtained window.

He drew in a deep breath, enjoying the cool summer air and preparing himself for the show of command he saw coming, and set off down the driveway.

He considered stopping by the neighbor's first. That was certainly protocol. But instinct and vanity pushed him toward the direct approach. He slipped between the pickup and the small sedan parked in front without checking their registrations, and climbed the worn wooden steps up to the narrow, homemade porch. He paused at the thin metal front door.

He certainly sympathized with the neighbor's complaint. There was a knock-down, drag-out screaming match taking place inside, accompanied by the thumping of doors and the smashing of crockery.

Kinney passed on ringing the bell and removed his flashlight from the slim pocket sewn into his uniform pants. He used it to smack the door three times.

"Brattleboro Police."

The immediate silence was like pulling the plug on an overly loud TV set—utter and complete. And in its sudden embrace, he felt abruptly and paradoxically defenseless.

The door flew open without warning, revealing a large man with a beard, a T-shirt, and an over-sized revolver in his hand pointed at the floor. "You get the hell away from here or she's dead. Got that?"

Kinney felt his stomach give way, along with his bravado. Transfixed by the gun, he imagined himself as the human-sized target he so frequently poked holes in at the range. He could see the barrel rising to the level of his eye, an enormous flash of light, and then nothing.

The door slammed in his face.

*   *   *

" 'You get the hell away from here or she's dead.' That's all he said. He had a gun."

Ron Kiesczewski closed his car door and leaned against the fender. He rubbed his face with both hands, still chasing the remnants of a deep sleep from his brain, before peering into the wary, almost belligerent expression, of the patrolman before him.

"You got the call? I mean, you were the one this guy talked to?" Ron spoke deliberately, hoping to project a calming influence. In fact, being the senior officer here, he felt his own anxieties beginning to roil inside him, a nagging insecurity he'd wrestled with all his life.

"Yeah. It didn't sound like a big deal from dispatch—a routine domestic. I knocked on the door, he opened up, delivered the one-liner, and slammed the door. There was a woman behind him, crying."

Kiesczewski took in the tight shooting gloves, custom gun grips, and strained nonchalance, and identified a neophyte's attempt to cover insecurity with accessories. "She look all right otherwise?"

To his credit, the patrolman became clearly embarrassed. "I guess. I was sort of looking at the gun. That's when I figured I better call for backup."

Kiesczewski studied him for a beat before asking, "You okay? Did he point it at you?"

There was a moment's hesitation, as if Ron had

asked a trick question. All traces of initial swagger vanished in the response. "No, I mean, yeah, I'm all right, but no, he didn't point it at me. It was a little scary, is all. Not what I was expecting. But I'm fine . . . And she's fine . . . I'm pretty sure . . . The woman, I mean."

Brattleboro's police department was known either as a lifer colony, where laid-back older veterans spun out entire careers, or as a turnstile agency, where baby cops hung around just long enough to decide between a flashier law enforcement job elsewhere or getting out altogether.

Ron wondered if the latter option wasn't circling this one's head right now. As it was, he was so new that Ron couldn't remember if his name was Paul or Phil. His name tag just said, "P. Kinney."

"How long ago did this start?" he asked him, deciding he looked like a Phil.

Kinney checked his watch. "Maybe half an hour ago." He keyed the mike clipped to the epaulet of his uniform shirt and muttered into his radio, "Jerry? It's Paul. You remember when I called for backup?"

"Twenty-three fifty-three," came the brisk reply.

Okay, Ron thought, so it's Paul. Things better improve from here. "The scene secure?"

Kinney nodded. "Only three sides to worry about. Jerry's covering the west and north. We're on the east, and Henry's got the south. Good thing the trailer park's half empty. Makes life a lot easier."

That last line was delivered with pale, leftover flair. Ron shivered slightly. Even summers in Vermont could get chilly, especially if you were fresh from a warm bed. "You've got more coming, though, right?"

"Oh sure. The state police are sending a couple. The sheriff, too. I asked dispatch to get hold of the chief and Billy Manierre, but no luck so far."

"They're both out of town," Ron said with some regret. He was head of a four-man detective squad and the department's only hostage negotiator, both positions put him closer to the upper brass than to the uniforms chasing taillights—the latter of whom he envied right now.

"You better show me around."

Paul Kinney stumbled over an exposed root as he turned, increasing his awkwardness. "Watch your step," he said needlessly. "It's just around the corner, past that fir tree."

They weren't using flashlights. The moon supplied just enough light to see by, and they didn't want to stir up the man in the trailer in case he was looking out.

Kinney lowered his voice as he drew abreast of the tree. "There it is."

Kiesczewski peered into the gloom. Looking slightly deflated, like a small grounded blimp needing air, the trailer sat alone in the middle of a narrow, hardscrabble yard. To one side of it was a blank rectangle showing where a similar home had once stood. To the other was a second trailer, some twenty feet away, lights blazing from every window. In the distance, a row of trees and a hill blocked off the scene like a set piece on a stage. A swaybacked pickup and a rusty compact were parked in front of the home they were interested in.

"Jerry's out behind?" Ron asked, pointing at the trailer.

"Right, and Henry's alongside the other one."

"Why're all the lights on in there? Are the neighbors still inside?"

Kinney answered more emphatically than the question deserved, making Ron think he might have addressed the problem later than he should have. "No, no. We got them out. And I talked to them, too. Got some good information. I guess we forgot about the lights."

"We can turn them off after the tac team gets here," Ron placated him, noticing the primary trailer had only one lighted window, its curtains drawn. "How did this go down?"

"Neighbors complained," Kinney explained. "Said they were screaming at each other next door and breaking things. That's sure what they were doing when I arrived."

"We know who 'they' are, yet?"

"Linda Purvis is the owner of record, and according to the neighbors, the man sounds like her ex, Matthew. That matches the two vehicle registrations and the physical descriptions I got."

"Any kids?"

Kinney's face turned toward him in the half-light, looking as blank as his expression. "I don't know," he stammered. "I didn't ask."

"So, there may be others in there." It wasn't a question.

"Yeah," the younger man admitted. "I guess so. If it helps," he added, "dispatch said this wasn't the first time, and Purvis is in the computer for prior domestics here, complete with a restraining order issued yesterday."

Which was probably what triggered this, Ron thought. One of the hallmarks of these kinds of situations taught during his negotiator's training was the so-called precipitating event. Almost without fail, it was lurking somewhere, usually acting as the proverbial one straw too many. In the worst cases, you got what they called the Triple—three cataclysms striking virtually at once, like a freakish planetary alignment.

"You smell liquor on his breath?" he asked.

Kinney nodded. "Big time."

Such as a drinking binge, Ron thought. He turned away and looked down the rutted road leaving the park. He saw the twinkle of blue strobes approaching in the distance.

"Get on the radio and tell everyone to respond

Code Two. I don't want to crank this guy up any higher than he is."

Kinney did as asked and they both watched the strobes wink out moments later, while the headlights kept bouncing toward them over the uneven ground.

Kiesczewski didn't look at Kinney as he continued, "As soon as everyone gets here, I want rat packs quietly placed under both Purvis cars, all other trailers within easy shooting range evacuated, and a perimeter established and sealed."

Rat packs were small tire spikes designed to prohibit a departing car from getting far.

"Who's the shift commander tonight?" he finally asked.

"Captain Washburn. It was supposed to be Lieutenant Capullo but he's out sick."

Ron looked up at the night sky, dread settling in. That made Washburn top dog for the duration, since the chief and his second-in-command, Manierre, were out of town. Negotiation by its nature was tough enough, especially when you had as little experience as Ron. Adding Washburn's built-in animosity for him wasn't going to make it easier.

The only missing stressor now was a gung-ho tac team, chomping at the bit to turn that trailer into the Alamo. And that much was a given with the team's new leadership—a transplanted Boston cop named Wayne Kazak. Ron smiled at the irony. Now he had his own Triple to deal with.

He sighed softly and said, "Okay, let's get the van down here and set up a command post. Better count on this taking a while."